STARTING FROM ZERO

LANE HAYES

For Bob-
You are my music between the notes. My inspiration and my love
song. Always.

1

JUSTIN

"Everything must have a beginning...and that beginning must be linked to something that went before."—Mary Shelley, *Frankenstein*

A SPOTLIGHT FELL over the lone microphone on the vacant stage. The dramatic illumination seemed unnecessary in a club as small as Carmine's, where the maximum occupancy topped out at one hundred, but size wasn't important. Of course, that was what all desperados said when making the most of a less than ideal situation. And things had definitely turned desperate.

My ragtag band of three was down a guitarist. Not good—especially tonight. Sure, our invitation to perform was last-minute and slightly suspicious. And yes, I probably should have waited for Johnny to confirm he was available, but no one turned Carmine down. His club might look like a basic dive bar...dim lighting, sticky floors, dark walls adorned with ancient concert posters, a tiny stage on one end, a busy bar on the other...but it was special.

Carmine's catered to music business hopefuls and professionals. On an average night you might bump into an A-list producer, an aspiring banjo player, or your neighborhood barista. The "invitation only" policy elevated the opportunity to an elite status that made me wonder how the hell Johnny, Tegan, and I made the cut. We'd only recently started playing together full-time. Johnny on lead guitar, Tegan on drums, and me on rhythm guitar and vocals. We were still missing some key components...like a bassist, a manager—and hell, a name—but we figured we'd work out the kinks. We were young, motivated, and we had nothing to lose. Literally nothing.

But we needed Johnny. If he didn't get here soon, we'd have to make some last-minute changes. Or bow out.

"What time did Johnny say he'd get here?" Tegan asked as he scanned the semi-dark area near the bar.

"He didn't say. He couldn't find anyone to close for him on three-hours' notice," I huffed. "I kind of hoped we'd catch a break and get a later spot, but Carmine said we're going on first."

"Shit."

"You can say that again. This is beginning to feel like a disaster." I tipped back my bottle and shot a weak smile at my brother, Rory, and his boyfriend, Christian, when they approached our table with a fresh round of drinks.

Rory slid a beer in front of me and patted my shoulder before angling his head toward the bar. "Heads up. Your ex is at the bar."

We all turned on cue.

Fuck. Me.

Xena was hard to miss with her trademark long and curly raven hair, ubiquitous Doc Martens, and cherry-red lipstick. She had a way of standing out in a crowd even dressed entirely in black. She married edgy style with innate confidence. Her shoulders were back, her head held high, and her eye was always on the next opportunity. Which definitely wasn't me—we were over and done six months ago. And there was nothing amicable about our split, so I had to wonder why she was here tonight. My luck couldn't be that bad, could it?

"Well, that kind of sucks," I groused, craning my neck to get a better look. She was talking to Carmine and someone in the shadows. "Did she say anything to you?"

"Yeah. She said 'Hi.' It freaked me out," Rory grumbled.

Christian slipped his arm around my brother's waist and kissed his cheek. "Poor baby. I'll protect you. Which one is she?"

"The dragon in black," Tegan replied, narrowing his gaze. "Hey, isn't that—"

"It doesn't matter. We're on first. We can't worry about her," I said.

"You're right. To new beginnings." Rory raised his glass of water. "Break a leg, boys."

I clinked my bottle to theirs and was almost ridiculously grateful when Rory changed the subject to the wicked LA traffic they'd battled to be here on a Wednesday night.

"Hey, we made a *date* of it," Christian teased.

"You're right. A romantic dinner at Chipotle," Rory intercepted.

Christian smacked Rory's bicep playfully, then chuckled when my brother winced and pretended to fall off his barstool. I rolled my eyes at their hijinks, though I appreciated the distraction. Christian and Rory were a cool couple: the football player and the math geek. They'd met when my brother tutored Christian for a statistics class last fall. Christian was a good-looking guy with brown hair, blue eyes, and broad shoulders. Rory was a couple of inches shorter than Christian's six foot four, but his muscular physique, copious tats, and general badass vibe made him seem taller. They looked good together. And happy.

I could almost be jealous. But after the drama of the past few months, I was more than fine with my single status. I had bigger things to worry about. Like how Tegan and I were going to perform without a real guitarist. I bit the inside of my cheek and shot a worried glance at my friend, hoping he had a plan B. Tegan had more band experience than Johnny and I, plus he'd been a member of Gypsy Coma too. He knew Xena well, though not in the same way.

Tegan was an über-masculine gay dude. He was a couple of inches shorter than my six two and built like an inked Mack truck. He had shaggy light-brown hair, green eyes, and a close-shaven beard that mostly hid the jagged scar that ran from the corner of his mouth to the right side of his jaw. I'd witnessed that particular bar fight and could personally attest that the other guy didn't fare nearly as well. Tegan had been a drummer for over a decade, and he was amazing. But he was also a muscular fitness freak who worked as a personal trainer and a bouncer when he wasn't chasing the rock and roll dream with me. Tegan had options and sound instinct.

Me? At twenty-six, I was beginning to feel like I was running out of time. I wanted my shot at the big time more than I cared to admit. And I was dangerous when I got desperate. I made split-second decisions and tended to leap without securing my proverbial safety gear. That was pretty much what was unfolding tonight. I'd agreed that four band members would play, then showed up with two on the night that my ex and—

Oh, no. I felt blood drain from my face so fast, I thought I might pass out.

"You okay?" Tegan asked, pulling me away from the high table.

"No. Declan's here too. This is definitely a setup." I gulped.

Tegan cast a wary glance toward the bar. "I figured. Shake it off, Jus. We got this."

"Do we? Fuck, this isn't good."

"Pull yourself together and take a deep breath. Relax."

I pushed my six-string behind my back and swallowed around the bile in my throat as I nodded. "I'm fine."

"That's the spirit. It's all about the music, man. The rest is just noise and—be cool. She's coming this way," he said before taking a swig of beer.

"Justin. Tegan. How are you?" Xena asked politely.

I gritted my teeth but somehow managed a civil nod. "Good."

"What are you doin' here?" Tegan asked.

"I was invited. Just like you. I bet Carmine is hoping for a round of fireworks...Justin style," she purred with an evil laugh reminiscent of Cat Woman, tossing her long, dark hair over her shoulder. "I'll behave if you do."

"I always behave." I flashed a tight smile that went nowhere near my eyes.

"We all know that's not true, but you might want to tonight. There's an important producer in the audience. Carmine thought it would be fun to show what's left of Gypsy Coma before I perform my new stuff. I wasn't sure it was a good idea, but it might be inspired. Publicity for all of us certainly can't hurt, right?"

"Yeah, right."

"Break a leg." Xena curled her red lips in a faux smile that went nowhere near her eyes, then snapped before adding, "I almost forgot. Declan says hi. We'll see you guys after the show."

I swallowed whatever I was about to say when Carmine stepped between us. Carmine was a skinny, shifty-eyed wisp of a man in his early sixties who used to play guitar in an LA punk band in the eighties. He'd rebranded himself as semi-relevant taste-maker with big Hollywood connections. Unfortunately, I hadn't considered that those connections might work against me when I agreed to this. Carmine loved drama. What could be juicier than an impromptu battle of the bands featuring the dregs of Gypsy Coma?

Carmine rubbed his bony hands gleefully and bumped my shoulder. "No introductions needed here! Xena, hang tight. I want to introduce you to someone. Boys, you're up first. Where's Johnny?"

"In the bathroom," I lied, pulling my guitar in front of me. "Don't worry. We're ready."

"Wonderful," Carmine said before stepping onto the stage to announce me.

I stared after them for a moment, then winced when Tegan pinched me. "*Ouch.*"

"Why did you lie to him?"

"I panicked. This doesn't feel right." I massaged the back of my neck and bit my bottom lip.

"Yeah," Tegan agreed, stroking his jaw thoughtfully. "It doesn't change anything, Jus. It's a distraction, nothing more. We'll get through their set, grab a drink after and—"

"No way. I'm not stickin' around for that."

"You *cannot* leave," he said sternly.

"I'm a big boy, T. I get to do what I want. C'mere." I inched closer to Tegan and spoke low enough for only him to hear above the din.

"What are you up to?" Tegan furrowed his brow before glancing toward the stage.

Carmine was an expert at revving up a small crowd. Any second now, he'd lift his right hand, signaling for the lights to dim and the spotlight to search the room before landing on the upcoming guest. Carmine's brief hello doubled as a means to let whoever was working the booth know who was next. The gimmick smacked of campy late-night TV. It should have seemed ridiculous, but Carmine pulled it off with panache. His goofy eccentricities were part of his charm.

"I have to go on alone."

"Wait. What?" Tegan asked, narrowing his eyes in confusion.

"You heard me. This isn't a chance for us, T. We're the sideshow. Let's be honest, we need Johnny. There's no reason for both of us to look like idiots."

"...and a few members of the funky but now sadly defunct Gypsy Coma. Give it up for Justin, Tegan, and Johnny!"

The spotlight searched the room like a spaceship landing in the desert. The second it found me, I grabbed Tegan's arm and slammed my mouth over his. I cupped the back of his neck, making it difficult to for him to escape, but then softened the connection so I didn't accidentally bite him. See? I'm not a total asshole.

Catcalls and wolf whistles broke through the thundering applause. I caught my brother's confused look when I finally stepped away.

"What the fuck?" Tegan whispered.

"We just gave 'em something to talk about. I'll wing the rest." I held his gaze, wordlessly begging him to trust me; then I pasted a smile on my face and headed for the stage with my acoustic guitar.

Sound came at me through a vacuum. My mind whirled at full speed, stumbling over every injustice I couldn't seem to shake and every stupid thing I'd done over the past six months. I had an unfortunate habit of taking a bad situation and making it ten times worse than it had to be. I overreacted, under-communicated, and tended to piss off anyone who tried to help. Words failed me unless I weaved them into a song.

I mentally blocked out the excess noise and did my best to ignore the eerie sensation that my past was literally closing in on me. I looked down at the strings for a beat and checked my fingers on the fretboard before I began.

"Walking into a quiet room, thinking I still can't hear
Thinking I still don't know the sound of my voice..."

It didn't take long for me to hit my stride. My guitar-playing skills might be suspect, but I didn't need precise notes to guide me. As long as the rhythm was there, I could get into my zone. I sang about lost innocence and disappointment, hopelessness and dreams of redemption. The music had a folksy vibe, but with additional instrumentation, it could fit any genre—rock, blues, country, pop. I'd been told my deep timbre and lilting arrangement sometimes sounded like early Springsteen. It was a nice compliment, but I didn't aspire to copy anyone. I just wanted to write meaningful songs. And I knew this was a good one.

"You can go. You can go. I'm gonna do this my way...."

I sang three songs back-to-back before pausing to thank the audience.

"Um, thanks for listening. You can find me at justincuevas-dot-com. I'm on Instagram and Twitter...when I remember to post. I'll share some info about my new band soon, so um... check it out. I have one more song." I strummed my guitar and gave a somewhat-feral smile. "But this one is from my last band. We used to do it as a head-bangin' rock anthem, but when you sing it acoustically, you can hear the words better. It's called 'Karma.' I'll just leave it at that."

I winked in Xena and Declan's general direction before belting out the lyrics to one of the best songs I'd ever written—in my humble opinion. I swayed as the tempo built and looked for a face in the crowd to focus on, so I didn't lose myself entirely. I avoided the corners and the bar and looked toward the back of the club where Carmine stood under a bar light with two good-looking men. One was tall and lean. The other was... hot, and he seemed vaguely familiar. I didn't think I knew him, but I had a feeling I was supposed to. And at the risk of sounding completely bonkers, it was lust at first sight.

He looked older than me, maybe in his late thirties. Of course, I could have been wrong. But he had the aura of someone who'd been around the block more than once and could tell a few stories of his own. That alone fascinated me. I noted his sharp features: his heavy brow, straight nose, and square, lightly-bearded jaw. He was tall, dark, muscular, and hot as hell in a well-cut suit coat and jeans. A cross between a businessman and a badass motorcycle man. *Sweet Jesus.*

I fought the sudden urge to stop midnumber, hop off the stage, and strike up a conversation with him. I was in the middle of a gig here. Sure, it was a crappy one meant to exploit my fledgling band and publicize my ex's new one, but I wasn't going to give anyone the satisfaction of losing control of my emotions and blowing it. As long as the stranger stayed right there, I had someone to sing to who didn't want more than I could give. He seemed interested, and that was enough.

I wrapped up the song with a guitar-hero flourish and raised my arms in the air to soak up the applause. Then I hopped off the stage and exchanged high fives with my brother, Christian, and Tegan.

"You were awesome, man. Rock god in the making," Tegan gushed. "I can't wait to see how Xena tops that."

I huffed derisively and pushed my guitar at him. "Hey, will you take this?"

"Where are you going?"

"I need some fresh air."

Tegan yanked my T-shirt and scowled. "Don't start something with Dec. He's not worth it, Jus."

I held my friend's gaze for a moment, then squeezed my brother's shoulder and waved to Christian before heading to the exit. I bumped fists and soaked in a few compliments of the "great job, man" variety as I weaved my way through the press of bodies. When I reached the main door, I paused to look for the man I'd had eye sex with during my last song. I spotted his friend at the bar, talking to a few patrons, including Xena. I wondered if he was someone important as I sidestepped a drunken couple entering the club and immediately bumped into Declan McNamara...my archnemesis.

So here's the thing about Dec....He was a world-class snake. The kind that lured you in with a killer smile, a great sense of humor, and a sexy body. I wasn't proud to admit it, but I'd fallen for his act. One minute we were laughing over a beer or ten—the next, I was sucking his dick. For the record, it was a big deal because I hadn't sucked anyone's dick in years. I liked it better than I remembered, and I was good at it. We were never going to be more than an occasional booty call, but we eventually became friends. Until he fucked me over. Big-time. It was a shame that all Dec's charisma and rock-star model looks, complete with long hair and a wardrobe that consisted mainly of ripped jeans and snug-fitted T-shirts, had been wasted on a not-so-awesome human.

"Justin. Hey, do you have a sec?" he asked, pushing a strand of his long, brown hair behind his right ear.

"Nope. See ya," I said maturely before slipping through the open door.

The blast of fresh air felt amazing. I sucked in a cleansing breath and got a lungful of secondhand smoke with it. A group of twentysomethings huddled under the eaves veiled in a cloud of e-cigarette exhaust. Their retro-punk look was kinda badass but they smelled like a bunch of fucking Strawberry Shortcakes. I rubbed my arms against the mid-January chill and stepped to the left to avoid the contact sugar high. And Declan.

"Hang on!"

I rounded on him as I stepped under the eaves. "I have nothing to say to you."

"Come on, Jus. It doesn't have to be like this. We were friends and—"

"And now we're not."

"Christ!" He rubbed his scruffy jaw absently, then held up his hands. "I'm sorry. But I really wish you'd move past this and—"

"Fuck you!" I shoved him hard. A few heads turned when he stumbled backward. I braced myself for attack, knowing he was more than capable of kicking my ass. Declan was built like a swimmer, with broad shoulders and a tapered waist. He was lean like me, but strong as hell. However, my surge of anger gave me a momentary advantage. I moved into his space and stabbed my forefinger on his chest. "You did your best to make me look like a fool once. It's not happening again. I don't know what you and Xena are up to here but—"

"Same thing as you, you fuckin' hothead. We want a break." His voice softened when he continued. "There's opportunity here, Jus. And there's room for more than one band. You were great up there, and those songs were amazing. Are they new?"

I furrowed my brow so hard, it gave me a headache. "What part of 'I don't want to talk to you again' did you not understand?"

"Fine. I get it. But I think we could help each other out. We could—"

"Am I the only one hearing this bullshit?" I yelled, raising my hands in the air. "This guy has the gall to screw me...literally, and then—"

"Shut the fuck up," he growled.

I gritted my teeth and glared at Dec. When the heated standoff went on for a beat too long, I glanced away and spotted the sexy older man from inside the club. He stood under a lamp-light, smoking a cigarette and observing me nonchalantly. The way you might a child throwing a tantrum on an airplane, with a measure of sympathy and annoyance.

I caught his stare and something in me went a little wonky. It was the best explanation I had for my bout of madness. I pointed at the stranger before jumping sideways toward him, while shooting a manic look at Dec. "Look, we're done here. If I don't kick your ass, my boyfriend will. Won't you, babe?"

The stranger lifted his brow and shrugged before replying in a deep, sexy voice. "I guess I'll have to."

"See? It won't end well. So, let's not pretend we're friends, Dec. Let's not pretend we ever will be. I'm nothing to you, and you should know the feeling is mutual."

"Listen to me, Jus—"

Xena stuck her head out the door just then and called for Declan. "We're on. Let's go."

Dec nodded before turning to me. "Come inside. We can talk after our set."

"No."

He growled angrily. "Fuck, you're stubborn. Remember tonight 'cause you're gonna need me someday, Justin. And you're gonna be very fucking sorry you didn't pay attention," he snarled before finally moving away.

I balled my hand into a fist and pulled my arm back. But before I could punch the wall like a real dumbass, the stranger called out, "Boyfriend. Cool it."

I jerked around and froze as if I'd been slapped. I raced through a series of breathing exercises and swallowed hard before moving toward the man under the lamplight. I paused a few feet away and stuffed my hands into my pockets. Damn, he was even more handsome up close. And a little intimidating.

"You're still here," I said lamely.

The stranger turned to me with a slow-growing smile that lifted one corner of his mouth. And fuck, I was right. He was hot.

"Well, I thought you might need someone to rescue you."

"Yeah. No, um..."

"Yes *and* no?" he teased.

"No. I'm fine. I just—can I bum one of those?" I asked, gesturing to the cigarette in his hand.

He nodded, then reached into his pocket. He slid one from the package and lit the end from his cigarette before handing it to me. I found myself watching his every movement—the bend of his head and the flick of his wrist. There was something old-fashioned and intimate in the ritual that made me think of black-and-white movies where a shared smoke and a drink were the ultimate icebreakers.

Truthfully, I didn't know why I asked. I didn't smoke. But I needed something to do with my hands. Adrenaline coursed through my veins, making it harder than normal to stand still. Between my solo gig and my run-in with Dec, my brain buzzed ominously. I wondered if I'd forgotten to take my meds.

"You okay?" the stranger asked.

I blew out a stream of smoke and nodded. "Yeah. Thanks. He's not my favorite person. No big deal."

The man studied me for a long moment. He made me nervous. The air around him seemed to crackle with electricity. Or maybe that was the switchboard in my cranium firing on all cylinders at once, because he wasn't really doing anything. He just stood there looking so...self-assured, put together and calm. Like a buoy in a storm.

"You done for the night, Boyfriend?" he asked conversationally.

I chuckled softly. "Yeah. Thanks for embracing your role."

"Anytime. You were good in there," he said, inclining his head toward the club.

"Thanks. I was."

The deep timbre of his laughter moved through me, warming me from within. "Modesty's overrated."

"It was four measly songs at a dive bar. Nothing to get excited about."

"Original material?" he asked.

"Yeah."

"Hmm."

We were silent for a moment. I watched the tendrils of smoke cross his features as he exhaled. He looked mysterious, like a detective or someone who knew things. The deceptively cool type who thrived under stress or—

"Are you a producer?" I blurted.

"No. Are you looking for one?"

"Fuck, no." I leaned my arm against the chipped stucco and gave him a thoughtful once-over. He was built like a football player, but he had the eyes of a poet. There was something earnest in his gaze that made me think he was taking internal notes. The way I sometimes did, but with a less manic edge. "I know I should say the exact opposite, but I'm not exactly ready for that stage in the game. I need a few other things first...like a bassist. Oh yeah, and a manager to take the reins from me before I sail this ship into an iceberg."

His eyes twinkled. "You're not dramatic much, are you?"

I huffed. "Unfortunately, it's all true."

"So you're in a band?"

"We're trying. It's safer to say I'm in between bands at the moment," I corrected.

"That's right. Gypsy Coma. What's your name again?"

"It doesn't matter," I sighed, feeling suddenly defeated. "That's not who I am anymore. I'm starting over."

"Without a name?"

"Yeah. Anonymous." I cocked my head. "What about you?"

"I'm not tellin'. I don't want a name either," he quipped.

I snickered. "Sounds fair. I'll call you Boyfriend or...Blue."

"Blue?"

"Yeah. You have pretty eyes." I winced. "Wow. I can't believe I said that out loud. I'm not flirting with you. I just—"

"Was that your ex-boyfriend?" he intercepted.

"No. He's my ex-girlfriend's new guitarist. Maybe they're together, but nah, I doubt it. They both need the spotlight. Sharing a stage for an hour or two is one thing. They'd never manage it in real life too." I waved impatiently. "Whatever. I don't want to talk about them. I'd rather hear about you. What do you do for a living? Or is that top secret?"

He blew a plume of smoke in the air and smiled. "I'm a writer."

"An author, a journalist, a blogger or...what? There're a million kinds of writers."

"True. I do a little bit of everything, but mostly in music. I'm good at jingles and hooks," he said with a wink.

"So are we talkin' commercial jingles or pop songs?"

"Like I said, a little of everything. Have you heard the Mason Hardware commercial on the radio?"

"Really? 'Mason's hardware helpers walk the aisle to make sure you leave with a smile...' That one?" When he inclined his head in acquiescence, I chuckled. "Wow. That's cheesy."

"What can I say? Velveeta pays the bills. What about you?"

"I'm a bartender. And a barista too. I like the coffee shop gig better, but it doesn't pay as well. I'm looking for something new."

"Can you tell me where? Or is that ambiguity infringement?"

"Ambiguity infringement," I repeated. "I oughtta write that down. Do I have to give you credit, or can I steal it?"

"It's yours," he said, turning so we faced each other.

The casual maneuver brought him fully into the light. Fuck, he was hot. And his eyes were gorgeous. I wanted to trace the lines at the corners but not smooth them out. They added character and hinted at untold stories. The tingle of awareness I'd felt when I first saw him in the bar was stronger than ever.

"Where do I work, or where do I want to work?"

"Yes. Tell me everything. This session is free."

I threw my head back, laughed, and felt my shoulders relax as some of the pent-up tension left my body. "Thanks. I'd take a part-time job almost anywhere except a gym or an office."

"Okay, I'll bite. What's wrong with a gym?" he asked, clearly amused.

I noticed his smartwatch light up and then vibrate like a cell phone. Someone wanted his attention, and I loved that he gave it to me instead. Any second now, our friends would come looking for us, and the real world would interfere. I wanted to keep him to myself for as long as possible.

"People exercise in gyms. And then they gloat about it," I scoffed. "I practically grew up at my local YMCA. I know what I'm talking about."

"I'm sure you do. But some people actually like to exercise... You know, for general health and well-being purposes." He chuckled when I rolled my eyes. "All right. I won't try to convert you. Where *do* you work?"

"I pour coffee at Aromatique and—"

"I haven't been there in a while, but I like that place."

"Me too. And...I bartend at Vibes." I paused for his reaction. A facial tic or a nod or something to indicate he knew it was a gay club. He looked seriously straight, but I hoped he was seriously bi. Not that it mattered—nothing was happening here. "Have you been?"

"No. Is it on Santa Monica?"

"Yeah." *Bingo.* I was right.

"Next to the new ice cream place," he continued. "I waited ten minutes in line for a scoop of designer mint chip."

Okay. Maybe not, I mused as my gaydar flipped back to neutral. Everybody liked ice cream. I couldn't work with that. And suddenly, it seemed like something I needed to know. I could have just asked, but he wasn't a random dude at the club. He had an air of sophistication and polish that demanded respect. Like a college professor or the sexy boss you secretly lust after even though you know you're out of your league. I had numerous fantasies of the high-powered executive, lowly employee variety all the time. The kind that usually involved staying late to work on a secret project...over a desk, on a conference table, in an elevator. Neckties and shirts undone, suit pants unzipped or lowered just enough to get his thick cock out and—

Oops. Now I'm hard.

I straightened from the wall and pretended to take one last drag from the cigarette before putting it out on the trashcan next to the parking kiosk. Then I clandestinely adjusted myself and rejoined him.

"Scoops is always packed. Even in winter," I said conversationally.

"True. I don't usually have the patience to wait, but I was with an eight-year-old at the time. It's amazing how cooperative that monkey can be when there's ice cream involved," he commented affectionately.

Talk about an erection killer. My X-rated daydream came to a screeching halt, quickly replaced by visions of a soccer-dad lifestyle complete with a house in the burbs, a hybrid SUV, three kids, two dogs, and a beautiful wife.

"You have three kids?" I asked, unable to keep the irritation from my voice.

"Three kids?" he repeated incredulously.

"Well, you said something about getting ice cream with your son and—"

"Nice try. I never said I had a son."

"Gee, I could have sworn you mentioned your wife and kids and...whatsa matter? Is this anonymity infringement?" I teased.

"The term was ambiguity infringement, smartass," he huffed without heat, turning to dispose of his cigarette. "And I was talking about my godson."

"My bad." I rubbed my arms and shot a faux-innocent smile at him. "I didn't mean to get too personal."

"Yeah, you did." He stepped in front of me, closer than he'd been before. "I'm single."

"Good to know," I said.

"What about the guy you kissed before you went onstage?"

I winced. "I probably shouldn't have done that. We're just friends. Tegan's our drummer. He was going to play bass tonight, but—*ugh*. I don't want to think about the mess I got us into. Let's talk ice cream. What's your favorite flavor?"

"I love it all."

I rolled my eyes. "Oh, please. Name two."

"Mint chip and chocolate."

"Good choices. I like chocolate chip and chocolate. But I like the basic real stuff. Not designer brands that claim to have fewer calories in fancy containers. I don't eat much of it, though. Ice cream is a luxury item."

He looked at me like I was an alien. "Ice cream is essential," he deadpanned.

I snickered as I folded my arms across my chest to ward off the chill when the wind whistled along the sidewalk. "When you're on a tight budget, it's a n-nice to have, not a need to h-have."

"Hmph. It's cold out here. Do you want to go back inside?"

"No," I replied quickly.

"Me either."

We stared at each other for a long moment, letting traffic and pieces of nearby conversation filter between us.

"If your friend is looking for you, maybe you should—"

"He's not," he replied quickly. "What about you?"

"My people know I'm weird. They probably figure I won't stick around."

His lips quirked in amusement. "Then come have a drink with me."

"Now?"

"Yeah. Why not?"

I grinned. The casual invitation delivered with the perfect note of nonchalance was hard to resist. "All right."

With a heightened sense of awareness, I watched him move to the valet kiosk and hand the attendant a ticket. Maybe this was crazy. Then again, that was all the more reason to follow him. 'Cause in my book, crazy was another name for adventure.

Of course, when his Porsche pulled up a few minutes later, I had second thoughts. He could be a psycho. Or a stalker. No, I wasn't stalker-worthy yet. Thankfully, curiosity kicked in before I could overthink. Wealthy older people who slummed it at dive bars usually came with a backstory. They liked places that reminded them of simpler times when being cool meant shredding their hand-me-down jeans and using lipstick for face paint. Now they found themselves following fashion trends from people half their age who paid big bucks for jeans with holes already in them. A night at a dive bar was like a temporary time machine for those who wanted to forget they had mortgages, car payments, and jobs with benefits to deal with in the morning. None of those were bad things, but they were so damn...adult.

Real adult. Not fake adult like me. My driver's license claimed I'd been a legal adult for eight years. Most days, I wasn't so sure. But the man whizzing down Sunset Boulevard knew exactly who he was. And what he liked.

I twisted in my seat and gestured toward the dashboard. "Your Silent Face" by New Order lit up the screen and a moment later, a synthesized violin track blasted through the stereo. "I haven't heard this song in forever."

"You like it?"

"Yeah. I grew up listening to this stuff. My mom was a teenager in the eighties. She liked seventies rock too. Led Zeppelin, the Stones, David Bowie. But New Wave British bands were her favorite. The Cure, Duran Duran, Depeche Mode. She liked some weird ones too, like Altered Images. Their 'Happy Birthday' was our official birthday song when we were kids. She would blast it first thing in the morning. Rory freaking loved it," I said with a laugh.

"Ha. I loved that song too. Your mom sounds cool."

"She used to be," I said, facing forward. "She's judgmental and unhappy now. She wasn't like that when we were kids. Life got to her. I don't know when exactly; it must have been a gradual thing. She was a kickass single mom. She didn't need or want my dad's help and when Rory's dad left, she seemed sad but still strong, you know? She masked her pain with alcohol, put a smile on her face, and did what needed to be done. When her drinking became an issue, she gave it up and found God. I'd be all for it if she was happy, but she's not. She won't let herself enjoy any of the things she loved when she was younger. It's like she's punishing herself and us, by association."

"Rory is your brother?"

"Yeah. He was there tonight with his boyfriend," I said.

"He's gay?"

"Bi. Like me. And I'm assuming you too. Or am I misreading this? I probably should have asked that before I jumped into your very fast car. Dude, feel free to drive within twenty miles of the speed limit," I chided as he whizzed around a slower-moving vehicle on Sunset.

He slowed behind a Prius at a traffic signal and turned to me with a cocky grin. "Yes, I'm bi. And we're just having a drink. I think you're hot as fuck, but I promise, I have no hidden agenda. I'm not trying to shake all your secrets out of you."

"Too bad," I sighed. "I'm easily shook. As you can tell, I don't do 'under the radar' well. I should probably just give you my social security number and the password for my bank account now. There's nothing in there so don't get excited, but still...I've compromised my anonymity, big-time. Remind me not to apply for a job with the CIA."

He chuckled. "You got it."

"Don't tell me your name or anything crazy like that, Boyfriend, but you should probably tell me something to even this out."

"I told you the name of the commercial jingle I wrote. You could always google it and—"

"That's research. Not happening," I huffed.

"Too much work?"

"Too annoying. You know my brother's name and that my mom is miserable and that I know the words to more eighties songs than I should admit. Fess up. It's only fair."

"Okay..." He pulled into the driveway of a posh boutique hotel on Sunset and parked behind a Tesla near the modern-looking entry. Then he unfastened his seat belt and glanced up at the valet rounding the front of his car before refocusing on me. "My favorite color is blue, I'm an only child, my parents both died five years ago within a month of each other and...I'm going commando right now. How 'bout that drink?"

I gaped at him with wide-eyed surprise before fumbling with my seat belt. I flashed a phony smile at the valet and hurried to catch up to my companion. He strode purposefully through the stark-white minimalist lobby to the elevator, signaling a bellman standing nearby. The young man jumped to attention.

"Top floor, sir?"

Apparently, the question was rhetorical. He swiped a card over the sensor and wished us a good evening as he held the sliding doors open.

I glanced at our reflection in the mirrored interior. We looked good together in the way contrasting people and things sometimes did. Other than our heights being similar, we were opposites—from our styles of dress to our ages and levels of self-confidence. I was confident for sure, but there were places I felt more at home than others. Boyfriend had the look of someone who belonged everywhere and anywhere he wanted to be.

Me? I wasn't sure I belonged anywhere in particular. The feeling was alternately freeing or lonely as fuck. It was kind of nice to be with someone who could navigate a dive bar and a swanky hotel bar with the right amount of swagger.

He flashed a wolfish grin in the mirror, then stepped forward and held the door open when we reached our destination. "This way."

2

GRAY

Justin followed me through a dimly lit corridor into the Skybar, one of my favorite spots in the city. I might not be a regular, but I came often enough with Sebastian that some of the staff knew me by sight. I could do without the LA glam crowd, but I loved the ambience. The space had a dark and sexy feel. The modern-style sofas and white leather ottomans anchoring the middle of the room were designed not to detract from the impressive skyline view visible through the massive wall of windows beyond the glass-and-steel bar. Outdoor heaters dotted the lounge area on the patio around the blue-lit pool. A few nights a week, famous deejays played hits for the elite crowd who danced under fairy lights well into the early morning hours—thankfully, not on Wednesdays. Tonight, a jazz quartet played a haunting melody from a raised dais in the corner.

Beautiful people posed like models in a fashion spread. Handsome men with artfully mussed hair and one too many buttons undone on their designer shirts chatted with gorgeous women who shared a similar look...model-thin with tight, short skirts and perfect curls in their well-coiffed, long hair. The uniformity was a tad off-putting, if you asked me, but it seemed to be the current style. And fuck knew, I was no expert when it came to fashion. I relied on my godson to keep me from pairing stripes and plaids. According to Charlie, that was a no-no. But I wasn't interested in impressing anyone. I was here to—

I had no idea what the fuck I was doing. None.

I gave Justin a quick once-over and gestured lamely toward the bar.

"What do you want to drink?" I asked.

"Uh...gin and tonic, please. Do you want me to grab a seat somewhere? It's kinda crowded."

"Sure. Or we can go outside."

"Dude, it's fuckin' freezing," he huffed.

I chuckled. "Okay, then find a seat for us."

Justin gave me a thumbs-up before wandering toward the band while I placed our order. I cautioned myself to not to stare at his ass in those tight jeans or admire his gorgeous ink or stunning profile. Damn, he was sexy. And I wasn't the only one who noticed. Men and women shot clandestine glances at the good-looking Latino standing to the side with his arms crossed, bopping his head to the beat. If I read his body language correctly, I'd guess he was uncomfortable but interested. Like he wasn't sure what he was doing, but he didn't mind. I felt the same way.

It wasn't like me to invite a stranger for a drink and whisk him to an exclusive bar in the sky to show him a different side of the city just for fun. Honestly, I didn't really like people that much. But from the moment Justin stepped onstage at Carmine's, I'd been intrigued.

He was a bundle of every contradiction known to man. Nervous and awkward, then cocky and self-righteous. And something magical happened when he smiled at the crowd and promised to sing a song they wouldn't forget. His guitar-playing was weak at best, but he had star power. He didn't have room to jump around and ignite the masses with over-the-top charismatic displays. He'd relied on his words and his passionate vocals. And damn, had he delivered. I was impressed. Hell, Sebastian was impressed. I sent my friend a quick text before slipping my cell back into my pocket and plotting my exit strategy.

One drink and then I'd call a taxi for Justin. I didn't want to take him home because I didn't want to know where he lived, and I certainly didn't want him to know where I lived. This was only okay if we knew as little about each other as possible. I didn't want to be Justin's champion or mentor or the guy who might introduce him to a bigger name. I wanted the anonymity he'd suggested earlier, and I wanted to give him his too.

Of course, I had an advantage. I knew who he was, and thanks to Carmine and Seb, I'd heard about the scandal with the ex and the drummer. Honestly, the whole story confused me. He seemed to be friendly with the drummer, but he hated the guitarist from the other band. Not that it mattered. I didn't care about the gossip surrounding him. I was interested in him. And for an hour or so, we could just be two guys who might be mildly attracted to each other but weren't going to do anything about it. Except have a cocktail.

"Here you go."

Justin smiled and thanked me. "These guys are good. They should be playing where they're appreciated. No one's paying any attention here."

"When you love what you do, you play wherever you can. Isn't that why you were at Carmine's tonight?" I asked.

"I guess," he replied before looking around the bar area. "Every seat is taken unless one of us is willing to hang a cheek off the edge of the sofa over there."

I shook my head. "Let's go outside. There are plenty of space heaters. You'll be fine."

Giant sliding doors opened onto the rooftop deck. It was blessedly quiet outside. No deejay in the middle of the week in January. No raucous crowds. Our only company was a small group huddled under a canopy on the other side of the pool. And they were far enough away that we couldn't overhear their conversation. I chose two comfy-looking lounge chairs near the glass and steel balcony under a portable heater. Our chairs faced the view and made it feel like it was just us, high above the city of angels.

"This is beautiful. So many lights." Justin flopped gracelessly onto one of the chairs and sipped his drink. "Good G and T too. The bartender in me is very particular about these things."

"That makes sense." I set my drink on a side table and sat on the chair next to his, under a space heater. "Do you want to switch, Jus—"

He snickered at my contrite grimace. "You don't have to avoid my name. I know you know it. In spite of my best intentions, I'm pretty much an open book. It's a curse. What else did you want to know?"

Talk about a loaded question. But I'd made a mental agreement allowing myself an hour with him, so I figured I should stick to professional inquiries. "Are you planning on going solo?"

My question seemed to surprise him. He shook his head vehemently. "No way. I need musicians who're better than me to back me up. Tegan's the best drummer out there, and Johnny's awesome on electric guitar. We've been playing dumps and dive bars for a few months now under JTJ when we can get friends to fill in on bass."

"JTJ?"

"Our initials. Once we lock down a full-time bassist, we can get more official. Waiting around for the stars to align has been frustrating. At first it was necessary because of all the fucking drama with Xena and Dec and...whatever. I hoped the invitation from Carmine tonight was a sign we'd all moved on. Sadly, I don't think that's the case. The truth is, I forced a situation because I wanted a chance. We were so unprepared, it wasn't funny. Tegan's a great drummer but a wonky bassist. We needed Johnny." He sighed heavily and jumped to his feet.

"Where was he?" I asked, joining him at the balcony.

"Work. He's a barista with me at Aromatique and works as a waiter in the evenings. We all have two jobs. Tegan and I both work at Vibes. Miraculously, we were able to get the night off together. Our boss-slash-Tegan's boyfriend makes sure that never happens. That must have been quite a blowjob," he huffed, looking out at the view. Before I could ask any probing questions, he turned back to me. "What about you? Were you ever in a band?"

"No."

"Do you play an instrument? You must. Songwriters usually play something."

"Piano and guitar."

"You any good?"

"I've been told I'm not bad." I smiled. "What about you?"

"Guitar only and I've been told I suck," he countered with a self-deprecating shrug.

I chuckled appreciatively. "I like your style. Your lyrics were poignant and fresh, with a perfect amount of relatable angst. The relatable part is important. A lot of songwriters regurgitate crap they hear about on the news or on social media."

"You're right. So many people want to sound woke. It's just a sales ploy."

" 'Woke'? What does that mean?"

"You really don't know?" he asked in surprise.

"I'm older than you. That doesn't mean I'm smarter."

"It means attuned to social injustice. Alert to what's happening around you. It's how I try to write. Sometimes emotional crap gets in the way, but words are therapy."

"Wise. The key is to draw from your own experiences. At least, it works for me sometimes. Who are your influences?"

Justin furrowed his brow and then grinned. The transformation was breathtaking, even in profile. "It's all over the map. Kendrick Lamar, Bob Dylan, Joni Mitchell. I like lyrics that paint a picture and use clever turns of phrase. I want to make people feel what I feel...but in a way that makes sense to them."

"Relatable."

"Exactly." He bumped his fist on the railing and shot a feverish glance my way before gesturing toward the glittering city below. "I don't want to write about bright lights and phony love stories. I want to know the people in those houses. The regular folks just trying to get by, not the ones taking selfies next to Porsches who hang out in sky bars. No offense."

I barked a laugh. "I'm regular."

"I'm not talking about your bowel movements," he snarked. "Hey, don't get me wrong. This is nice, but...the city lights from a fancy hotel...it's not real."

"Sure it is. It's a perspective from above. Sometimes I can imagine flying close enough to see and hear what's happening behind closed doors."

"Like a peeping Tom."

I smirked. "Something like that. Minus the creepy connotation."

"Hmm. I'm the opposite. I want to be on the street. I want to be part of the story, not just the guy recording it. I'm not exactly a success story, though. Maybe I should think about changing my approach," he huffed with a laugh.

"Okay, let's try something." I pointed toward the hillside.

"Check out that house. The one with the telescope in the window. See it?"

"Yeah."

"What's the first thing that pops into your mind?"

"I wonder if they have a dog," he replied.

"Really?" I asked incredulously. "You just said you wanted to be part of the story. Don't you wonder about who lives there, what they do, and if they're happy or sad or if they're lonely as fuck?"

He squinted in the distance, then shook his head slowly and bent to pick up his drink. "Nope. Don't care. Right now I'm worried about the dog."

"They might not have a dog," I countered.

"If they do, I hope it's small and doesn't need a ton of exercise. Look at that fucking driveway. It would be hell to take a big dog on a walk up those hills too, but I'm guessing people do it and—why are you looking at me like that?"

"You're either very odd or this is a not-so-subtle way of changing the subject."

Justin raised his glass in a toast and grinned. "Both. If we talk about music and songwriting, I'm gonna want to know more about you, and that might ruin tonight. I like the mystery. Let's keep it shallow."

I chuckled. "Okay. Do you have a dog?"

"No. I can't for now, but you should get one."

"I'm not getting a dog," I deadpanned.

"What kind? Big dog, little dog? Purebred, mutt? C'mon. I can help you with this. Don't be shy. We're just spitballin' here."

"Um, okay...well, I'd probably get a wirehaired pointing griffon," I replied matter-of-factly.

Justin widened his eyes. "What the fuck is that?"

I threw my head back and guffawed at his comedic expression. "I don't know. I was watching the *Westminster Dog Show* a couple of months ago, and the name stuck with me. He was probably some goofy-looking guy who was doing exactly the opposite of what he was supposed to be doing. That seems like the kind of dog I'd end up with. I'd say 'Chester, come,' and he'd either give me a bored 'whatever, man' look or run down the hill chasing cars."

"So we're naming him Chester, eh?" he asked. "I like him already. Sounds like me."

"A pain in the ass?"

"Occasionally...yes. Depends on who you ask."

I cocked my head curiously. "Are you saying you're attracted to uncooperative types or that you are one?"

"Both. I'm attracted to people who are a little out there, you know what I mean? People who aren't afraid to look silly or take chances." He flopped back onto the chair and motioned for me to sit. Then he leaned over the armrest and absently brushed his hand against mine. "But not completely insane and ideally, not malicious."

"Your bar is a little low."

Justin snickered and then took a sip. "I don't really have a bar. I'm terrible at relationships. I could never write a believable love song."

"Sure you could. You just pretend you're writing about ice cream or Chester and let your feelings go."

"But that's fake and contrived. I'd rather write about things everyone can relate to, like isolation, frustration, loneliness."

"That sounds bleak," I commented. "Don't you think people need songs about hope, friendship, romance, love?"

He scoffed. "Friendship and hope...sure. But romance and love are bullshit."

"What's wrong with romance?" I hiked my knee on the cushion to get a better look at him. His expressive facial features fascinated me. He was scornful, then thoughtful, and always passionate.

"Romance is the perceived gateway to love. It's a front. You can woo someone with flowers, nice dinners, return text messages in a timely manner, and pay extra attention to their boring-ass stories, but let's be real...you do it for sex," he proclaimed.

"Me?" I pointed at my chest and gave him an innocent look.

"Yeah, you. And me. And every single person in this bar and the one we just left. We all want something. 'Everybody's in it for their own gain.' " He jumped to his feet again and snapped his fingers. "That's a line from a Joni Mitchell song, by the way."

" 'Free Man in Paris,' " I said automatically, impressed that someone his age knew Joni Mitchell well enough to quote lyrics from a relatively obscure song.

"Yeah. That's it. And it's true. We do this casual exchange of emotional currency all the damn time without thinking twice. Tell me I'm special, I'll give you a blowjob. That kind of thing. Maybe there's real affection involved, but if channels of reciproca-tion and communication fail, you're fucked. Not in a good way."

"You are very cynical for a guy who hasn't hit thirty yet."

"I'm realistic. My brother and his boyfriend are the only exception I've seen lately. And I can't even tell you what makes them different. It's not flowery bullshit like romance or love. It's something more elusive, like the right balance of respect, affec-tion, friendship...and still wanting to fuck whenever they can."

I barked a quick laugh, then stood to join him at the railing. "Cynical *and* eloquent. I should be writing this down."

Justin shrugged nonchalantly. "Go ahead. It's the truth. I've never had that before. Definitely not with Xena. We were a series of gives and takes. That sounds okay, but mental and physical bartering without respect wears thin after a while. We broke up six months ago, and it still feels like a chess game. I just don't want to play anymore. With anyone."

"What *do* you want to do?"

"Start over," he said in a low tone. He pointed meaningfully toward the sparkling city lights and continued. "You can do anything in LA. This city is so diverse. It's a little phony sometimes, but the truth is there...if you're brave enough to look for it. You won't find it hanging out at the Grove or Universal Studios or hiking Runyon Canyon or—"

"Slow down. What's wrong with Runyon Canyon?"

"Nothing. It just reminds me of my dad. When I was a kid, my dad went through a brief phase where he decided he wanted to get to know me. I was eight, so Rory would have been six. The timing was kind of brutal because Rory's dad had just left...as in, we woke up one morning and his shit was gone. We never saw him again. Anyway, I rarely saw my bio dad. Even when he picked me up to hang out, he'd end up dropping me off at my grandmother's house. Which I didn't mind. She only spoke Spanish, and she was an amazing cook."

I chuckled at his dreamy expression. "What does that have to do with Runyon Canyon?"

"Nothing. Or maybe everything. See, when he said he was taking me to Dairy Queen, I knew what to expect. Ice cream and then a day of speaking Spanish with my grandmother and eating tamales until my stomach hurt. But a real hiking trip with Dad? That was special." Justin snorted derisively. "I should have known better. The entire trip was a disaster. No one spoke on the drive from Long Beach to LA. Mom had tears in her eyes and Rory looked upset, like he was afraid I was leaving for good too. By the time we got there, I wasn't excited anymore. My mom must have noticed I was upset, 'cause she smiled and said, 'Don't worry. He's trying to do the right thing.' Except he wasn't. He showed up late with his new girlfriend and her son."

"Oh."

"Yeah, oh," I repeated derisively. "I sat in the back seat of his crappy Chevy, staring out the dirty window and tried to believe in his alternate reality for a few minutes. I thought maybe I could pretend we were a regular family...a dad, a mom, and two boys who shared the same skin color and spoke two languages. It was a nice fantasy, but something wasn't right. At eight, I couldn't quite put my feelings into words. I just knew the whole thing was a setup. I was a prop. My dad was using me to piss off my mom and woo a pretty girl with a single-dad sob story. It made me miss my real brother, the blond kid with blue eyes back home in Long Beach.

"That was the first time I remember being aware of the lies so-called grownups tell each other. The fake smiles, pretty words, empty promises. As a species, humans are hypocritical assholes. We give away pieces of ourselves every day...for recognition, for money, for affection." Justin turned to me with a fiery expression and gestured toward the glittering lights below. "Everyone here wants more than what they have. And I guess I'm the same. I don't need recognition and I sure as fuck don't want love, but I wouldn't say no to a few bucks," he commented with a laugh. "What about you?"

I did a double take. I was two steps behind, struggling to keep up and if possible, memorize every word he'd said. I hadn't been around anyone so raw or so honest in a long time. Justin made rules and broke them at whim, letting me in and then shutting me out. He had a way of revealing himself that made me feel as though he was holding a mirror to me, daring me to acknowledge my broken pieces too. He was either slightly insane or incredibly gifted. I suspected it was the latter. The cadence of his speech lured me in...and made me want more. I'd tell him anything he wanted to know, just to be near him and this intense spark of...newness, creativity, and wonder.

"What about me?" I asked in a low, raspy voice.

"What do you want?"

"Nothing."

"Liar," he said without heat. "Try again."

"Okay. I want everything that you just said was bullshit. Romance, love, a little recognition and...I want to write the perfect song," I replied.

"There's no such thing."

"Maybe, maybe not. But it would be nice to leave something that felt special."

Justin held my gaze, then inclined his head in agreement. "Yeah. I want that too."

We stared at each other as whispers of conversation floated from the far corners of the rooftop deck. We weren't alone, but we might as well be. I couldn't remember ever feeling intimately connected to someone I'd never really touched. It was puzzling and enchanting at the same time.

He shivered when the breeze kicked up. I took it as a sign from above and pulled him against me. I had to touch him. I studied the sexy indentation in his bottom lip before giving in to impulse and resting my hands on his hips. He gave me a funny look but didn't push me away.

"You shouldn't be anonymous. You have too much to share. Too much to say."

"I do. I don't know if it's all wise or good, but I have a firestorm in my head some days, and I can't get the words out fast enough."

"There's no hurry. Remind yourself to take it slow. The real music is in between the notes and the words," I said.

Justin snaked his arms around my waist and stared out at the city lights below.

We were still for a while. The lingering quiet was deceptive. A casual observer might have mistaken us for old lovers engaged in a tender moment. Or maybe they'd guess we were tentative strangers anxious to make the right moves. Not too fast, not too slow. Neither was correct; there was no quiet here. An electric current sizzled and hissed between us. Intense sexual awareness and something more. Something fiery and passionate that had nothing to do with pretty words or music. He was wild and rough with jagged edges and a sharp mind. And he was so close now, I could feel his breath on my lips when he turned to face me.

"I want to kiss you," I whispered, inching closer so our noses brushed.

Justin gave me a crooked smile and tugged at my belt loop. "Then do it."

I stuck my tongue out and licked his bottom lip from one corner of his mouth to the other, then gently pressed my lips to his. He was deceptively tender at first. He closed his eyes and hummed into the connection. When I tilted my head, he let me in without hesitation. I couldn't get enough. He tasted like gin and nicotine with a hint of peppermint. I pulled him against me, cupping the back of his neck, to kiss him harder and deeper. Our tongues twisted in a growing frenzy until everything and everyone around us dissolved into white noise. Justin lulled me into complacency and let me think I was in control. But when the unexpected sweetness threatened to pull me in, he held my face between his hands and drove his tongue into my mouth.

At first I was too surprised to do more than hang on, but the slide of his obvious hard-on against mine in steady rhythm with his hungry kisses spurred me into action. I angled my head to deepen the kiss as I raked my fingers down his back. Our feverish make-out session wasn't sustainable. The moment we broke apart for air, I knew I had to come up with an alternate plan. We weren't exactly in the middle of a crowded room, but we were still in public. And while Justin didn't seem like the type to care about getting arrested for public indecency, I couldn't risk it.

I broke for air and wrapped my fingers around his neck to keep him in place when he leaned forward to nip my bottom lip. Justin grinned like a madman and then lowered his eyelashes in a show of faux subservience. I didn't trust him to stay still or obey for a second. He was wild and headstrong. He wasn't going to do anything that wasn't either his idea or a bad idea.

I ran my fingers through his hair and tugged it to get his attention. "Dammit, you're a sexy fucker."

Justin grunted his approval when I tilted my hips suggestively. The brush of our hard cocks, even through two layers of denim, felt amazing. I hadn't been this horny in a long time. Hell, I hadn't been this close to a man in a long time. I'd forgotten how much I liked it.

"Fuck, that feels good," he whispered.

That was an understatement. I didn't know how much longer I could hold back. My cock swelled against my zipper, and my skin tingled everywhere...my fingers, toes, and along my spine. Every part of me ached with desire for someone I barely knew. I wanted to devour him. Suck him, lick him, taste every inch of him. My hands trembled and my pulse raced. I cupped his chin and ran my thumb over his stubbled jaw as I grinded my thick shaft alongside his.

Justin's eyes fluttered shut for half a second, and his Adam's apple moved lustily in his throat. "Let's go to your room," he purred.

"I don't have a room here."

He pulled away and cocked his head thoughtfully. "Oh. I'd invite you to my place, but I don't really have one. Do you think anyone would notice if I got on my knees?"

"Christ," I hissed. I grabbed his wrist and pulled it behind his back. I gave him a sharp look before glancing around the almost-empty deck area. "Come with me."

I dropped his hand and headed inside.

The bar wasn't overly crowded now. I couldn't remember how late it stayed open during the week, but I didn't think we had a lot of time before closing. I stopped at the elevator and pressed the button.

Justin glanced at me. "What are we doing?"

"We're getting a room."

"Wait. I want to, but...I don't think..." He shook his head and stepped back. "The truth is, I talk a big game. I haven't been with a guy in a few months, and I'm still dealing with the aftereffects from that experience. I should just...go. I'm sorry."

I held his gaze, then nodded slowly. "Okay. Um...do you need a ride?"

"No, I'll figure it out." Justin shoved his hands into his pockets and bent his head. The awkward affectation made him look younger than his age. He seemed overwhelmed and completely out of his depth, and though I wanted to reassure him, I felt suddenly unsure. "Thanks for tonight. You were exactly the person I needed to meet."

I smiled and then glanced toward the bar. "Take care. I love your words and I—"

"No." He stared at me for a long moment, but he didn't move a muscle.

"No, what?" I asked furrowing my brow.

He opened his mouth as if to speak, before launching himself into my arms. I stumbled and hit the wall just as he crashed his mouth over mine. Some semblance of propriety had me scrambling for new options. I backed us into a short hallway, cradling his head as our tongues glided and twisted passion-ately. We broke apart when one of the restroom doors creaked open. I smiled wanly at the startled young woman and then frowned when my companion snorted in amusement.

Justin wound his right arm over my shoulder and bit my bottom lip. He looked like he was about to say something, when the door opened again. He let out a low growl of frustration before slipping his hand in mine and pulling me into the men's room.

The restroom was dimly lit by a pair of modern sconces on either side of the sinks. A single private stall with a floor-to-ceiling partition was located on the far end of the row of urinals. The space was well appointed, but small. And other than the sexy man leaning against the marble counter, it was empty. Justin caught my gaze in the mirror and grinned.

"What are you—"

Justin sealed his lips over mine and shoved his tongue in my mouth in a sexy power play. I met him thrust for thrust, deepening the kiss as I tilted my hips, grinding my shaft against his in a quest for friction. I ran my fingers along his spine and then squeezed his ass and rocked my pelvis. He groaned, licking my lips before burrowing close again and driving his tongue inside my mouth. The press of our bodies mixed with feverish groping and deep, hungry kisses made me crazy.

I gasped for air. Then I pushed him against the wall and wrapped one hand around his throat. We were so close now I could see flecks of gold in his eyes. When his expression morphed from surprise to amusement, I tightened my grip and licked his lips. He shivered and sighed in a sexed-out feverish way.

"What now?" he asked huskily.

"I don't know. You're the one with all the ideas."

"Yeah, but they're all very X-rated. Maybe you should take over. I don't want to get us arrested."

I nodded sharply, then tugged his elbow, bypassing the

empty row of urinals before heading for the stall at the far end of a short marble wall. I closed the door, clicked the lock into place, and drew him against me. We made out in the semi-dark bathroom. But I dictated a slower pace. When he reached for my belt, I held his wrists and sucked his tongue before licking the column of his throat. Every time he pushed for control, I reset the tempo. It was sweet torture, and every second we denied ourselves, the fever rose higher until we were panting for more.

I raked my fingers down his back and buried my face in his neck. "God, I want you."

"Fuck, yes," he whispered. This time when he reached between us to unbuckle my belt and unzip my jeans, I didn't stop him. "Can I touch you?"

I lowered the denim over my ass in response and finally released my aching cock. Then I grabbed his hand and wrapped his fingers around my shaft. "That's right. Feel me, baby."

"Oh, fuck."

We stroked my cock together while we licked and sucked at each other in a frenzy. After a minute or so, I let go of his hand so he could free himself. I felt his leather belt slide against my lower abdomen and his fingers graze my cock as he unzipped. I wanted to watch the show, but his hungry kisses were all kinds of distracting. He effortlessly took over and this time, I let him. He angled his head to deepen the connection, plundering my mouth while he stroked me from base to tip and back again. He brushed his thumb across the precum leaking from my slit, then met my gaze as he sucked the digit clean.

"Mmm. You taste good," he hummed.

The wild, erotic look in his eyes had to be the hottest thing I'd ever seen. Coherent speech wasn't possible. I bit his chin, clutching his T-shirt for support as I gripped his shaft, grunting my approval when he reached for mine again and stroked us together. A public bathroom hand job never felt so damn good. I could have happily done this all night, but I was greedy as hell. I wanted more. And I was pretty sure he did too.

I lowered his jeans and briefs out of the way and squeezed his bare ass before sliding a single digit along his crack. Justin broke our manic kiss with a groan and bucked into my touch, wordlessly telling me what he was looking for. I pushed two fingers between his lips and then reached behind him to pull his cheeks apart and tap his hole. Justin released his hold on us and rested his forehead against mine as he humped my pole, then pushed back on my finger.

"Tell me what you want," I whispered.

"Put your finger inside."

I massaged the sensitive skin around his entrance, loving the feel of his weight against me. It was fitting that I was the one with my back to the wall while he called the shots. I wanted to claim this was an equal exchange of power, but I would have done anything he asked at that moment. He tensed when I added a second finger and went perfectly still.

"Do you want me to stop?"

"No," he said quickly. "Just give me a sec. And lube if you have any."

"I don't. Maybe I should—"

"Fuck me," he intercepted. "You have two fingers in my ass. No way are you walking away now.

"I'm not going anywhere, but I don't want to hurt you."

He gave me a pointed look as though daring me to use an alternate meaning. "You won't hurt me. I won't break. I think I have a lubed condom."

Justin fumbled in his pocket for the latex. He held up a shiny square wrapper a moment later with a grin and then made a production of opening it with his teeth. He raised his arm above his head when I reached for the condom and *tsked* playfully before dropping to his knees and swallowing me whole.

"Fuck."

He fondled my balls as he worked me over. Up and down, up and down. I grabbed a handful of his hair, barely curbing the desire to let loose and fuck his mouth. But I was already close to the edge, and he obviously had other things in mind. He pulled off me with a popping sound, then stood again and slid the lube-slicked condom down my thick cock.

"Do it. Just go slow at first." He licked my lips before shuffling to face the wall next to me.

"I'll be gentle." I switched places and moved behind him, running my hand under his shirt and along his spine before smacking his left ass cheek.

He chuckled appreciatively when the obscene sound bounced off the walls in the quiet room. "I don't want gentle. I want—*oh, fuck yeah*."

I finger fucked him, twisting my wrist slightly and pressing soft kisses along his neck as he jacked himself. He wiggled backward, riding my fingers like a pro before begging for a third. I obeyed. I was aware of a few things at once. The sound of the door opening, a bright light followed by darkness, and the click of a lock. And then stillness.

We were locked inside the bathroom.

The grownup, responsible part of me figured this was a wake-up call. I gently removed my fingers from his ass and straightened. Justin growled and reached back to stop me.

"We aren't done here. Fuck me," he whispered insistently.

I gulped, but I didn't require any persuasion. Fuck grownup responsibility. I felt for him in the dark and moaned aloud when I realized he was holding himself open for me. I lined my cock up with his hole and slowly pushed inside my lover. I took my time, moving inch by inch, until I was balls deep.

"God, you feel amazing," I said.

He bucked his hips backward just as I reached for his dick. "Yeah, that's good. I'm ready. Move. Please move," he begged.

I did. Slow and steady at first before picking up the pace and giving him exactly what he asked for. Faster, harder, more.

The silence and heavy darkness added a sensual layer. Our sweat-slicked skin and lusty groans of pleasure echoed and reverberated around us, wrapping us in a carnal cocoon that felt a little dangerous but much too good to stop. When he bent farther at the waist, I let go of his cock and set one hand on his hip and the other on his shoulder, chanting a litany of praise. The "Your ass is so tight, baby" kind that seemed to drive him crazy. When he reached down to lift his balls and feel my cock sliding into him, I knew it was over for me. Moreover, I could tell the wave of pleasure coming for me would drag me under and hold me down. I was right. I cried out as the first rush of orgasm hit me. I wrapped my arms around his waist and thrust into him over and over until he joined me a moment later.

Neither of us moved. And if he spoke, I wouldn't have been able to hear over the rush of blood to my head. Even in the aftermath, I felt like I was falling through space, somersaulting at a breakneck speed while tethered to a stranger I desperately wanted to know. Maybe that was why I held on longer than necessary. Once I let go, he'd fly away and I'd be left wondering if this was a dream.

"That was…"

"Yeah…wow." Justin gently nudged me to disengage.

I stepped backward, pulling my cell from my pocket to use my screen as a flashlight so I could see what I was doing. I disposed of the spent condom and grabbed some toilet paper, handing a wad to Justin before cleaning myself up as best I could. He playfully licked his fingers, then wiped them on my stomach, chuckling when I swatted his ass. We redressed in silence, opened the door, and headed for the sink. Light streamed from under the main door, providing enough illumination that we didn't need to use our cells to guide the way.

"What are you thinking?" I asked as I met Justin's amused expression in the mirror.

"I wonder what the procedure is for breaking out of a hotel restroom in the middle of the night."

"Hell if I know." I glanced at the time on my phone. "I can't believe it's after two a.m."

"Hotels don't sleep. The light's on out there. Maybe if we bang on the door, the janitor will come and free us. I don't know about you, but I don't want to spend the night in here."

I grabbed his elbow just as he raised his fist. "Hang on. I'll call the reception desk. We'll do this the civilized way."

"Civilized? We just fucked in a bathroom stall at a hotel bar. Somehow bangin' on the door seems like the logical escape route, but hey...let's hear you spin this."

I shot him a dirty look before scrolling the hotel's website and contact info. I found the number and pushed Call.

"Hello, can I speak to the reception desk?...Thank you." I gave him a quick thumbs-up sign as I waited for the call to transfer. "Yes. I'm currently locked in the restroom outside of the Skybar. The one next to the elevators....Men's Room....Yes, I'm not sure how it happened, but I'd appreciate it if you could send someone with a key....Perfect. Thank you."

I disconnected the call and slipped my phone into my pocket. "They'll be here shortly."

Justin regarded me with a thoughtful nod. "Are you famous?"

I chuckled and shook my head. "No. Why?"

"You know they're gonna know what we did in here and if you're famous, it could be a thing for you."

"Well, I'm not. Why are you looking at me like that? Don't you believe me?"

"Sure, I do. You just look important. Like someone I should

know but don't. I never recognize anyone, though. It used to be you could look at a *People* magazine and know the actors, models, and musicians on the covers. Now I have no fuckin' clue."

"You read *People* magazine?" I asked dubiously.

"Fuck, no. My mom does though, and she knows every so-called celebrity on the planet. 'Oh, he's from *The Bachelor*. She's on the Food Network,' " he said in a woman's falsetto. "I've never watched those shows. If you have, don't tell me, 'cause I'm seriously infatuated with you right now. Don't ruin my crush."

I laughed. "So you like me, eh?"

"Oh, yeah. I'm totally hot for you. My ass hurts, my dick is sore, and my heart rate just returned to normal. I'm in that post-sex euphoric stage, planning a big romance."

"I thought you were against love and romance," I reminded him.

"I am. I'm thinking more along the lines of future sexcapades. Nothing too crazy. Change of location and position, that kind of thing. Bathroom sex wouldn't be my first choice, but this was swanky. As far as position goes, I'd want to top next time... and I'd want to see your face. Missionary style, legs over my shoulders." He grabbed his crotch and winked.

"Jesus, I'm getting hard again." I adjusted my cock.

"Me too. Let's try doggy-style...on the floor."

"The floor's filthy," I said primly. I rolled my eyes when he chuckled.

"I'm kidding. I—hey, I think someone's coming. I hear whistling." Justin moved to the door and knocked before calling out, "Hello!"

"I don't hear anything," I said, squinting as though that would help.

"I do. *Hola!*"

Justin spoke Spanish to someone on the opposite side of the

door and gave me a thumbs-up sign just as the lock clicked. A short Latino man pushed the door open and flipped the switch on a moment later. The sudden light was blinding. I blinked as my eyes adjusted to the glare and thanked our rescuer. He nodded in acknowledgment but thankfully didn't ask questions when he relocked the restroom door and led the way to the elevator. He swiped a key card over the inside panel and pushed the Lobby button before exiting the elevator with a friendly wave.

We were silent on the way downstairs. I wondered what he was thinking, but I was afraid to ask. And the closer we came to saying a final good-bye, the more anxious I felt. I could chalk it up to dealing with real-life stuff, like getting my car from the valet in the middle of the night, but I knew it was something else entirely. I didn't want to leave him. I smiled wanly when the elevator door opened.

"Let me take you home."

"No, thanks."

"Justin..." I wanted to argue, but I stopped in the middle of the empty lobby and motioned toward the front desk instead. "I have to get my keys and...let me give you my number. Please. You don't have to call me, but if you want to, you'll know how to reach me."

Justin regarded me for a moment, then pulled out his cell and typed something quickly before handing it over. "Here you go."

I smiled at the contact heading "Boyfriend." I added my info and returned his phone. "Call me. Or don't. But either way, write magical songs, do amazing things, conquer the world. I want to tell everyone I knew you when you were just starting out."

"Starting from zero."

I grinned. "Gotta start somewhere."

He gave me a crooked smile, then headed for the wide glass

door. I watched him until he disappeared into the shadows like a vampire returning to his lair or a fallen angel. He was unruly and wild and infinitely unique. And though I was grateful we met, tonight was an anomaly. We had no history and we had no future. This was a good place to say good-bye.

So why did letting him walk away feel like a big fucking mistake?

———————

AN INCESSANT BUZZING yanked me from sleep the following morning. I flung my arm toward the nightstand, blindly groping for whatever was making that awful noise. I breathed a sigh of relief when it stopped on its own, then rolled over again and pulled the duvet over my head.

Buzz. Buzz. Buzz.

I sat up and reached for my cell, growling at the caller ID flashing on my screen.

"Are you decent and are you alone?" Seb asked, sounding far too peppy first thing in the morning.

"What time is it? I'm pretty sure I have a gag order on you till nine. At least," I snarked, flopping back onto my pillow.

"It's eight. Close enough. And if your bed is empty, I'm coming upstairs. We gotta talk," he chirped.

"Are you in my house?"

"Yeah. I dropped Charlie off. He said he's helping you organize your new collection. What the hell were you thinking? He hates getting dirty, and we both know he prefers delegating."

"Stop yelling," I groaned.

"I'm not yelling. Are you hungover? Do you have someone up there?"

"No and no."

"Good. I'm coming upstairs."

"Bring coffee," I grunted before disconnecting the call.

I rubbed sleep from my eyes, then stared unseeing at the ceiling, willing myself to wake up enough to deal with tsunami Seb. I loved the guy, but he was a force of nature; gregarious, friendly, funny, and scathingly honest when necessary. Those qualities made him a natural in Hollywood. High-profile producers had to know how to get the most out of every team member to deliver to expectation. "Summer blockbusters don't get released in fall" was one of his favorite sayings. He had a dozen of them. And he had a million ideas whirling around his brain on any given day and a fierce need to bounce them off others. Particularly me. That was probably because he could trust me to tell him the truth. Even if he didn't like it.

Of course, that worked both ways. I frowned as pieces of last night filtered through my sleep-hazed mind. Justin onstage with his acoustic guitar, singing in that sexy, soulful voice about peace and karma. Justin in my car. Justin on the rooftop with the city lights behind him, talking about writing and romance and... Justin in the bathroom. My dick twitched at the memory of being inside him. Fucking in the dark. He was hungry and curious and vibrant. And for a few hours on a normally run-of-the-mill evening, I'd willingly made a host of questionable decisions with a man who didn't even know my name.

"Knock, knock. Are you decent?" Seb bounded into my bedroom, kicking the door closed behind him before setting a cup of coffee on my nightstand. "That's hot. Give it a second."

"Did you put cream in it?"

"Nope. It's as black as my heart." He narrowed his eyes suspiciously and tapped his Rolex impatiently. "Why are you still in bed? You never sleep in. Are you sick?"

I let out a half laugh when he slowly retreated to the end of my king-sized bed. I shook my head, then leaned over to pick up the coffee cup. "No. I'm fine. I went to bed late."

"You? Was there a *Friends* marathon on TV last night or something?"

"Ha. Ha. Fuck, this is hot."

"It's coffee, idiot." Seb skirted the bed and sat beside me. "You ditched me after the first act at Carmine's last night without a word."

"I texted you."

"Yeah, and I told you to call me back. We have to talk. Shit is going down, my friend. And I need you to come save the day."

I scowled over the rim of my cup and took a leisurely sip while I studied my oldest friend and former lover. Sebastian Rourke was six three and built like a runner; long, lean, and muscular. His short, dark hair and well-trimmed beard were liberally streaked with gray. I'd heard him referred to as a silver fox and I wholeheartedly agreed. Seb was a very handsome man. Of course, I'd thought he was pretty damn sexy a few decades ago too. The difference was, I didn't want him naked in my bed now. Or even sitting on my bed while I was half-naked under the covers.

Actually, I didn't care anymore. We'd navigated a painful breakup from deep within the closet. So deep and so long ago that very few people knew we were once much more than friends.

And why did it just occur to me that Justin would have been a toddler when I met Seb? My forehead creased hard enough to give me a headache. I pushed the errant thought aside and sipped my coffee while Seb barreled on about a theme song.

"...should be a love song. Kinda syrupy. Audiences love schmaltz and we gotta give 'em what they want, but with a twist they don't expect." He paused to pull my cup from my fingers. He took a healthy swig, then set it on the nightstand and inched closer with a wily look in his eyes before continuing in a low theatric tone, "The warrior princess."

"Huh?"

"The girl from last night." He snapped his fingers and frowned. "Starts with an X but sounds like a Z."

"Xena," I replied.

"Yeah! Were you still there? I thought you'd left. She wasn't bad. Needs some polishing for sure, but her voice is strong. Well...strong enough. I dig her look. What do you think?"

I cocked my head. "About what?"

Seb sat up taller and gave me a thorough once-over. "What's going on with you? Did you get laid last night? You've got that dopey look in your eyes like you either got the blowjob of your life or..."

"Stop."

"Ooh. I'm right. Who was it?"

"For fuck's sake, Seb. I'm not telling you who—"

"That's okay. I can guess," he said, picking up the coffee cup again and taking another sip. "The pretty blonde at the bar with the big tits. No? Um...oh. The guitar player! Carmine said he left after you went out for a cigarette. I thought you quit, by the way. You know I fucking hate it when you smoke. But yeah, that guy was pretty good. He was your type too. Dark and broody. So, what happened? You got five minutes here. I gotta give you my spiel and get to the studio before my secretary sends someone out to look for me. Go on."

See what I mean? Seb the tsunami. The man was exhausting.

"I have nothing to say...other than it was one cigarette. Leave me alone and give me my coffee."

He furrowed his brow as he handed the cup back to me. "Fine. I'll get it out of you later. Here's the deal." He raked his hand through his hair, then tugged at his designer trousers as he twisted to face me. "I need you to add a couple of songs for the Baxter movie."

I sighed heavily. "So that's why you dragged me out last night. I knew you had an agenda. The score is almost complete."

"Yeah, but I'm not talking about the music. I need a song. A hit song."

"Oh, right. That's easy," I huffed sarcastically.

"It's easy for you. You're a fucking genius at this stuff," he enthused.

"Save the ego stroking and give me specifics. How much time do I have?"

"You've got a few months before it has to be in production. I wanna release a big blowout, serious smash-hit love ballad, you know, something corny but cool...by July. The movie is sched-uled for an August release. That'll give us a month of pre-release hype. I want a new recording artist. Not an established big name. It's been done over and over. Let's go back to basics this time. Bring in a fresh face with a ton of attitude and sex appeal." Seb paused for dramatic effect, then said, "I want Xena."

"No."

"What do you mean no?" He frowned.

"You heard me. My contract is for the score and a theme song. Find someone else to do the rest."

I put the mug down and kicked at his leg until he scooted aside and gave me enough room to get out of bed. I scratched my nuts as I made my way to the adjoining bathroom. Of course, Seb followed. He leaned against the counter with his arms crossed and watched me pee. Or maybe he just wanted to examine my dick for clues.

"So, you fucked this guy and you don't want to deal with the ex-lover situation," he said after a long moment.

I met his gaze in the mirror and blinked. "Where do you come up with this stuff?" I bluffed.

"Number one, you've got dried cum on your stomach. That's grade-A weird for a clean freak like you. Number two, you never stay in bed after six a.m. during the week, seven on the weekend. If you're not sick, you did something or someone after you left the bar. Timing adds up to the hot guy with the guitar. Am I right or am I right?"

I rolled my eyes, then headed through a small alcove to the shower and turned on the water. I stepped out of the briefs I'd changed into when I got home and examined the dried mess on my stomach. Seb was right. About everything. But it still wasn't his business.

"Does it matter?" I asked, tossing my black boxer briefs at him.

He caught them before they hit him in the face and glared at me. "What are you doing? I'm talking to you."

"No, you're dictating. I'm not writing you a love song, and I don't want any part of jumpstarting a mildly talented singer's career when we both know there are better options. Now, if you'll excuse me...I need to wash the jizz off my belly." I winked because I knew it would bug him, then stepped into the glass-and-marble spa-like enclosure.

My house was freaking beautiful if I did say so myself. It was a contemporary estate nestled in an exclusive section of Hollywood Hills. A long driveway lined with palm trees led to the two-story modern glass and stone house. I loved the clean lines and minimalist decor. But the real draw for me had always been the view. I'd specifically asked the architect to showcase the impressive cityscape from every window, and she'd more than delivered. The property's elevation ensured a level of privacy that made it possible to have perks like floor-to-ceiling windows in my shower.

I glanced at the puffy clouds as I reached for the soap before turning to Seb. His silence was nice, but kind of disturbing too. He had one of those wickedly brilliant minds. And he didn't understand the meaning of the word "no." He took it as a mild suggestion or an outright challenge. I mentally prepared my rebuttal even though I didn't really know how he'd convince me that writing a few forgettable songs for an action flick would be in my best interest. No doubt, he'd think of something.

"Get the boyfriend to write 'em," he said in a faraway tone that indicated his brain was whirling at warp speed.

"What boyfriend?"

"Xena's ex—aka, the guy you fucked last night. Was he here?" he asked, setting his hands on his hips as he looked around the bathroom.

"No, he wasn't here and—"

"So I was right!" Seb clapped and let out a whoop that didn't quite seem to fit the situation. "It was the guitarist. You know, he wasn't that great on the guitar, but I loved his voice."

"Okay, well I'm gonna go ahead and finish up here. Feel free to mosey downstairs and grab some coffee on your way out." I moved under the spray and closed my eyes. When he didn't move or speak for a full minute, I opened them again and reached for the soap. "You're creeping me out. Why are you still here?"

"I'm thinking."

"Oh. That's bad."

"No. It's good." He snapped his fingers and paced to the doorway and back. "I've got it! You write the music and get him to write the words. Xena said he wrote all the songs for their band. Get him to collaborate with you on one or two songs. Like the love song."

I barked a quick laugh and shook my head. "He wouldn't do it."

"Of course he would. He's a struggling artist. He'd make fucking bank and get the chance of a lifetime to work with a Grammy-winning composer and songwriter. What's the downside?" He furrowed his brow and then pointed his finger at me.

"Don't even think about flicking water at me. I've got a meeting in twenty minutes."

"Then you better get going."

"Not until you tell me you'll talk to him."

"Seb, there are a lot of talented singers, songwriters, and composers who would happily jump through all the Hollywood hoops for you. Why are you fixating on these two?"

" 'Cause they're real and fresh and new. And their story complements the movie very nicely. Check this out." He splayed his hands wide and went into Hollywood dream spinner mode. "Baxter's busting up a drug ring in LA, meets a gorgeous punk chick whose brother runs the cartel. He suspects her ex might be involved too and guess what?"

"The ex just happens to be the guitarist in her band," I replied, flicking water at him. I chuckled when he hopped backward like he'd been stung, then turned off the faucet and reached for my towel. "Really?"

"That's the story. I shit you not. How crazy perfect would these two fit in? Not as actors, but as a side note that draws in the curious crowd that likes to wait till the movie comes to Netflix."

"So this is a publicity scheme."

Seb shot a wounded look at me. "It sounds so dirty when you put it like that. I prefer the term 'interest-added incentive,' " he said with a wide grin. "Everybody wins. Two nobodies get a chance of a lifetime to launch their careers, my movie crushes the box office, and you get musical creative license and make a fuckton of money for your effort."

"I'm not messing with their private lives. Neither of us can guarantee them fame or fortune. And I don't know about Xena, but Justin didn't seem like the kind of guy who'd get excited about a Hollywood movie. He's an indie artist, a nonconformist. He wants to make his mark his own way."

"Oh brother," he scoffed. "Trust me on this one, Gray. Hippy virtuosos change their tunes when a recording contract falls out of the sky. Ask him."

"No."

We engaged in an intense standoff, sizing each other up in a heated way that once upon a time had led to hot, angry sex. Wrestling for dominance, careening against walls before tumbling into bed and fucking like mad. Those days were long gone, but Seb still had an uncanny ability to get under my skin.

"Fine. I'll ask him myself," he huffed.

"Fine. You do that. But leave me out of it." I gave him a sharp look before drying myself off and wrapping the towel around my waist. "Why are you staring at me?"

"You really like him." Seb cocked his head thoughtfully. "You always push people away when you like them. Odd habit and not a good one. If someone is special, you gotta let them know how you feel so—"

"So you can use them for your own gain," I finished.

Seb glared. "What about for their gain? Xena and Justin are nobodies. Their band...what the fuck was it called?"

"Gypsy Coma."

"It was a glorified LA garage band. They weren't special, but their blow up was epic...lies, deceit, and a gay lover. The public devours this sort of thing. You know it as well as I do."

"Nature of the beast." I sighed irritably before heading back to my bedroom with Seb close behind.

He sat on the edge of my mattress, observing me like a bug under a microscope as I stepped into a pair of black boxer briefs. I might have seemed unfazed, but I was on high alert. A pensive Seb usually meant trouble for me.

Seb's drive and boundless enthusiasm were instrumental in his success. He was the well-respected and sought-after producer responsible for the wildly popular Baxter franchise and a string of mainstream blockbusters. I'd seen him in action, alternately browbeating and cajoling to get his way...just like every other big-time Hollywood exec. He had a gift for seeing what others couldn't and the skill to communicate his ideas on a global scale. But I knew his quiet, introspective side was infinitely more dangerous.

"I need you to write the song," he said softly. "You're the best there is. I'll look for other singers, but Xena is my first choice."

"And Justin?"

"I want him too, but you're right. He may not want to write for his ex. I should be cautious when I approach him."

I groaned. "I did not say that."

"Close enough. If he agreed, would you work with him?"

"He doesn't know who I am."

"You didn't tell him?"

"No. He didn't want to know anyway."

Seb chuckled. "He's going to think he won the fuckin' lottery!"

"But I don't want that."

"Why? Are you afraid he'll fall for your money instead of you?" Seb rested his elbows on his knees and shot a rye lopsided smile at me. "I hate to break it to you, but it's always about the Benjamins, baby. Don't go looking for love in a bar or—"

"Fuck you. I'm not in love with the guy."

"Then give him a chance." He stood abruptly and moved to my side. He nudged my arm. "Fine. I'll ask him."

"You already told me you were going to, and I told you he'll say no," I replied.

"A challenge! All right. We shall see. I'll find a way. And if he says yes...which he will or he's a fucking moron...you'll do it, right?"

"He won't."

Seb furrowed his brow. "I want to wring your neck. I hate when you don't blindly agree with me."

I chuckled at his comedic delivery, though we both knew he wasn't really kidding. "You should be used to that by now. Don't you have a meeting to get to?"

"Yeah, yeah. Give me a minute. Did I tell you I'm going to Toronto next week? We're filming a—"

"Ask his band to do it," I blurted. "They're new and they're looking for a break. He might be interested then."

Seb looked at me like I'd grown a pineapple from my head. "I don't want a band. I want two star-crossed lovers. The only thing loosely resembling a band last night was Xena and her guitarist, Declan. He was hot and...you know, a love triangle song could work. Xena and two guitarists. I like that. I think the actual story involves the drummer, but I loved that guy's looks. Great idea, Gray."

"No, it's a bad idea. Forget it. When are you going to Toronto?"

I pulled a pair of jeans from my drawer and listened with half an ear as Seb droned on about a location visit for another film. I was grateful for the topic switch. I grunted occasionally in acknowledgment as I dressed and silently mulled over the series of landmines Seb had planted.

Writing another song or two for the movie wasn't a big deal. Seb knew I could do it in my sleep. But writing a song with Justin for his ex to sing felt...cheap. Like I was willfully feeding him into the Hollywood machine, exploiting his weaknesses for gain. And though he hadn't shared what happened with Xena's guitarist, I had a feeling that adding him to the mix would be even worse for him. I knew how the business worked. It was cruel and callous, and no one did anything out of the goodness of their heart. There was always a bottom line at stake.

3

JUSTIN

My dreams were very fucking weird lately. I was on a sailboat, leaning against the railing, staring at the horizon where blue skies met turquoise water with a seductive sense of calm...no worries, no responsibilities. And I wasn't alone. The sexy stranger was by my side. The gentle, rocking motion seemed indicative of smooth sailing and an aura of peace. It didn't last long. The boat teetered precariously, the sky darkened...and then my phone rang.

I blinked rapidly and glanced around. Light streamed through the dirty window, reflecting in a rainbow prism off the ancient glass coffee table. I squinted at the Pink Floyd poster above a cast-off forest-green recliner and swiped my hand across my face before glancing up at my roommate, aware that his lips were moving.

"Jus, wake up!"

"Wha-what the fuck?"

Tegan tossed my cell on my chest. "It's your mom."

I rubbed my eyes as I scrambled to sit up. When the fog cleared and reality seeped in, I let out a sigh that was equal parts relief and defeat. *Fuck me.* The good news was that I wasn't in the middle of the ocean, bopping around in a tin can. The bad news was, I lay sprawled on Tegan's sofa. And yeah, my mom was on the line.

"Hey, Mom," I said in a groggy voice.

"Hi. I'm just leaving for work, but I had the strangest dream about you last night."

"I just had a weird dream too. What was yours?"

"You were at the Y after school. I think I was home, and I got a call to pick you up because you were running around like a chicken with its head cut off, and no one could stop you. Not even your brother."

I bristled when she didn't call Rory by name. It was on the tip of my tongue to supply it when she continued, "I woke up in a sweat, worrying about your medication. Have you been taking it? I read a terrible report linking the one they prescribed when you were a kid to depression. You know you can't mess with depression, Justin. It's serious."

"I know, Ma. Don't worry about me."

"Worrying is my job. What medication are you taking? I think my dream was a sign we should do some research on it and make sure it's safe. Studies were done recently showing…"

I closed my eyes and buried my head in my free hand. *Fuck.* These were the days I wished Rory was still part of our original circle of three. My mother was a lot for me to handle on my own. Especially pre-caffeine.

"Mom, I'm fine."

"Well, I'm glad about that, but I still need to research. So which one is it?" she asked before listing a few names that easily had twenty consonants apiece.

I named the medication I'd been prescribed and added, "But I'm weaning myself off of it and going for a holistic approach."

Silence.

"Does that mean you're smoking the devil's lettuce?"

If I'd been drinking anything, I'd have spit it out for sure. I threw my head back and laughed like a loon. I couldn't stop. There was something really fucking funny about my formerly-hip-turned-religious-fanatic mother primly reciting a slang name for marijuana. When she said my full name three times in a row, I sobered. "Oh man, that was hilarious. No, Mom, I wasn't referring to weed. I do breathing exercises and I try to eat right. I cut brussels sprouts out entirely."

"Vegetables are good for you. How does cutting out brussels sprouts help?"

"They make me gassy and fart jokes make me laugh. And once I start laughing, my brain kicks into third or fourth gear. I want to laugh more, do more, talk more. Honestly, I exhaust myself. So there you have it…no more brussels sprouts. And you probably should never say devil's lettuce again." I chuckled.

"Hmph. Do you enjoy making sport of me?"

"Yeah, sometimes I do," I teased. "C'mon, Ma. I'm twenty-six. I've been living with a spacey brain my whole life. I got this."

"You don't have a spacey brain. You have a condition."

"Millions of people have ADHD, Mom. I'm not special. And I'm doing just fine."

"Are you? The band, the part-time jobs…you sleep on a sofa, for goodness sake. That's terrible for your brain. You should move back to Long Beach, Justin. You can stay here until you get a real job."

I pulled my cell from my ear and gave Tegan my best "*Help!*" look. He chuckled softly, then made a drink gesture I hoped meant he'd made coffee before he headed toward the galley-style kitchen. "Thanks for the offer. But if it makes you feel any better, I have a job interview this morning. It's for something clerical. It sounds boring as fu—fudge, but I think it pays well."

"Oh, that's great news! Good luck, honey," she gushed.

"Thanks. I should get going. Bye, Mom. Oh, hey...you should know Rory's doing well too."

The line went quiet for a second before she said a curt, "Good-bye, Justin."

I sighed and was about to toss my phone aside and search for coffee when a new message lit up my cell. From Declan. I thought I'd deleted him from my contact list for good. What the fuck was happening in the universe?

We need to talk. Xena's signing a contract you might be interested in.

"Good times with Mom?" Tegan snarked, setting a mug on the coffee table.

"The usual." I thanked him for the coffee, then tossed my phone at him. "Read that text."

"Whoa. What do you think that's all about?" he asked, dropping my phone into my lap.

"No idea."

"You can't trust him."

"No one knows that better than me," I huffed. When Tegan narrowed his eyes and crossed his arms, I added, "And you."

I wanted to chuckle because he didn't look nearly as fierce as he thought. Then again, I was probably the only person on the planet who wasn't intimidated by him. Further proof, if needed, that I might not be dealing with a full deck, 'cause Tegan was anyone's idea of a badass. He was also a good friend who got a little more than he bargained for when he offered me his sofa for the night...a few months ago. I was currently renting the right to be there until I could afford a place of my own, which I hoped would be soon. I sighed when a fresh wave of despair hit me out of the blue.

I'd been in a serious funk during the two weeks since my set at Carmine's. I hadn't expected much from the gig. The invitation to play in the first place was cool, but everything that happened after I stepped outside was even better. Well, after my run-in with Declan. That part sucked. But meeting a hot stranger, talking under a starlit sky on a fancy rooftop overlooking the city before having incredibly hot bathroom sex...had been worth the flood of doubt and misgivings that set in when I returned to my real world.

So yeah, I wasn't sure what to think when I received an email offering a job interview for clerical work out of the fucking blue and now a cryptic message from Declan. I'd add the conversation with my mom to the mix, but her worried calls were a biweekly occurrence, if not more.

I was tempted to call the newest addition to my contact list if only to hear a friendly voice. I'd stared at his number more often than I'd ever admit, but I didn't call. I studied the word "Boyfriend" and conjured his face before turning my cell facedown on the coffee table. What the hell was wrong with me?

Tegan perched on the corner of the sofa and sipped his coffee. "Did you text him back?"

"No. I'll do it later. Maybe. I need to get through this interview first."

"You'll be awesome. Just wear something nice-ish. At least something that's not a T-shirt. Take deep breaths when you need to and try to relax. And after you nail it, text Declan and see what the fuck he's up to."

I raised my coffee mug in a toast with what I hoped passed for enthusiasm. I didn't feel particularly hopeful or enthusiastic though. I felt restless and weary, and a little concerned for my own sanity. Obsessing over a stranger wasn't healthy. I had to either call him or delete his number. Neutrality didn't suit me. I had too many worries and too much going on in my brain. It was time to get my life on track. Or try anyway.

After this interview.

FORTY-FIVE MINUTES LATER, I parked my crappy old Toyota behind a sleek Range Rover at the end of a long driveway, then pulled out my cell to confirm the Hollywood Hills address. While I was at it, I decided to read the initial email one more time to make sure I wasn't about to make a fool of myself.

Dear Justin Cuevas,

I have a unique job opportunity to offer you. It involves the organization of a large collection of. You were highly recommended by a mutual friend. Please let me know if you're interested.

Sincerly,

Charles Robertson

Right off the bat, I noted a couple of weird things. First of all, he addressed the letter "Dear Justin Cuevas." "Dear" was reserved for family members and close friends. And then there were a few missing words...a collection of what? Highly recommended by whom? And he spelled "sincerely" wrong. For some reason, that last one really bugged me. Everyone had spellcheck on their fuckin' computer.

I'd replied, thinking whoever was behind this would give himself up and admit the whole thing was a hoax.

Hello Mr. Robertson,

Thank you for your offer. I have a few questions regarding your collection. I'm interested in learning more about the scope of the job, the compensation scale, and how soon you'd need me to start. Also, I'm curious about who might have recommended me for the position.

I look forward to meeting with you soon.

Sincerely,

Justin Cuevas

Mr. Robertson replied immediately and suggested meeting at his home to work out the details. We went back and forth before agreeing to this date and time. Nothing seemed overly suspicious and yet, something didn't compute. Like who in their right mind would recommend me to organize anything?

I squinted against the glare of the late morning sun, then pulled my Ray Bans from my shirt pocket and checked the number marked on the modern style mailbox at the curb with the one I'd been given one more time. *Five four three zero.* Yep. This was it. The forest of palm trees hid the actual house from view, but even I could tell we were in the high-rent district. This was a quiet, respectable neighborhood. The kind where residents avoided eye contact in an effort to discourage unnecessary conversation with neighbors whose names they couldn't remember to save their lives before parking their zero-emission vehicle in their garages next to a gas-guzzling Cadillac Escalade. Pretentious pricks.

Not like I knew what I was talking about. I'd never lived in an actual house or a real neighborhood. Ever. I was from the other side of the tracks, where you heard more than you ever wanted to know about your neighbors through paper-thin walls in an ancient apartment building adorned with graffiti.

I hiked the palm-lined driveway toward the two-story modern home, pausing to admire the mini garden of succulents surrounded by pristine white pebbles. Everything was so damn clean. Like Disneyland or someplace where they had someone assigned to jobs like "rock caretaker," I mused with a laugh as I raised my hand to knock. The massive glass-paned front door swung open before I had a chance.

I jolted and stepped backward to check out the golden curly-haired vision posed with one hand bracing the jamb and the other on his hip. For some reason, I had assumed Charles Robertson was much older. This guy was young, blond, and very fabulous.

"There you are! For fuck's sake, I've been waiting for you!"

"Hey there. I'm Justin. Nice to meet you," I said, extending my hand.

"Yes, I know. Come in. I wanted to brief you beforehand, but I'm running out of time. This way." He clapped aggressively, then grabbed my wrist and pulled me across the threshold.

I yanked out of his hold and scowled as I removed my sunglasses. "Hang on. What do you mean, 'brief me'?"

He huffed impatiently and set his hands back on his hips. I amended "fabulous" to "bossy" in my head and gave him a thorough once-over. He was roughly my age and kind of petite. No more than five eight, tops, with a compact physique. His floral shirt was see-through in parts and tucked into a high-waisted pair of khakis he'd rolled at the hem. I noted his bare feet in the red leather loafers and absently thought he might be the only person on the planet who could pull off that look. He reminded me of a frustrated tango dancer waiting for his partner to catch up.

He pursed his full lips and regarded me thoughtfully before shrugging. "I mean, I want to give you a little background."

"Okay, but who are you?"

"I'm Charlie. And I'm going to change your life!"

"Charles Robertson?"

"Yes and no. The important thing is, I know all about you and what happened with Gypsy Coma and…I'm going to help you. Think of me as your fairy gaymother. Come on." He spun away, leaving me in a cloud of expensive smelling cologne in the middle of the foyer.

I glanced up at the enormous contemporary glass chandelier hanging above a round marble-topped table, then caught my reflection in the ornate mirror leaning against the wall. I looked confused as fuck and so out of place, it hurt. My borrowed blue oxford shirt was too big across my shoulders and my "nice" jeans were worn at the crotch. Everything about this situation was off.

How did someone who looked and acted like Charlie, aka the Mad Hatter, know anything about Gypsy Coma or me? This world didn't mesh with dark indie bands with cult followings. This house belonged to the country club set meets so-called respectable business elite. And Charlie looked like a pampered West Hollywood pretty boy. But what the fuck did I know? Nothing yet.

I moved into the adjoining great room and scanned the bookshelves flanking the wide bank of windows. I paused to admire the grand piano before fixating on the impressive views of LA in the distance. The vibrant water met the blue sky at the horizon, showcasing the city in a picture-perfect light.

"Oh, my God. Are you coming or not? It's like I'm talking to my ex!"

Charlie tapped his foot and motioned for me to hurry up.

"Are you really sharing secrets about your sex life?" I asked impatiently.

He snickered lightly and shook his head. "I don't have much of a sex life, and that's fine for now. My former one was a bit too zealous...if you know what I mean. My ex popped Viagra the way a yoga mom drinks kombucha. He was one of those four-hour-erection guys."

"Um...o-kay."

"I read up on the phenomenon once. Apparently erectile dysfunction drugs shouldn't affect stamina, but for him, it did. I swear I don't know how many times I stared at the ceiling, willing him to finish the fuck up." He held up his hand and lowered his eyelashes dramatically. "I know what you're think-ing. And you're right. I have no filter. It's like I accidentally drank truth serum at birth. It's a real problem every once in a while, although occasionally it works in my favor."

He spun away and disappeared around the corner. I hurried to catch up to him, craning my neck to take in my surroundings.

The house was unreal. It had high ceilings, light wide-planked flooring and seemingly more windows than walls. Modern art and prized instruments were displayed on any free wall space or in random nooks. Guitars, violins, a stand-up bass. I was pretty sure I saw a harp too. I didn't know anything about furniture, but nothing looked particularly comfortable. Chic black leather sofas with clean lines but no real cushioning juxtaposed with funky, bright-colored chairs. Every room looked like something out of a fancy magazine or a TV show about ridiculously beautiful people who had more money than sense. If Charlie told me we were on a movie set, I would have believed him. It was hard to imagine that anyone actually lived here.

Charlie sailed into a wide corridor surrounded by windows on three sides with his head held high and flashed an encouraging smile before pointing at the pool.

"Gray is on the roof. I'll call him down now."

Yep. He was nuts.

"Who is Gray?" I asked, frowning.

"Your future employer. This is his house, his collection. He can tell you all about it."

"And how is this going to change my life?"

Charlie cocked his head and set his hands on his hips. "I don't have time to go into that now. I'm running late for class. We'll have to chat another time. Let me introduce you."

I moved to the window and tapped my finger against the glass and squinted. "Is he the naked man playing guitar?"

"Where?"

I gestured toward the figure sitting with his legs crossed on the pool house roof. His head was bent over an acoustic guitar, which might have hidden swim trunks or a Speedo. I couldn't be sure from the distance.

"Ugh. Why does he do this? It's January, for fuck's sake!" Charlie groused as he stomped outside and yelled to the man on the roof. "He's here, Gray. Can you come down?" No answer. "Gray?"

"Give me a sec," the man replied.

I crossed the pool area and glanced up but couldn't see anything. The light was directly behind Gray, sending long shadows across his face. But he had a nice voice. Deep and raspy...and vaguely familiar.

I shaded my eyes against the glare to get a better look. It didn't help.

"Who is this guy again, and why am I here?" I whispered as the man headed for the ladder attached to the side of the pool house.

"Gray Robertson," Charlie said.

"And he's your dad who needs help filing...what?"

"No, he's my godfather, and he needs someone to organize his record collection. It's a recent acquisition and it's massive. He wanted me to do it, but I suggested you."

"Why? You don't know me."

"I know *of* you, and that's almost as good." Charlie gave me a tight-lipped smile and lowered his voice. "Here he comes. Remember, we're friends from the club."

"What club?"

"Vibes," he hissed.

I was about to respond, when the man approached, holding an acoustic guitar in one hand. He was still hidden in the shadow so I couldn't quite make out his features, but I could tell he was tall and muscular and...not naked.

He wore blue swim trunks with a funky print and a pair of beat-up black-and-white checked Vans. And he wore them well. In fact, he seemed to be in really good shape. *For someone his age*, I added in my head to lessen the weirdness of admiring a potential employer. Whatever. It was true. He had a thicker build reminiscent of a football player with broad shoulders and sun-kissed skin. I fixated on the dragon tattoo that wrapped around his torso and the gorgeous Gibson guitar he held before pasting a smile on my face when he stepped into the light.

"Hi, there. I'm—holy fuck. It's you."

I dropped my hand and stared at the guy I'd thought about nonstop for the past two weeks. Hell, the guy I'd woken up in a cold sweat dreaming about a couple of hours ago. And though my brain was already working out logistics of probability and quickly coming to the conclusion something weird was happening here, the rest of me...including my dick, was incredibly pleased to see him again.

"What are you doing here?" he asked, sounding equally baffled.

"I don't know," I replied in a daze. "Um, Charlie said something about a job and—you live here? Gray. This is...odd."

Gray shot a curious glance at Charlie and rolled his tongue along the inside of his lower lip. "Yes. Some kind of strange coincidence."

Charlie opened his mouth in a comical O and cast a wide-eyed look between us. "You know each other? Well, this is crazy. Just nuts. I'll let you two catch up while I—"

"Not so fast." Gray grabbed Charlie's elbow before he could escape. "What's going on?"

"You need someone to organize those records, and Justin is the perfect candidate. He's friendly, organized, bilingual...and he knows the alphabet!" Charlie's bright grin dulled when Gray didn't respond. "The bilingual part will come in handy with all those Brazilian albums."

"Except I don't speak Portuguese," I interjected. "And to be honest, I'm only sporadically friendly and never organized."

"He has a great sense of humor," Charlie assured Gray with a nervous laugh. "But you probably already know that."

"I remember." Gray held my gaze intently.

I was instantly transported in time to that night, chatting about everything and nothing at all with a handsome stranger, high above the lights of LA. The latent romantic in me wanted to claim this was fate...like we were supposed to meet again. Maybe we were even supposed to mean something to each other. I'd be lying if I didn't admit the idea appealed to me on some level.

Gray Robertson was the stuff of modern fairytales. He lived in a castle on a hill and played guitar shirtless on his roof in the middle of the day. Normal people were at work now and—oh, right...music was his work. He wrote commercial jingles. I couldn't decide if I should google him first to find out more or if I should just start running because none of this seemed real. When I needed fantasy, I played video games and watched porn. And yeah, lately I jerked off to the memory of what we did in that bathroom. But our one-night stand didn't give me any special rights here. In fact, in a weird way, it made me feel more uncomfortable. I didn't belong here.

"Me too," I said, pushing aside my growing anxiety. "So you're Gray Robertson."

"I am. And you're Justin..."

"Cuevas. Did you summon me or something?"

"No." Gray let go of Charlie's elbow, then lifted his forefinger in a silent command for him to stay put in an authoritative manner. Charlie frowned but didn't move.

I glanced between them before refocusing on Gray. Well, on his tattoos this time. I didn't realize he had so many. The dragon's tail wrapped around his side below script that was too small to read at a distance and a set of Roman numerals. I suddenly wished I'd paid better attention to shit like that in school. *M equals one thousand, right?* I had no fucking clue. But I wanted to know. In fact, I wanted to know everything about him. Not just his favorite ice cream. I wanted to know his birthday, where he was from, and if he watched *Game of Thrones*. Important stuff.

But I wasn't supposed to know him or even see him again. So what the hell was going on here?

"So this is just a crazy coincidence?" I asked dubiously.

"Or the stars have aligned! You need a job and Gray needs help." Charlie danced out of Gray's reach and gave me a look I couldn't read without serious help before hiking his thumb toward the house meaningfully. "I have to print out an assignment before I head to class. I'm sure Gray won't mind giving you a tour of the library. Text me if you have any questions. See you later."

"Hold on a second," Gray said.

"No can do. Gotta run!" Charlie pivoted on his red loafers and hurried for the house before either of us could respond.

Gray let out a rush of air and raked his hand through his hair in frustration. Then he pulled his guitar strap over his head and pushed his instrument behind his back. I noticed a fresh set of details at once. Weird things like his muscular calves, his trim waist, the smattering of hair on his broad, sun-kissed chest, and the rip in his ancient Vans.

"Okay. This is...odd. Just so we're clear, I don't know what's going on. But it's good to see you again."

"It's good to see you too," he replied softly.

I stuffed my hands into my back pockets and looked around the sprawling yard and the LA skyline beyond the low hedge. "Nice place. I bet this view rivals the one at the Skybar at night."

"Yeah, it does."

He smelled like sunshine and mint. The combination seemed extraordinarily appealing. I fought the urge to lean in and lick his bare shoulder when he stepped closer. It would have been a bad move. We weren't strangers flirting over gin and tonics in the dark now. We were fully exposed. Sunlight reflected off the pool and the second story windows. It revealed more than his hot dad bod and ink. It revealed our differences. Our ages, experiences, and our places in life. Gray was obviously successful and accomplished. And I was obviously not.

I swallowed hard against the ugly impotent feeling roiling in my gut. I'd spent a few hours with this man sharing things I rarely did because he felt like a safe harbor on a night when I needed to connect to someone who didn't know me. Someone who wouldn't look at my past or present and wonder when the fuck I'd grow up. For a few hours, we'd been friends and then lovers. I didn't believe in forever. I'd had my ass kicked by real life too many times to get any flowery notions about "happily ever afters." But I'd hoped to keep those few hours with him sacred. I didn't want to know him and be forced to acknowledge he wasn't just out of my league...he was in another galaxy.

I cleared my throat and inclined my head toward the house. "Look, here's what went down. I got an email from a Charles Robertson saying he needed someone to do some clerical work. I showed up for an interview, and here I am. I don't know if there really is a job, but—"

"There is," he intercepted with a lopsided smile. "Charlie agreed to take it on, but he's hard to pin down, and it looks like he came up with another idea."

"And he just happened to call me?"

"I didn't ask him to contact you, but I'm not sorry he did. It's good to see you. I've thought about you a lot. I was hoping you'd call."

"I wanted to, but I didn't know what to say," I admitted awkwardly. I pursed my lips and willed myself not to tell him I'd been staring at his number like a lovesick weirdo for weeks. God, I felt like an idiot. I had to get outta here. I hiked my thumb toward the house and stepped backward. "You know, this probably isn't a good idea. I should go."

"Don't you want to see my records?"

That stopped me. He sounded so...unsure. And kind of nerdy. I tilted my head and I wondered if I was being punked or if "see my records" was code for something else. The hint of vulnerability I'd heard was gone in an instant, replaced by the careless disinterest I expected from a successful music guru.

I met his nonchalant gaze and shrugged. "Why not?"

Gray nodded curtly and motioned for me to follow him. He led the way across the pool deck to the main house via the wide glass door I'd come through with Charlie. He paused to make sure I closed it behind me before turning down the wide corridor and opening the first door on the left to what looked like a bedroom-slash-gaming room. There was a queen-sized bed in the corner but the giant television, a comfy-looking sofa, and a coffee table littered with controllers and discarded games indicated that the real action happened in front of the flat-screen.

"I'm gonna grab a shirt," he said, heading to the walk-in closet.

"Okay."

I perused the games while I waited. *Grand Theft Auto, Fortnite, Call of Duty.* I picked up *Dragon Ball FighterZ* and read the back of the box. Nice collection.

"Do you play?"

I glanced up with a wry grin and started to give a smartass reply about my videogame expertise, but I immediately forgot whatever I was going to say. Fuck, he was hot. His red plaid flannel shirt stretched enticingly as he slipped it over his shoulders. I wanted to laugh at his wardrobe choices. He should have looked like a test pattern gone wrong with the long-sleeved plaid, checked shoes, and printed swim trunks...but somehow the combo worked on him.

Gray bent his head briefly to deal with the buttons before

giving me an expectant look to let me know he was waiting on a reply. I averted my gaze from the sexy trail of fur leading south from his bellybutton and swiped the back of my hand across my mouth, hoping I caught myself before I drooled.

"Yeah. I'm in the middle of *Assassin's Creed Odyssey* right now with my roommate. He's obsessed and he doesn't seem to care that I kick his ass every night," I said with a laugh before gesturing toward the bed and closet. "Is this a guest room or your room or...what?"

"It's supposed to be a guest room, but it's mostly a place to hang out. My studio is down the hall, and the library is next door. I keep a few things in the closet, so I don't have to traipse from one end of the house to the other to look for a shirt or a clean pair of underwear. When I get deep into a project, I sleep here or in the pool house. It's easier to be close to the music."

"The music?" I asked, casting a curious gaze around the space. It was a teenage boy's dream room. The only things missing were a stocked mini fridge and obligatory pics of sports idols and rock gods.

Gray flashed a smile. Then he grabbed his guitar and inclined his head in invitation. "Come this way."

If the house was a fraction of its size, I would have been impressed. The modern architecture, breathtaking views, and the pervasive sense of solitude were awe-inspiring. I didn't think it could get any better, but I was dead wrong. Gray's in-home studio was the stuff of dreams. It was chock full of more instruments and sound equipment than I'd ever seen in person, outside of a music store. I didn't know where to look first.

The far left side was set up like a stage in front of a wall of acoustic and electric guitars. Any band could walk in and be ready to rock at a moment's notice. An elaborate drum kit sat in the far right corner near a collection of bass guitars, and a series of keyboards. A gorgeous grand piano anchored the space. On the opposite end of the room, a massive array of computer screens and engineering equipment were positioned in front of a real live sound booth. I noted the acoustic panels on the stone walls and the comfy sofas along the perimeter as I turned in a slow circle, taking in as many details as possible. The studio was clean and orderly but had a lived-in feel lacking in the rest of the house. It was fucking incredible.

"This might be the coolest place on the planet. Do you work here? Stupid question. Of course you work here. Wow. Just fuckin' amazing," I blabbered.

"Thanks."

He crossed his arms, fixing me with an amused chuckle as I moved around the room like a kid in a candy store. "Do you play all these instruments? You probably do. That's another stupid question. Wait. I think you told me. Guitar and piano."

"Right. The rest I can fake with varying degrees of success." Gray met me in front of an elaborate wall of guitars and pulled a beautiful mahogany Gibson down. "Try this one. She's got a true sound. Clear and strong."

"That's okay. I don't want to mess it up."

Gray scoffed. "Unless you smash it against the wall, I don't see how you can mess it up."

"Uh, all right..."

I held his gaze in a strange standoff of sorts before taking the guitar and sitting on the stool next to the drum kit. I settled it over my knee and fingered the strings idly, hoping something amazing would come to me. I drew a blank. When in doubt, start at the beginning.

The first song I ever learned to play on the guitar was Neil Diamond's "Sweet Caroline." It was an inspired choice because it was easy to learn, and everyone loved it. If you could fake it well enough on a popular song, people tended to fill in the rough patches and not notice the guitarist needed a tune-up.

However, I'd never played an instrument that belonged to a real songwriter and potentially cost more than everything I owned put together.

I liked to think of myself as a fairly confident guy, but nothing felt familiar. I was a nerve-wracking combination of edgy and horny around Gray. This would have been a hell of a lot easier if I didn't know how rough and tender he could be and how amazing it felt to have him inside me.

I sucked in a deep breath and strummed the first few chords. When I flubbed the intro, I covered it up by singing. Loudly. It was a habit I'd developed to cover my mistakes when I was in Gypsy Coma. If I sang above anyone else, they might overlook my amateurish guitar skills. It had worked in my favor. For a while, anyway.

My philosophy applied to everyday life too. If I distracted someone with a laugh, I could temporarily make them forget the color of my skin, my lack of education, my sexuality, my social inadequacies, and the fact that I didn't have a dime to my name. It was a perverse kind of magic. I could fake anything for a short time, but I wasn't a comedian and I wasn't much of a musician. The one thing I did pretty well was sing. Hopefully well enough to distract Gray from my fumbling fingers. Fuck, I was nervous.

I powered through the song, then flattened my hand over the strings when I reached the chorus and belted out, "So good, so good, so good!" like I would in a karaoke bar.

"That was inspired," Gray enthused. "You have an amazing voice."

His smile morphed into a wide, luminous grin that stopped me in my tracks like a car skidding off the road into a brick wall. Cue sound effects—screeching brakes, metal-on-metal, glass shattering, and *boom*! My heartbeat reverberated in my head, making me feel dizzy and dopey. I felt warm and then hot. Too hot. And maybe a little punch-drunk, 'cause *wow*, I'd never seen a smile quite like his. It started in his eyes and took over his face, radiating from him like sunshine.

"Um. Uh...thanks." I covered my mouth and coughed to hide my embarrassment as I stood and looked around the studio. "So you have records?"

He pulled the strap over his head and set his guitar on a nearby stand. "It's the library next door. I have to warn you, it's a disaster zone. If you're a type A neat-freak, you may find this disturbing."

I snorted. "I'm not actually sure my socks match. Bring it on."

"This way." He paused with his hand on the doorknob to the adjacent room and then winked before slowly pushing the door open. He stepped into the cavernous room, his arms spread wide. "Welcome to the library."

"Holy fuck."

My notion of what an enormous record collection might look like didn't jive with reality. I wasn't sure why, but my mind conjured neatly stacked vinyls waiting to be alphabetized and stored on a shelf. My mom kept a few of her favorite albums from the eighties in a cabinet under the TV when I was a kid. Rory and I used to pore over them, checking out the covers and reading the lyrics while listening to them on her ancient turntable. This was that version on steroids. And Gray was right. It was a fucking mess.

The room itself looked like a recent addition. The ceilings were high and vaulted like a chapel. Light streamed through the skylights above and from the series of small windows located above the shelves that lined every inch of wall space. There might have been seating on the other side, but it was impossible to see much beyond the forest of boxes stacked high on every surface...floors, tables, chairs...everywhere. The sea of cardboard reminded me of a storage facility. If he'd told me UPS was using his home as an outpost, I would have believed him. Some of the boxes were ripped open, but most were taped shut, waiting to be shipped out or put away.

"Those are all filled with records?" I asked in an awestruck tone.

"Yeah. I just purchased this collection. Mine was decent-sized to begin with, but this takes it to a whole new realm." Gray headed for the table and popped open the top of a box and pulled out an album. "Check this one out. It's a rare jazz recording from the early thirties. Oh. And this is a bossa nova classic."

"Mmm...cool," I replied.

I took the albums he handed me and glanced unseeing at the faded artwork on the covers as he went on about the lush sound and how each record provided an incredible glimpse into history. Not just about the music but the people who bought the music as well.

"...music is a mirror into the soul. The words, the beat, and the arrangement provide clues about the human experience. But the physical vinyl record tells you about the owner too. You can't get a more in-depth picture of who we are as a species. This is history!" he insisted excitedly. "You can get to know..."

I tuned him out when he detailed the impact of fashion, social commentary, and poetry through the vinyl disc medium. His enthusiasm was charming as hell, but I was more fascinated about his transformation from cool musician to history geek than the amount of records he owned. It was...cute. Weird adjective because Gray wasn't cute. He was sexy and a little scary. Almost as scary as the sheer number of albums in this room. I tried to think of a formula to estimate how many might be in each box, but I didn't have my brother's mind for math. The direct approach worked best for me anyway.

"How many records do you have?" I interrupted.

"A few hundred thousand. There's a bit of every—"

"A few hundred thousand?" I repeated incredulously.

"Yeah." Gray shot a wry grin at me. "I need to organize them by genre and alphabetize them. It's a daunting but necessary job. I'd love to do it myself, but I don't have time."

We stared at the sea of boxes together like a couple of sailors analyzing the impact of an iceberg in the distance.

"How long would you say a project this size would take?"

Gray put his hands on his hips and gave a cursory glance around the space before answering. "A few months. Are you interested?"

He seemed as surprised by his offer as I was. He narrowed his eyes and twitched his lips. I could practically hear him thinking of a way to unask the question.

"Really?"

"Yeah. Why not? I bet you could have it done by summer. It's not a bad gig. You can stay in the bedroom I showed you, swim or use the hot tub when you feel like it, and I'll even let you use my studio when I don't need it if you want to practice." When I didn't immediately jump at the opportunity, he added, "Think about it. No hurry. This mess isn't going anywhere."

"That's a very generous offer, but no."

Gray frowned. "Why not?"

"Because I like you."

"That doesn't make any sense. If you like me, you should stay."

"But I don't casually like you." I shook my head and reached for a Patsy Cline album. I pretended to study the liner notes while I gathered my thoughts. If I walked away not feeling like an idiot, it would be a minor miracle. "I've played that night over in my head a few times a day for two weeks straight. I stared at your number and almost pushed Call more than once. In fact, I almost did it before this meeting."

"I wish you had," he whispered.

"But see, I'm glad I didn't now. We were equals that night. I knew you were older and probably wealthy and successful too, but in the dark, you were just a normal guy. Better than normal. You were interesting and funny, and sexy as fuck. And maybe this sounds paranoid or shortsighted, but I need that night to stay complete. I don't want to ruin it with reality. I have a lot of shitty things to deal with that stress me the fuck out and I need this...need to be able to take that memory out of a box in my head and just remember things aren't always crappy. Does that make sense? I hope so, 'cause I feel like a real moron, getting all moody and sensitive here."

"No, it doesn't make sense." Gray licked his bottom lip and looked away. "I want you to stay. We can pick up where we left off. This time we know who we are."

"Employee, employer. Top dog, little dog, alpha, beta. How old are you?"

"Forty-four."

"You're eighteen years older than me. You were probably in college when I was born. That's a whole lifetime. There's a built-in huge divide between us, and working for you would only widen it. If I was smart, I'd take the job and laugh at the irony of someone paying a guy who gets distracted halfway through the alphabet to organize this insane collection. It wouldn't take me months, it would take me years to get through it. And then what happens? I lust after my boss from the sidelines and hope he drops by to chat about something silly he watched on TV, like *The Westminster Dog Show*, while I try to remember if M goes before N."

"Okay, first of all, *The Westminster Dog Show* is not silly. But pretending you're stupid is and—"

"I'm not stupid. I have concentration issues."

"ADHD?" he asked with a frown.

"Yeah. Whatever. Not a big deal. I make it work. But I know my limitations. And this is one of them."

He regarded me thoughtfully with a hard look I couldn't read to save my life. "So what I'm hearing is...you're an ageist with trust issues."

I snorted. "I am not! I mean...yes, on the trust part, but I don't care how old you are."

"You just said you did. You walked into my house and judged me before I could judge you. Then you put a label on me and decided the idea of me is better than the real thing."

"You know, you're making me sound like a real asshole," I huffed.

"Really? Because I think you're fucking amazing." He moved in closer and grabbed my hand. "And I'm so glad you're here."

I grinned like a fool. When I tugged my hand away, he tightened his hold and then lifted my fingers to his lips. I tried to act cool and unmoved by his unexpected gallantry, like I was used to hot guys making romantic moves on me. It didn't work. I wasn't just moved, I was swept away.

I didn't argue when he slipped his arm around my waist and pulled me against him. And I didn't turn away when he cupped my chin and gently pressed his lips to mine. I went completely still and tried to find a balance that would allow me to enjoy this with enough distance to not lose sight of reality. The moment he licked my lips and pushed his tongue inside, I knew it was useless. I wrapped my arms around him, moaning when he backed me against the wall.

Gray set his free hand above my head as he deepened the kiss. I fucking loved having him over me. He was big and imposing, but his size didn't overwhelm me. Somehow, I felt safe, which was strange. I was bi, but my experience with men was limited, hurried, and usually involved some measure of regret.

Gray didn't give me room to overthink, but he was careful not to suffocate me.

We made out leisurely with twisting tongues and roving hands for a while. When we finally broke for oxygen, Gray smiled and pointed at the album I'd dropped.

"How do you feel about Patsy Cline?" he asked.

"Love her."

"Good. That was a test. You can stay. Let me show you around." Gray winked before playfully pulling me into the room.

His library was impressive. Any music lover with an appreciation for vinyl would have been in heaven. But I was more enchanted with him. And yeah, I was fully aware "enchanted" was a goopy word to even think about a guy. But it fit because I didn't recognize my thought process. It was like I was under a spell that put a dreamy look in my eyes and had me hanging on his every word. Of course, it was a matter of time before my brain tripped my internal wiring and asked me to clarify what the hell I was doing here with someone like him.

"...this is an original Fats Domino recording from—"

"Why did Charlie call me? I mean, I get that he's your godson, but I don't know him. He seemed to know about me, though." I furrowed my brow in distaste. "Did you tell him about us?"

"No. But his dad is my best friend. He knew."

"And decided to play matchmaker?" I asked incredulously.

"No. Seb is a producer. He was with me that night and...well, he's interested in switching up the music for his next movie. He talked to Xena about contracting a—"

"Whoa!" I raised one hand, then paced back toward the door to lean on the jamb for support. My legs felt like jelly, and the roaring noise in my ears made it difficult to hear. That was probably a good thing. I pulled out my cell and read the text Declan sent me that morning. *We need to talk. Xena's signing a contract you might be interested in.*

I couldn't believe it. This really *was* a setup. I had no idea what they wanted from me, but something told me my starry-eyed infatuation was like fish bait to a shark. Gray might have remembered that night fondly...who wouldn't? But he hadn't called me here to rekindle something or even give me a fucking job. He was working for his friend. Writing him jingles...and somehow Xena and Dec were involved? *Fuck this shit.*

"Justin, whatever you're thinking, you're wrong."

"I don't think so. You're using me. I don't know what you want but—"

"Don't be ridiculous. Let me explain," Gray said in a rational, mature tone.

"No. Don't."

There had to be twenty perfect comeback lines, but I couldn't think of one. Nothing funny, nothing snarky, and certainly nothing intelligent. Surprise warred with pride and made it difficult for me to see through the fiery red haze clouding my vision, let alone think of a pleasant way to tell him to shove his record collection up his ass.

A little voice in my head told me I should take advantage of this not-so-chance meeting. But using sex and making the right connections to get ahead wasn't my specialty. Hell, anyone who knew me agreed I was an expert at destroying opportunity, not exploiting it.

And just to prove it, I pushed Gray's chest and backed him against the wall before capturing his face between my hands and sealing my mouth over his in what I referred to as a "fuck you" kiss. Something sexy but harsh that should have said everything I couldn't without sounding delusional.

Unfortunately, my "fuck you" backfired.

My body responded to him like a match to a flame. It was

instant and all-consuming. The scrape of his stubbled jaw, his soft lips, and his hard body. The wicked combination and his immediate response made me horny as fuck. I moved between his open legs and tilted my hips, moaning aloud at the feel of his shaft alongside mine. The friction felt amazing through his flimsy swim trunks. I lowered my hands to his waist, then nipped his jaw before cupping his ass and grinding against him like I was riding a pole at a strip joint. We made out in a furious tangle punctuated by rhythmic thrusts until I dipped my hand under the waistband of his trunks and traced his crack.

"We can't do this here." He gasped for air and shook his head.

I blinked in surprise. Holy crap. What was I doing?

"Save your speech. I don't need you to tell me this is a bad idea. I don't need your special treatment, I don't want any favors, and I don't want your fucking job," I huffed humorlessly. "Thanks for wasting my time and ruining a perfectly good memory. It's been fun."

I flung the door open and hurried along the maze of sunlit corridors and posh living spaces, retracing my original path to the main entry as quickly as humanly possible. I sucked in a breath of fresh air on the landing, then pulled my keys from my pocket and raced down the path. I made a mundane to-do list to keep from spinning over the disastrous meeting. Something bigger than a chance meeting with a former hookup was at play, but I couldn't begin to make sense of anything in my current state of mind.

I paused at the bottom of the driveway to stuff my cell into my pocket when I noticed Charlie next to my car, posing like a superhero in training with his hands on his hips.

"How did it go?" Charlie beamed.

I scoffed. "Peachy fucking keen. Later, dude."

He chased me to the driver's side and flattened himself against the door. "Wait! What happened?"

"Let's just say it didn't work out." I gestured meaningfully, then added, "Now, if you'll excuse me."

Charlie shook his head vigorously and spread his arms wide. "You're not going anywhere until you tell me what you did. You must have done something or said something. You owe me an explanation. By the way, your car is filthy. I'm sending you the dry-cleaning bill for this shirt."

I snorted in disbelief. For a little guy, he had big balls and a lot of nerve. "I don't owe you shit. You, however, owe me the last hour of my life back. Let's make that two hours. I'm charging you for gas money and the beauty rest you interrupted."

Charlie gasped in outrage. "You needed a job. Alphabetizing records has to be the cushiest deal ever. How could you possibly blow it?"

"Look, thanks for thinking of me, Charlie, but I don't need your so-called help and I don't want your charity. You aren't my friend. You aren't my fairy gay guy either. Now if you'll excuse me." I picked him up like a toy doll and set him a few feet away before opening the car door.

"Fairy gaymother," he corrected.

"Whatever. Stay out of my life. Stay out of my business. I know something else is going on here, but I'm not participating in this BS. Don't call me, don't email me, and don't talk to me in the club. Try me and I'll have you banned for harassment. Got it?"

I didn't wait for his reply. I put my sunglasses on my nose, James Dean-style, and then climbed behind the wheel of the battered yellow Corolla like a badass. The engine sputtered a couple of times before it revved to life, ruining the vibe. But I pretended it was part of my mystique as I rolled down the window, flashed a peace sign, and drove away.

4

GRAY

I waited in the entryway, with my arms crossed. I had to nab Charlie before he escaped, and I knew from experience he was a slippery one.

"What the hell just happened here?"

Charlie closed the front door with a start. He widened his eyes and shrugged. "I don't know."

"You do know," I corrected. "Your dad obviously brought you into this. Explain."

"Come on, Gray. I'm sure you can guess. He's in Toronto and he's freaking out about that publicity angle for the Baxter movie. You know how he gets. He can't let anything go."

"So he asked you to interfere."

"He asked me to help." Charlie copied my pose and cocked his head in a gesture that instantly reminded me of the little boy who'd followed me around when he was two years old. "He wanted me to talk to Justin at Vibes, but I have zero time for clubbing. I'm stressed out of my mind with the project I'm working on for my Creative Management Course and—"

"Charlie…" I tapped my foot and gave him my best "Quit the BS" look.

"I thought I could kill two birds with one stone. Get Justin here to meet you so you could ask him about the song yourself. I thought once he saw the studio and heard my spiel about representing his band, which you'll be thrilled to know ties in with my master's course...he'd realize his cup runneth over. You can't sign up for this much good luck at once!"

I let out a deep sigh. "Char, you can't force people to do what you want them to do."

"You're telling me. You and Dad are the most uncooperative duo ever. I'm going to have gray hair before I'm thirty at this rate," he huffed theatrically. "And before you say anything, I'm not having a *Parent Trap* moment. I'm trying to fulfill my father's request, work on my master's project, and help a struggling artist all at once. I'm working harder than the button on my skinny jeans, and it wouldn't hurt for someone somewhere to give me a little slack!"

"Don't get dramatic on me," I warned, pointing a parental finger at his chest.

"I am not dramatic. I'm at my wit's end! I've been commissioned to save the world, and it is not easy. What could possibly be so hard about asking Justin to—*gasp*!" Charlie put his hand over his mouth. "You like him."

He stepped backward, then sank theatrically onto the uncomfortable bench in the entry.

"It's not like that," I lied.

Charlie ignored me. "This is...different, but good. I think. I mean, he's only a little older than me, but that's okay. Dad isn't going to like this. He's all about having fun, but you're the one he loves."

I rolled my eyes. "You've officially gone off the deep end. I met Justin once. I'm not in love with him. I like him. That's all."

He patted the space beside him. When I sat down, he looped his right arm around my shoulder. "What are we going to do about him? We have to get him back. Dad wants to talk to him about that song and I—"

"He isn't business to me, Char. He's personal."

"Oh."

"What's in it for you anyway? Did your dad promise you a cut in commission?"

Charlie scoffed as if offended by the idea, then nodded yes. "Of course, he did. You know how he operates. No story is exciting unless you sensationalize it. Xena was more than excited to cooperate, but I saw them play live. Justin was the best thing about Gypsy Coma. I think he's got it."

"I do too," I said softly.

Charlie laid his head on my shoulder. "You know, I worry about you. It's not healthy to spend so much time alone."

"Don't worry about me, Char. I'm fine."

"Sometimes I wonder." He sighed; then he kissed my cheek and hugged me before hopping off the bench. "I've got to go. I have class in twenty minutes."

"What about the records? I thought you came by today to work on them."

"No. I said I'd come by to help you. And I did. Now you just need to help yourself. Love you, Gray."

He spun gracefully, pausing to lift his man bag over his shoulder and set his giant sunglasses on his nose. Then he opened the door and waved one last time before closing it behind him.

The silence was deafening. It always felt this way after Charlie or Oliver or Seb left, but Justin was new. And very unexpected. When he didn't call, I assumed he was adamant about keeping that night a one-time-only deal. I'd thought about him constantly. If Seb hadn't come up with his grand publicity ploy, I might have sought him out on my own. But I wasn't going to play a game where the only winner was a record label or a studio box office. I'd been there, done that too many times. But maybe Charlie was right. I had nothing to gain, but if I could help, that might be enough.

———

Justin

DESPERATE TIMES CALLED for desperate measures...and research. I spent the rest of the afternoon doing a little homework of the Google variety on Gray Robertson. I was prepared for almost anything. He could have been a burned-out musician from the eighties or a tech genius who retired too young and had nothing better to do than sit on his roof all day playing guitar. I typed his name, pushed Enter, and gaped at the results.

Gray Robertson was a musician-slash-songwriter virtuoso originally from St. Paul, Minnesota. He attended NYU before moving to Los Angeles to write commercial jingles for children's shampoo ads when he was twenty-one. By the time he was twenty-five, he'd written his first top ten hit. A year later, he had his first number one song and a Grammy nomination. At thirty, he'd made his mark as a highly acclaimed songwriter credited with writing some of the biggest songs for a few major recording artists. And according to Wikipedia, he turned forty-four last November. I did the math in my head and realized I was twelve when he turned thirty. I think I'd still been into my Pokémon phase when he was just hitting his stride. His most recent credits included writing musical scores for big-budget Hollywood movies like *The Baxter Chronicles.*

The man was music royalty. So what the fuck was this all about?

"If you'd stuck around and asked a few questions, you'd know," Tegan snarked around a mouthful of pasta.

"It doesn't make sense that Charlie would insert himself in my life out of nowhere. And who the fuck is Charlie anyway? He said he knows me from Vibes, but I've never seen the guy before in my life. Do you know him? He's short with curly blond hair and he's cute...but nuts."

Tegan set his bowl on the coffee table and furrowed his brow like he was deep in thought. "Did he put his hands on his hips a lot?"

"Yeah."

"Mmm. I know him. He's at Vibes a couple of times a week. Not lately, though. I heard he went back to school. Maybe he met someone or just doesn't have as much time."

"Then why wouldn't I recognize him?"

"You're behind the bar, dude. Other than bathroom breaks and occasional trips to get supplies from storage, you don't see anyone unless they come to you. I'm a bouncer. I see 'em comin' and goin'."

"He did say he didn't come to the bar much," I said before taking a bite of my burger.

"He doesn't have to. Sean lets him in for free 'cause he's well-connected and travels with an exclusive entourage. And he's colorful. He dresses up in funky clothes and dances the entire time."

I set my burger on the battered coffee table, then twisted to give Tegan a sideways "What the fuck?" look. "Exclusive entourage?"

"You know...Instagram influencers, wannabee actors, and models. Some of them are idiots, but there are a few super-brainy types too. Sean says they're good for business. They post the club on social media in exchange for complimentary drinks and free entry. Every time Sean places a special order at the bar, it's usually for one of Charlie's posse. He loves Charlie."

"Oh." As in "Oh, fuck."

"I don't really get the appeal, but people eat that crap up," Tegan huffed. "They want to see pictures of boys kissing boys and video clips of them dirty dancing with their buddies. It's all staged. They get paid to wear designer jeans and hang out with a bunch of guys they barely know. Then they post their photos on Instagram and everyone goes crazy over them. Including Sean."

"So he's a big social media guy and he helps club owners like Sean by hyping his brand online?"

"Nice way to make a living, huh?" Tegan leaned back on the sofa and rested his hands behind his head before continuing, "We should ask Charlie to help us. You know, we gotta up our social media game too. We have to hash out some details and put a plan into action. We've got some good new material. Email him. You have his contact info, right?"

"Uh, yeah, but we don't know it's the same Charlie for sure."

Tegan sat up and fixed me with a shrewd once-over. "What did you do?"

"What makes you think I did anything?"

" 'Cause you're acting shifty. The way you do when you've fucked something up," he deadpanned.

"Who me?"

"Uh huh. You know, his dad's a big-time producer. He—" Tegan bolted upright and pointed at my laptop. "Holy fuck. His dad is Sebastian Rourke. He does those spy thrillers. So that's why he was at Gray Robertson's house. That's awesome! If he was at the show at Carmine's and then contacted you through Charlie, he's gotta be interested. Maybe he wanted Charlie to feel you out before he offered assistance."

"Nah, I don't think so," I bluffed.

"It fits. They saw you play, they liked you. You disappeared after your set like an asshole, but they tracked you down and asked Charlie to help. I know you're suspicious, but it makes sense now. Call him back. This could be great for JTJ!"

"Our name is not JTJ," I huffed. "We need to get away from the Gypsy Coma drama and focus on our own music with a new name, a new direction. Oh, yeah. And we need to line up some new shows."

"I bet Charlie can help us."

I puffed my cheeks out and slowly let out a rush of air followed by a weak chuckle. "I told him to fuck off."

"Then un-tell him to fuck off. Apologize. Tell him you were surprised or that you weren't feeling well or that your goldfish fucking died. He's our ticket to real exposure. To guys like Gray. To—"

"I told him to fuck off too."

Tegan deflated like a sad balloon. He slumped forward and braced his forearms on his knees. "Of course you did."

As far as Tegan knew, the email-slash-job offer was an odd stroke of luck. He didn't know about my evening with Gray, and I wanted to keep it that way. By mutual unspoken agreement, we didn't talk about our sex lives. I knew he was with Sean. He knew I wasn't exactly a monk.

We were mostly back to normal, and neither of us wanted to dredge up something we couldn't fix overnight. Our short-term side trip into "more than friends" territory was a good example of what happened when I let my brain go on vacation and put my dick in charge of major decision-making. I was grateful we'd emerged with our friendship intact.

I set my laptop on the sofa cushion and paced the short distance to the big-screen TV. "We don't need Charlie or anyone else."

"We can't do it all on our own, Jus. We're going to have to ask for help once in a while, and we're going to have to trust that not everyone is like Dec or Xena. It's the only way to get ahead in this business. We gotta stop bracing ourselves for the next blow and start making our mark. It's time to move forward and start to—"

"Zero," I blurted.

"Huh?"

"Our name! Zero. Starting over. Like a new beginning."

Tegan scratched his jaw thoughtfully. "Zero to Hero? Zero to Sixty?"

I rolled my eyes. "No, asshole. Just Zero."

Tegan smacked my hand and then held it briefly. "I like it."

"It's fucking perfect!" I nodded like a puppet on a string. "This is it. Let's call Johnny. The three of us have to be sure we're on the same page. You call Ky and—"

"And you'll call Charlie," he intercepted.

"Yeah, yeah."

"Don't let your pride get in the way, Jus," he warned. "Short-term satisfaction isn't gonna pay the bills. If we're in this for the long haul, we have to be in it one hundred percent. And occasionally, we have to be willing to make sacrifices."

A WELL-TIMED PEP talk can work wonders. I called Johnny and invited him over for an impromptu jam session and a last-minute power meeting. We opened a bottle of Jack and the three of us brainstormed all night. We muddled over mundane but important details like leasing sound equipment and pulling our resources to come up with more studio time.

Johnny leaned his guitar against the sofa, then fell into the plush beanbag chair near the window. "We have some great songs and a lot of dysfunction. Both are probably key ingredients, but it takes more than occasional practice sessions and coffee shop gigs to become something special."

I liked Johnny the first time I met him at Aromatique. We'd bonded over music and commiserated about how damned hard it seemed to catch a break in the business. He had an expressive face. Big brown eyes, full lips, a pointed nose, and a lot of hair. His wild curly mane, black jeans and T-shirt chic, and the hint of eyeliner were his trademark. Johnny was roughly my height but even leaner. He was good-looking, personable, and perpetually upbeat and friendly. He offset the dysfunction he mentioned between Tegan and me very well. In fact, it disappeared when we played.

"We need to be diligent about practice, and we have to get a couple of real gigs. Let's ask Carmine if we can play his club. I know he was a little pissed I left after my set, but—"

"He was a lot pissed," Tegan corrected.

"And he's invitation only," Johnny added. "He invited you because of Xena. I heard he was hoping to stir up some commotion, but you walked out and killed his fun. The only way he'd be marginally interested in your new band is if you came with a new scandal. Oh, and speaking of scandal...Declan told me Xena signed a movie contract. I think he's pissed because they don't want him too. Do you guys know anything about that?"

"When did you talk to him?" I asked.

"He came by the coffee shop. I think he was looking for you. He seems like he's mellowed out. You know he plays bass, right? Maybe we should ask—"

"No fucking way," Tegan growled. "I'm calling Ky. I think he's interested in trying something new."

I nodded in agreement. "Dec stirs up trouble just for fun. I want Zero to be about real music. No hype, no drama. I've been in bands since I was a teenager. I was happy to play covers in the beginning, and I didn't mind hopping around stage doing a mediocre Dave Grohl impression while Xena pretended to be Exene Cervenka with Gypsy Coma. But I don't want to be a retro bullshit cover band or a fucking poser, hiding behind people who're braver than me. I'm done with that. I want a do-over and I want to do it the right way this time...in my own voice. My words, you on lead guitar, T on drums, and Ky or someone who's not Dec on bass. And I know it's not gonna happen overnight, but it will happen. We're gonna be big someday."

"I like that attitude." Johnny's cautious smile morphed into an ear-to-ear grin. He slapped high fives with us, then snapped his fingers and pointed at me. "Shoot, I forgot to tell you...someone else came by looking for you today. A sexy older guy. His name was...um...fuck, it's a color."

"Gray?" I asked, furrowing my brow in surprise.

"That's it! Hot-as-fuck daddy, if you know what I mean."

I let out an amused huff at his over-the-top lecherous expression. I'd gone months thinking Johnny was straight. He wasn't. It cracked me up when he went gaga over a sexy man. "Right. Thanks."

"He said you have his number...text him or call him."

Tegan gave me a sharp look. "That's perfect. Text him."

"I will. Later."

Johnny cast a wary glance between us before suggesting that we outline a schedule and made a list of LA clubs we wanted to play.

Tegan set his hand on his chin thoughtfully. "Moonlight, The Hole, Porcelain Doll—"

"No. Those places are dives, dude," Johnny said, shaking his head. "We need a goal. Something to shoot for, so we know we aren't just spinning our wheels."

"An invitation to Carmine's. Just Zero," Tegan replied.

I shook my head. "No. Bigger...the Troubadour."

Johnny and Tegan grinned and raised their glasses to mine.

"To Zero."

"To Zero." We clinked our glass and then exchanged bro-style handshakes and fist bumps that felt like ink on contract. And a new beginning.

———

Aromatique was a hipster coffee shop within walking distance of Tegan's apartment and Vibes in West Hollywood. The tiny shop married a French bohemian ambience with European class. Soft blue-and-gray walls contrasted nicely with the black-and-white tile flooring while tasteful photographs of well-known landmarks like the Eiffel Tower and the Louvre hung beside rock gods like Jimi Hendrix and Queen. The sophisticated yet bohemian atmosphere appealed to the chic-meets-cool clientele who enjoyed sipping lattes while listening to live music.

Every afternoon aspiring musicians were invited to play to a small but enthusiastic audience. Guitarists, violinists, keyboard players...any instrument that fit was welcome. The space near the window served as a mini stage. It was a little cozy, but it worked okay. I played a few times myself before I mustered the courage to ask the owner for a job. My confidence was gutter-level low after my breakup with Xena and the demise of Gypsy Coma, so I was pitifully grateful Michel hired me on the spot. I needed every dime I earned serving lattes, and I was willing to wake up early after a long night bartending at Vibes. But I was more excited about the additional perk of performing for customers on a regular basis. I didn't want to lose my edge.

I'd learned a few humbling things about myself from those initial solo gigs. First of all, playing electric guitar behind a diva indie rock goddess with a dramatic side was completely different than going solo with an acoustic guitar. Secondly, I was a better singer than guitarist. I had a ton of energy, and I could be theatrical when I got swept away by the music, but I'd never wanted to be a front man. I'd grown more as a performer in the past few months than I had in the two years I'd been with Gypsy Coma. My songwriting was better too. And late morning after my shift was the perfect time to unwind in a quiet corner to write.

I hefted my backpack over my shoulder, then tugged at my apron string and glanced around the mostly empty shop. A young couple sat at a table for two under an artsy black-and-white photograph of Freddy Mercury, and three middle-aged women chatted quietly as they perused the Parisian treats in the corner display. My timing was good. The early morning rush was over, and the pre-lunch crowd hadn't descended yet. I sidled behind the counter and swatted Johnny's ass as I headed for the commercial-grade coffeemaker.

"What time are you off?" I asked casually.

"Two o'clock. Who's that for?" Johnny asked, gestured toward my latte.

"Me. I need more caffeine."

He held up the steamed milk and fluttered his eyelashes. "Would you like a leaf on your latte?"

I snickered. "Tempting, but I'll pass on jizz in my mug today, man."

Johnny chuckled. "You're nasty. How about a heart? I made one for the hot guy in the gray Hugo Boss suit this morning. 'Member him?"

"Barely."

"I was testing the waters to see if I got a glimmer of interest."

"And?"

"I think he likes me. Or he liked my jizz art anyway," he assured me. "I can't decide if I should try to learn how to make something cute like a panda or a fat cat, or if I should go straight to dick. Thoughts?"

"Why hold back?" I cradled the mug in both hands and leaned against the marble counter.

"Good advice," he agreed with a laugh before gesturing toward the far end of the coffee shop by the window. "Better grab your table before the yoga moms arrive and ask you to move your stuff."

I made a peace sign and headed for the corner table for two near the window. I set my backpack on the free chair and pulled out my notebook. I tuned out the background noise with practiced ease while I sipped my latte and jotted song lyrics down. It was an odd habit that morphed into a lifeline of sorts.

When everything around me fell to pieces, writing kept me sane. I'd filled dozens of notebooks over the past decade. Some days, when the words wouldn't come, I wrote a line or two about the color of the sky or the smell of baked bread. Silly things to remind me that even on days when nothing was going my way, there were still puppies and cupcakes and good things in the world. Other days, words poured out of me faster than I could get them on paper.

Yesterday, I wrote about fear and frustration.

You told me we'd be fine

You told me that we'd make it through the fire

Okay, that kinda sucked. Thankfully, I felt more hopeful today. I pulled my guitar from my case and mulled over what I'd written until I could hear the music. I bent the notes to fit a melody that could work for a rock ballad or even a country song. I stared into space and let it play out in my head like I was listening to a tune on the radio. Halfway through the song, my mind wandered and the song became part of a daydream. I was on the road with my band, touring the US to support our hit album. We were on a tricked-out bus, and then onstage in a huge arena...in Texas. I didn't stop to wonder why; I just let the story unfold. Screaming fans, lights, cowboy hats and fancy boots. I raised my shiny black Gibson in the air before settling on a stool to do a solo rendition of our recent hit. I strummed the first few chords, scanned the audience, and the only face I recognized was Gray's.

He stood out in his beach bum chic...swim trunks and an unbuttoned plaid shirt, but no one else seemed to notice. They swayed to the music while I stared at Gray. He gave me a knowing look before unfastening the fly on his trunks and freeing his cock. He crooked his finger and next thing I knew, I was on my knees, fumbling with my belt buckle with my mouth wide open and—

What the hell? I flattened my hand over the strings and cast a wary glance around the now-bustling café before reading over what I'd written.

I want you over me, inside of me, hands in my hair, mouth everywhere

The words jumped from the page and immediately suggested a beat. Something sultry and bluesy. As the music built inside me, the imagery sharpened. And it was all Gray. I could practically feel his hands and his lips. I didn't stop to wonder why I was so obsessed with him. I learned not to question the process when the words flowed and the song practically wrote itself.

I don't want you to take your time
I don't want to make you mine
Take it harder, take it faster, take it—

"Sounds sexy."

I started in surprise and frowned. "What are you doing here?"

"Coffee." Gray lifted his to-go cup as proof. "Mind if I join you?"

"Why?"

"Because I'd like to talk to you," he replied patiently.

"Uh..." I held his stare as I tried to get my heart rate under control.

This was weird. It was like I had a magic pen that somehow conjured what I'd written. Or maybe I was still dreaming. If I blinked and found myself on a giant stage in a noisy arena with a raging hard-on, I might just drift back to sleep and—

"Are you okay?" Gray cocked his head and gave me a concerned look.

I nodded before dropping my backpack on the floor. "Be my guest."

Fuck, he was hot. He looked like a construction worker in his plaid shirt and Levis. His dark hair was mussed like he'd just rolled out of bed, and his beard was thicker, like he hadn't bothered shaving. It didn't cover his dimple, though. And nothing could hide the obvious humor in his twinkling eyes. I wondered what the hell he was smiling about. We hadn't exactly parted on friendly terms. And in spite of what I'd told Tegan, I hadn't called Gray. My pride kept getting in the way. *Ugh.* I was such an idiot sometimes.

I cradled my guitar and reached for my lukewarm latte as Gray pulled out the chair next to mine. And then presented me with a bouquet of mini red roses. "These are for you."

"You bought me flowers?" I asked incredulously.

"Yeah." He gave me a bashful shrug and looked away. "I'm sorry about last week. I was wrong and I apologize for offending you."

"You didn't offend me," I bluffed, brushing my thumb over the tiny petals. "Okay, fine. You did, but you didn't have to buy me flowers. Ice cream would have worked."

Gray chuckled. "Believe it or not, I brought a pint of Häagen-Dazs chocolate chip for you yesterday and the day before. You weren't here, so I had to eat it myself. I was on track to gain ten pounds if I kept missing you, so I switched to roses. The florist was very specific about the type and the color. She said red is for lovers, and since we don't know each other well, she suggested the miniature ones. Don't let this freak you out, though. They're just flowers."

"No one's ever bought me flowers in my life," I assured him with wide-eyed wonder. "I'm totally freaked out. But in a good way."

"So, you forgive me?"

"Yeah. I might have overreacted. I'm a hothead sometimes. I get anxious and lash out when I don't know what's going on and...you know, I had no fucking idea you were famous."

"I'm not famous, Justin. I'm just a writer."

"I googled you, dude. You're famous. You've written tons of songs. Good ones too. I heard the one they're using for the Apple commercial the other day. It usually pisses me off to see a good song ruined by the corporate machine, but it was pretty well done. So don't tell me you're not famous. You are. Christ, you even have a Wikipedia entry. Why didn't you tell me your name at Carmine's?"

" 'Cause you didn't want to know it," he reminded me. "You wanted anonymity, remember?"

"I was having a bad night. But it got better."

"Mine too. You know, I didn't want to go to Carmine's that night. Seb's always trying to drag me out of the house. I love live music, but I don't like going places where someone wants a piece of my time to further their career. I didn't know why he wanted me there until the next day. He mentioned Xena, but I didn't know about the contract. And once I did, I figured I'd wait to see if you called me. But you didn't."

I frowned as I tried to unravel his logic. "But if I called, you'd have assumed I wanted something from you. So I really couldn't win."

"I suppose I wanted to keep that night in a box too, Justin. I didn't want to ruin it." Gray brushed his hand across his stubbled chin and pursed his lips. "I've been thinking about you every day for weeks now. When you showed up at the house, I knew Seb was up to something, but I didn't have time to process it. Or maybe I didn't want to. I was just happy to see you. At the risk of sounding romantic..." He smiled when I rolled my eyes and then continued. "I'd give anything to relive that night. To be on a rooftop with the city beneath us and feel free for a while... and yet connected. It was magic."

"Yeah. It was," I said in a low voice.

"It seems unfair to let anyone else in. I don't want anyone to take that away from us."

I nodded but didn't speak. We sat quietly, letting the café noises fill the empty space between us. Edith Piaf played through the speaker system under the din of conversation, clinking silverware and the occasional hum of the espresso machine. After a long moment, I set my instrument in the case before clicking it shut and shifting to face Gray.

"So, who's Seb?"

"He's my best friend, Charlie's dad...and yes, he's a successful producer. He's one of those hands-on, über-innovative types. He's always thinking of a new twist to keep his projects fresh and relevant with younger audiences. I won't delve into his résumé, but it's impressive."

"*The Baxter Chronicles.*"

"Exactly. The most recent one will be released this summer."

"And you're working on the soundtrack." I tried to mentally connect the dots, but I still couldn't figure out what this had to do with me.

"It's finished, or nearly there. But nothing's ever really finished with Seb. He decided he wanted to add a couple of songs. In Seb's mind, these unwritten songs are already smash hits. He can hear them on the radio, see them climb the music charts and hang around for weeks on end. Hell, he can hear the cellular ringtones and commercial ads ginormous companies will purchase the rights for later. And while he knows the lyrics and music are crucial, he's a movie guy. He wants a backstory that loosely complements the scripts. So one night at dinner, Charlie tells his dad about a band that just blew up. It's a compelling story…bisexual love triangle, beautiful singer catches her boyfriend fucking the drummer and goes ballistic and…"

"Oh, my God." I swiped my hand over my jaw, then slouched in my chair and crossed my arms. "So he asked Carmine to invite her and her idiot ex to perform. Wow. And Xena knew about the producer and the movie stuff all along. No wonder Declan was pissed."

"No. Not exactly," Gray hedged, biting his bottom lip. "She knew Seb would be there but to be fair, she didn't know what he wanted."

"They must have struck an agreement of some kind, 'cause I haven't heard a thing from her since," I snarked. Because I was kind of an asshole, I made a tongue-against-cheek gesture, complete with a hand motion.

"Not that kind of agreement. He wants her to sing the song."

"The hit ringtone song?"

A ghost of a smile flitted at the corner of his full lips. He nodded slowly, then said, "And he wants you to write it."

I gaped. "Me?"

"Yes, you. You're a good songwriter. The material you played was strong. Seb was impressed."

"I don't know how to write a song for a movie. Geez, I'm just trying to get my band off the ground," I replied in a bewildered tone.

"You wouldn't be doing it alone. We'd cowrite. He wants two or three songs, but the big one is a ballad. A love song."

"A *love* song?" I repeated, making a "yuck" face.

Gray chuckled lightly. "Yes."

I propped my elbows on the table and leaned forward. "Let me get this straight. Your friend wants you and me to write a love song for his movie...for my ex-girlfriend to sing."

"That's correct."

I cautioned myself not to make any hasty decisions. I glanced over at Johnny helping a customer behind the counter, and I could practically hear Tegan begging me to think before I said anything stupid. This could be the break we were talking about. People made bank writing songs for movies. I could fund Zero and hire a manager. I could pay back the ridiculous amount of debt I inherited when Gypsy Coma imploded. Geez, I could get my own apartment and maybe a car too. I could be set. And working with a well-respected songwriter for a big Hollywood movie was the chance of a lifetime. Even if it sucked, I'd probably learn something in the process and network with smart people who knew other aspects of the business. It was a no-brainer. An automatic "Fuck yeah. Where do I sign my name?"

But something stopped me.

"No, thanks."

"No?" Gray repeated incredulously. "Just like that? Don't you want to think about it?"

"What's the point? I don't know how to write a love song. I don't want to learn how to fake it for a buck. I want to write music I can be proud of, not homogenized crap some Hollywood prick I don't know will use against me to further my ex-girlfriend's career. I'm not being spiteful here. I sincerely wish

Xena the best. But I didn't fuck her over. It was the other way around. I don't see how this works in my favor."

"It's good money."

"Well, that house on the hill and your sweet ride are nice, but I'd rather have my integrity," I blurted unthinking.

Gray glared at me for a long moment. "Don't be a fool, Justin. And don't for one second think you know anything about me. I've worked my ass off for years. I've paid my dues and done my time and no one...I repeat, no one offered me any cushy gigs to make my life a little easier."

"I don't want your fucking charity."

"It's not charity. It's work. Hard work." He glanced away, then fixed me with an intense stare. "I told Seb you'd say no. I've known you for a handful of hours, and somehow I knew your pride would get in the way. I'm not saying I blame you. I told him about you the morning after...you know."

"We fucked," I supplied belligerently. "I thought we agreed— no names and no blabbing."

Gray huffed irritably. "He knows me, and he figured it out on his own. I told him I wouldn't ask you, so he enlisted Charlie. I was as shocked as you were. And I was pissed. Then I said all the wrong things because I was also very distracted."

"By what?"

"You! Jesus, I don't do that kind of thing. Ever. I don't talk to strangers. I don't memorize the cadence of their voice and write down everything I can to keep it fresh and alive. You mentioned that Joni Mitchell song, and I swear I listened to it on repeat for days. And it might sound crazy, but I would have given anything to do it over again with a new set of rules."

I gulped. "What kind of rules?"

"No anonymity. I would have demanded to know everything about you before I took you home with me. And I wouldn't have let you go."

"Because you fell madly in love with me?" I asked sarcastically.

"No." He smirked. "Because I'm madly infatuated with your insanely hot body. Better?"

"Much."

Gray flattened his hand over my notebook and gave me an intense look. "You're talented and you're smart. If you thought about it, you'd realize there's a way to write a song so beautiful, it turns the table on everyone...your ex or anyone else who thought they had you figured out. Use the element of surprise in your favor. Create something that surpasses anything you thought you were capable of. That's how you win."

"So you want to do this?"

Gray shrugged. "I'd be willing to give it a try. What about you?"

I took a deep breath and slowly released it. "Honestly, I don't know. This is a weird curveball. I want to concentrate on getting Zero up and running. We need to get in the studio more often and—"

"You can use mine," he intercepted.

"In exchange for what?"

"You can help organize the records. Think about it. You don't have to decide today. But this doesn't have to be a huge time commitment. We can start with a couple of sessions and see if our styles are compatible. If it's not going to work, we'll know immediately. No harm, no foul."

"When would you want to start?"

"Right away."

I regarded him curiously. His sudden enthusiasm clashed with his puzzled expression. It made me think he hadn't planned on asking me to consider the offer. It was the same look he'd given me when he invited me to go for a drink.

"What if we had a trial period? Something to be sure we

could work together before I sign anything," I suggested.

"That's fine," he said.

"Okay. I can start Thursday."

"Great. One more thing."

"A catch! I knew it."

"Can we keep *us* separate?" he asked, sounding a little unsure.

I furrowed my brow. "You don't want me to tell anyone about you? Won't they already know?"

"No. I meant...the song is work, we're personal. I think they'll entwine on their own, and that's good. But the contracts, the musicians, sound engineers, producers, family and friends...I don't want to share you with them. It would be nice to have a space that just belongs to us."

I narrowed my gaze thoughtfully, then inclined my head. "Are you asking me to be your boyfriend? 'Cause I'm gonna want bigger roses for that."

Gray chuckled. "I'll keep that in mind."

I brushed my thumb over the soft petals and listened to every other word of his speech about schedules and syncing calendars. I figured he'd remind me if I missed anything important. And at that moment, when the urge to jump up and pace the coffee shop was so strong my knees twitched, the sound of his voice soothed me and kept me grounded. I didn't feel the need to remind him I wasn't committing to anything. He knew. And I couldn't pass up a day in the studio with a songwriting legend. "Thinking about it" would be a waste of energy. I'd consider it research and report back to my bandmates if I agreed to the song. I wasn't sure how, but maybe we could spin this for Zero's benefit. I liked that idea far better than being an opening act for Xena again. I trusted Gray. He wasn't interested in cashing in on my past. In fact, he might even help me get around it.

Gray

My CELL BUZZED in my pocket the second I stepped out of Aromatique. I glanced at the caller ID and sighed.

"Seb, you're a pain in the ass. I told you I'd call you later. What do you want?"

Seb chuckled. "What do you think I want? Did you talk to him?"

"Yes."

"And?"

"He said maybe."

Seb groaned. "Maybe? I can't work with maybe. I need an answer. I need a song. I need—"

"Don't you have a movie to make and other people to hassle?" I griped.

"Always, but I'd like all the loose ends tied up on this one before I head back to Toronto. Xena signed her contract. If you can get Justin to at least agree to writing the song, I'll worry about his contract later."

"He may be willing, but it's not gonna happen overnight," I replied as I turned to stare into the café.

Justin had taken his instrument out of its case again. He straddled the chair with his head bent as he strummed his guitar with his eyes closed. My fingers itched to tuck the loose strands that had fallen across his face behind his ears so I could look at him while he played. Maybe he wasn't a skilled musician, but his soulful voice and innate charisma set him apart. I'd never heard anyone make "Sweet Caroline" sound like a hot new single. I wanted nothing more than to slip inside the café and listen to him perform for the gathering lunchtime crowd.

"Why not? Don't tell me he wants to think about it," Seb huffed incredulously. "Did you tell him how much he'd make? For fuck's sake, the guy is broke. What does he have to lose?"

"I think it's more a matter of trying figure to out what he has to gain. And by the way, I have no idea what you're offering him or his ex, and I don't want to know."

"Does he know who you are?"

"He does. And he doesn't care."

"Bullshit. He cares. Don't let him play you and don't—"

"Enough. I told you I'd ask him and I did."

Seb sighed heavily into the phone. "How much time does he need?"

"We're getting together this Thursday to see if we're compatible cowriters. I'll let you know how it goes."

"Please do," he said sarcastically. "Is Charlie having dinner with you tonight?"

"Charlie is twenty-four, Seb. He doesn't check in with me about his dinner plans. Why?"

"He's acting funny. Funnier than usual," he amended quickly. "I wonder if he's mad I haven't been around as much lately and..."

I headed down the street toward my car, listening with half an ear as Seb confessed his guilt-laden fears that he was the world's worst dad. The familiar speech sometimes made me sad, and other times it made me want to smack him upside the head. I let him talk because he seemed to need to hear his own voice. But for the first time in a while, I wondered if he was jealous or staking a claim. Maybe he brought up his son to remind me of our past. To remind me that we were connected and we always would be...on the off chance I forgot who we once were to each other. I cast one last look at Aromatique before handing the valet my ticket. Why did everything feel so damn complicated?

5

GRAY

The doorbell scared the hell out of me. I couldn't remember the last time someone actually used it. I hurried to the door and opened it with a flourish.

"Hi, there. You made it," I said lamely.

"We said Thursday at seven, right?" Justin replied. "Is it Thursday?"

"It is. Come on in."

He stepped into the foyer and looked up at the high ceiling before setting his guitar case down and heading for the wide bank of windows beyond the contemporary wood-and-steel staircase. He was dressed in his ubiquitous jeans and leather jacket over a plain black T-shirt. And damn, he looked and smelled amazing.

"It must be awesome to have your own pool," he said in a dreamy voice. "Do you use it a lot?"

I met him at the window and pushed my hands into my back pockets to keep from touching him. "When the weather is warmer. I spend more time on the roof of the pool house than in the pool lately, though."

Justin chuckled. "You're a weirdo. We talked about writing love songs on the roof at Skybar, didn't we?"

Gray smiled. "We did. You said, and I quote, 'Love and romance are bullshit.'"

"I still believe that, so how are we gonna do this?"

"Well...I was thinking we'd hang out in the studio, play around with some melodies and see if we can get the ideas flowing. Are you hungry? I can order a pizza or something," I offered.

"Uh, yeah. That sounds good."

"Okay." I pulled my cell from my pocket. "Pepperoni?"

"Sure. And onion, olives, and anchovies too."

I gave him the "What the fuck?" look he deserved. "Are you serious?"

"And pineapple."

"You know, I think this may have been a mistake," I deadpanned.

Justin marched back to the foyer and picked up his guitar case. I was half afraid he was really going to leave when he barked a quick laugh and gave me a Cheshire cat grin. "Pepperoni is perfect. Are you ready to do this?"

"I am."

Two hours later, we sat across from each other in the studio, playing with harmonies and ideas. But mostly, we talked. Not necessarily about anything relevant. He asked me about the lights in the pool, if I used the Jacuzzi often, and if I knew my neighbors. We stopped to eat pizza and chatted more about topics ranging from Harry Potter books to a Jimi Hendrix documentary he'd watched recently. Then we pushed the pizza box aside, grabbed our guitars, and got back to it. As much as I looked forward to spending time with Justin, I had low expectations about collaborating with a newbie. However, I was impressed. Justin could fashion lyrics out of a hint of a melody.

He was a quick-witted wordsmith whose biggest weakness was the guitar. He skipped chords regularly and became easily frustrated when it slowed him down.

"I suck," he griped, pulling the strap over his head and setting his instrument on a nearby stand. "I should stick to pouring beer."

"Only for now. You're gifted...and don't argue with me. I know stuff." When the urge to gush became strong, I cleared my throat and looked away for a moment. "I was surprised you didn't have to work."

"I asked for the night off at Vibes. My boss kinda hates me, so it didn't go over well, but he'd hate me if I showed up too," he said with a self-deprecating laugh.

"Why does he hate you?"

" 'Cause he and Tegan are sort of together and Sean hates knowing that anything happened with Tegan and me. He's a possessive motherfucker. He's not in love with T. He just wants to own him. And that's a good example of why I don't understand the concept of 'love.' It seems like there's a fine line between love and lust and the desire to possess and control. That's fucked, if you ask me."

"It *is* fucked," I agreed.

"I've never been in love. Have you?"

"Once. Years ago," I said vaguely.

He cocked his head as though waiting for me to continue. When I didn't, he shrugged. "Hmph. I didn't love Xena. I'm not sure I ever really loved any of my girlfriends. We were friends or just lovers, but not both. That's the problem with this love song stuff. How do you draw experience from real life when you've never experienced it?"

"You take any strong feelings you've had and work through them in words. I've written plenty of love songs while I've been single. It's a matter of being in the right mindset. I wrote 'Midnight Love' after my divorce. Do you know that one?" I hummed, then sang the first line, *"Your sweet smile in the moonlight..."*

"I like that song. You wrote that?" he asked with a dopey grin.

I nodded. "I did. And at that point, I hadn't been in love in years."

"So you faked it?"

"I wouldn't say that. I just...drew from other experiences and when that didn't help, I did some research. I watched old romantic comedies, read sonnets and poetry, and I observed."

Justin raised his eyebrows. "I see. The old creepy voyeur technique. I've never tried it."

"Everyone people-watches."

"Not me," he singsonged.

"Bullshit. I have an idea. We'll do it together. That'll be a good way to get started and put words down to some of the melodies we've worked on tonight."

"O-kay...where does one go to people-watch lovers?"

"Places you'd go on a date. Movies, dinner, the park, the beach, the mall."

"Seriously?" he gaped incredulously. "If you were gonna ask someone out, you'd take them to the mall? Dude. Even *I* know that's lame."

"Okay, but I'm not writing about only things I like. I want to write in a language everyone understands. Get it?"

"But the mall?"

I sighed in mock defeat. "Pretend you just landed a hot date with the guy or girl of your dreams. Where are *you* gonna go?"

"Somewhere free. I'm on a tight budget."

"The mall is free."

"And boring," he countered. "And what's the point of going someplace where you can't afford anything?"

"You can window shop," I suggested cheerily.

He held my gaze until I laughed. Then he shook his head and lifted his water bottle to his lips to hide a smile like he thought I was kind of a dork and didn't want to hurt my feelings. Fuck, he was cute. Well, mostly hot...but cute too.

"What about you?" he asked. "Where would you take a hot date?"

"Dinner, movies..."

Justin slumped in his chair, closed his eyes and fake-snored before sputtering awake. "Remind me never to go out with you."

"Deal," I agreed with a half laugh. "I'm a terrible date. I don't like going anywhere. I'm perfectly happy to stay home and play music and video games all night."

"Is that an adorkable way to ask me to play *Assassin's Creed* with you?"

I chuckled. "No, it wasn't, but let's do it."

"You sure you can handle me?" he taunted.

"No, but I'm willing to try."

Justin kicked my ass. I could make excuses about being distracted by his contagious enthusiasm and childlike sense of fun. That was all true. But I also liked the sound of his laughter and the feel of his body next to mine. I'd lost track of time a while ago. The house was quiet, and as the night stretched on with nothing and no one to interrupt us, we seemed to drift closer on the sofa. Knees touching, then thighs and arms. When he annihilated my last man, he tossed the control onto the coffee table and let out a victory cry. Then he draped his leg between my thighs and crashed his mouth over mine.

Maybe the maneuver was meant to be playful. I knew a lot of people who were capable of meaningless kisses and offhanded flirting. I wasn't one of them, but maybe it was a generational quirk. However, when he licked my lips in a wordless request for entry, I figured we'd moved past "casual." We made out with slow kisses and roving hands. There was a sweetness in the unhurried give and take of twisting tongues and soft sighs...until he pulled my shirt from my jeans and raked his fingers along my sides.

"Fuck, I want you," he whispered.

I pulled back slightly and shivered at the glint of desire in his eyes. He wasn't kidding. He wanted me. Maybe as much as I wanted him. I willed myself to reset the balance before either of us got swept away, but my body wouldn't cooperate. My dick hardened as my gaze followed the tip of his tongue across his bottom lip. Nope. I wasn't going anywhere.

I pulled him to his feet, then sealed my mouth over his. His breath hitched in surprise. For a half second, I thought he might push me away, but he cupped my face with both hands instead and bit my lip. I was immediately consumed. The heat and electricity we'd been dancing around exploded in a fiery fusion that was all about getting as close as possible in record time.

Justin grabbed my ass and rocked his pelvis. The feel of his denim-clad cock against mine felt incredible. Justin was a full-body sensory experience. He was everywhere. His hands in my hair, fingers raking my back, then fumbling with my belt. He tried to do everything without breaking the kiss. Although it was more of a tongue fuck than a kiss now. An erotic push and pull that mirrored our frenzied humping.

I yanked my shirt over my head before pulling Justin's off and molding my bare chest against his. His skin felt warm and damn, he tasted amazing. Like winter and peppermint and something uniquely Justin. Whatever it was, I wanted more. I grabbed a handful of his hair and pulled his head back to lick the column of his throat. He growled and reached for my belt.

I stilled his hand, panting for air as I tried to read his expression. "Wait. Are you sure you—"

"Are you fucking kidding me? Yeah, I'm sure." He yanked my

wrist and roughly set my palm over his erection. "Do something about this before I come in my jeans."

I heard the challenge in his tone and wanted to laugh at his arrogance, but I fucking loved it. My nostrils flared appreciatively.

"We can't have that," I purred.

I pulled him toward the bed and pushed him onto the mattress. Then I kicked off my shoes, straddled his thighs, and immediately reached for his belt. I unbuckled and unzipped him before slipping my hand into the opening and flattening my palm over his length. I held his gaze as I curled my fingers and stroked him through his boxer briefs. The thin barrier should have been annoying, but the flimsy cotton accentuated his impressive cock. I tightened my grip, loving the feel of his girth. He was thick and long and very responsive. He whimpered when I rubbed my thumb over the tip in a lazy circle, making a mess of his precum-soaked briefs.

"Fuck. That feels good." Justin licked his lips.

I watched his Adam's apple slide in his throat lustily. He was hot and horny as hell. He wanted whatever I was willing to give. And just knowing he was in the same state was a major turn on.

"Take them off," I commanded in a deeper than normal voice.

I rolled sideways to give him room to remove his shoes and undress as I unzipped my jeans. I thought about folding the comforter back, but then I glanced over at Justin and all my good ideas abandoned me. God, he was beautiful. Long, lean, and naturally toned. And the colorful ink on his arms and torso seemed to highlight his sexy physique. The rope of thorns around his biceps, the flames along his lower left hip, and the tiny script on his V line that seemed to point to his gorgeous cock.

Justin kneeled on the bed next to me, gripping himself at the base. He looked like a rock god with his longish hair, tattoos and badass pout, languidly stroking his dick instead of a six-string.

"What are you waiting for?" he asked huskily.

I pushed my jeans and briefs over my ass, watching him through hooded eyes as I wrapped my fingers around my shaft. I wondered what he saw. I knew I was considered fairly attractive, but maybe I was delusional. I hadn't cared about fashion trends or hanging out with the "in-crowd" in years. I figured if I worked out, ate right, and still fit in my favorite jeans, it was a win. But a young man in his prime might see things differently.

Justin's reverent gaze indicated that wasn't the case. I stroked myself as I watched him. He fixated on my chest for a long moment before zeroing in on my languid motion. Up and down with a slight twist of the wrist...then repeat. I smiled and patted the mattress. "Come here."

Justin scooted closer and lay beside me. He set his left hand over mine and stroked himself with his right. I slipped my leg between his and covered his mouth, kissing him in time to the rhythm he set. The slight tug and twist in his technique sent tingles along my spine.

"You like that?"

"It's okay," I said, gritting my teeth.

He barked a quick laugh and continued the sweet torture while he sucked on my tongue. I rested my hand on his hip, then slowly lowered it to squeeze his ass. I traced his crack as I nibbled his jaw. Justin groaned and climbed over me, covering me like a blanket. He held onto the headboard with one hand and rocked his hips so that my dick slipped between his cheeks. When the tip nudged his hole, Justin backed off and reached between our sweat-slicked skin to jack us together.

"Do you like this better?" Justin asked mischievously.

"Fuck, yes. I—"

He drove his tongue between my lips before I could finish.

Not that I had much to say. This was perfect. He was perfect. His weight, his intensity, and the friction of that primal slide of our thick shafts. I felt like a starving man being fed for the first time in years. I wanted everything at once. I could tell Justin felt the same. He writhed over me, wantonly sucking my tongue and licking my lips as he moved, twisting his wrist and stroking. Up and down. Over and over.

When I grabbed his ass and planted my feet flat on the mattress, he bit my bottom lip and straightened slightly. I glanced down at his smooth inked skin against my hairy, more muscular chest. Damn, we looked good together. Our rigid cocks glistening with precum were a thing of beauty, and I had to have a taste. I swiped my thumb over our slits, then sucked it clean.

"Oh my God," he moaned.

I did it again, staring into his eyes as I set my thumb on his lower lip. He rested the tip of his tongue on the digit before sucking it ravenously. That was it. I pushed at his chest and rolled on top of him, rutting like a madman before sitting back between his knees and stroking my cock furiously.

"Fuck, I'm gonna come."

And I did. Ropes of jizz spurted across Justin's hand. He didn't hesitate to use it as lube. Two pumps of his fist and he was gone. He roared as his release hit him a moment later.

I held on to the top rung of the headboard and surveyed the mess we'd made as I fought to catch my breath. I met Justin's gaze and gave him a lopsided smile.

Now came the awkward part.

The last time we'd done this, we agreed it was a one-time thing. Everything was different tonight. Straddling an invisible line between nonchalance and gratitude felt like a big task.

I glanced out the window at the moonlight reflected on the pool before gazing down at my lover. "Justin, I—"

"Mmm. Lie down," he commanded, closing his eyes.

I swallowed hard and licked my lips. "Stay here. I'm gonna clean up."

I hiked my leg over him and then hurried to the bathroom to grab a towel. I wiped the sweat and cum off my chest and hands quickly, making sure to avoid the mirror as I headed back to the bedroom. I set the towel on Justin's stomach and studied him. He lay with one arm over his heart and the other over his head. His eyes were shut, but his mouth was open and though he wasn't snoring, he was making a funny noise as he exhaled. He looked peaceful and serene. Neither were adjectives I'd use to describe him. Justin was a manic fireball. All energy and momentum, with no clear direction. He barreled forward, crashing and burning yet somehow emerging in one piece. With a modicum of direction and discipline, he could be dangerous. I watched him for a moment before gently cleaning the mess on his stomach.

When he opened his eyes and smiled, I knew I was fucked. Whatever happened here wasn't ending anytime soon. We'd only just begun.

Justin

"MMM. THANKS."

"You're welcome." Gray smiled and tossed the cummy towel onto the floor before reaching for his jeans.

"Don't go."

He dropped his jeans, then pulled the duvet back, motioning for me to lift my ass and get under the covers. Then he lay down and rolled to face me. "I'm not going anywhere."

"Good. It's gonna be weird between us if you go."

"How would it be weird?"

I propped myself on my elbow and laid my hand on his chest. "Taking our clothes off, rubbing against each other, and running away is a bad habit to get into. I'm all for the first two, but we can't work together if we can't talk freely about..." I twirled my finger between our naked bodies. "This."

"What do you want to talk about?"

"Nothing. I just want to look at you." I peeked under the duvet and whistled. "Damn. I can't believe that was in my ass. You're big."

"All right. Now you're just being crude," he huffed primly.

I snickered. "It's a compliment. But you should know I was sore for twenty-four hours after. Totally your fault."

"You want me to apologize?" he asked, reaching over to massage my left ass cheek.

"No. I want to do it again. Tonight."

"We will. Though I don't know about tonight," he said with a laugh.

"Why not do it all night? That's romantic, isn't it?" I joked. "We can probably get some great material just lying here in bed. This isn't even your bed, is it? We can pretend it's a hotel room and that we met at a bar and—oh wait, we did that."

"You're hysterical." He smacked my ass, then pushed his leg between mine. "I think we agreed to do research at a mall next."

"Ugh."

Gray smirked. "Hey, at least I'm coming up with ideas. You haven't told me anything you like...only what you don't. C'mon, work with me."

"I don't know. I guess I'd go to a park or something."

"Where'd you go with your girlfriend?" he prodded.

I frowned. "Nowhere, really. We hung out. We didn't have money, and we both worked a lot. She'd come by my bar after her shift at the restaurant, and then we'd walk back to my place or hers and just...talk. I liked that fifteen-minute walk in the dark more than a lot of the things we did. Even though we weren't looking at each other, we listened. We shared stupid stories about our day and talked about new bands and songs we liked. Sometimes we held hands, sometimes we didn't, but we connected, you know? I miss that. I miss being connected."

I cringed at the note of melancholy in my voice. Ripping my guts open and spilling weird, vulnerable stuff most people didn't share with strangers wasn't smart. It made me want to belch or say something obnoxious to push him away and dim that glimmer of understanding in his eyes that wordlessly told me he'd been there too.

But just as I was about to open my mouth, he nodded. "Yeah."

I wasn't sure I'd heard more pain or loneliness in one word in my entire life. It stopped me in my tracks. I cocked my head and studied him for a long moment like I was seeing him for the first time. Not simply admiring his ruggedly handsome exterior, but really seeing him...and noticing things I hadn't before. The telltale lines of humor around his eyes were laced with a profound sadness I wanted to examine and run from at the same time. The fact that he hid it so well with that beautiful smile and proud posture hinted at a strength of character I found intriguing.

The problem with being a writer was that I saw all that beauty and was rendered speechless. I needed to write what I saw. I couldn't speak it. I couldn't tell him he reminded me of a Hank Williams song or better yet...a work of art. The lonely kind that draws you in with colors and keeps you standing there for hours, memorizing the cracks in the paint and the fuzzy lines next to the razor-sharp ones. He'd think I was crazy, or he'd wonder what someone like me knew about old country songs or modern art. He'd think I was pretentious or—

"You look like an Edward Hopper painting," I blurted in a

small voice.

Gray widened his eyes and opened his mouth in surprise. "Which one?"

"The one with the guy looking out a window or into a window. Doesn't matter." I waved dismissively. "That was weird. Hey, I—"

"No, it wasn't," he said with a smile. "You just made me want to look up Edward Hopper or visit a museum. Not weird at all. More like thoughtful...and interesting. You don't give a lot away, do you? But I can tell you're smart as fuck and very intuitive."

"Thanks." I flung my hand over my forehead and yawned. "I should go."

"No. You should stay. Go to sleep. We'll talk in the morning."

"Are you going somewhere?"

"No. I'll stay too. C'mere." He tugged me against his chest and kissed the top of my head, then pulled the covers around us. "Rest now."

I burrowed against him, closed my eyes, and fell fast asleep.

OF COURSE, I woke up alone.

I didn't overthink it. My bladder wouldn't let me. I used the adjoining bathroom, pulled on my jeans, and padded down the hallway through a maze of sunlit rooms toward the main entry. I paused to listen for voices or the smell of coffee. The quiet was eerie as hell. It was almost noisier than being freeway-close, I mused before moving into the great room.

"Good morning, Justin. You're looking very well...rested. Coffee?"

Charlie set his enormous rainbow unicorn mug on the kitchen island and flashed a bright smile. His blond curly hair framed his face sweetly, but the spark in his eye was full of mischief. He wore a blue checked oxford shirt with a pair of fitted yellow chinos and black loafers. And somehow he pulled the peculiar combination off.

"Um...hi. Yes, please." I pushed my right hand through my hair and rubbed the back of my neck. Okay, this was embarrassing.

He chuckled at my awkward greeting, then motioned for me to take a seat at one of the black leather barstools. I obeyed, thanking him when he set a plain white mug in front of me. "Cream or sugar?"

"No, thanks. This is good. Where's Gray?"

"He had a meeting. I'm here to work in the library for an hour before I head to campus," Charlie replied as he rounded the island and perched on the barstool next to me. He caught my dubious look and chuckled. "Okay, the alternate truth is, I dropped off a key and ran into the man of the house making a mediocre pot of coffee. I remade the one you're drinking....You're welcome for that. Anyhoo, he mentioned he had a sleepover party and that his guest wasn't awake yet. I think he said, 'Leave him alone, Char,' but it sounded vaguely like, 'Grill him, Char,' so here I am."

I took a sip and set the mug down slowly before answering. Charlie was a lot before noon. "Right. So are you leaving me alone or grilling me?"

"What do you think?" he snarked, cradling his coffee. "I'm a master griller and you, my friend, are a kabob."

I chuckled softly. "What do you want to know?"

"Did you ask him to help you?"

"Help me do what?"

"Put your band together, pull you out of the gutter...you know, break the Gypsy Coma curse and move on," Charlie replied irritably.

"No."

"Good. That's my job. It will be anyway. Please just tell me you agreed to write the love song."

"Not that it's your business, but...I agreed to try."

"Try?" He twitched his nose comically and furrowed his brow. "Amateur! You don't tell a Grammy award winner you're going to think about working with him, you seize the opportunity!"

"In a normal world, maybe so, but Xena being part of this makes me very leery," I said, raising my mug in a mock toast.

"Understandable. But as your manager, I think you should do it."

I barked a quick laugh. "Manager? When did this happen?"

"At our first meeting. Don't you remember? I want to launch a band. Or help, anyway. I'm more interested in brand management. I'm finishing my master's degree right now, so I don't have a ton of time, but there's no reason we can't start talking about your social media presence. You need a slow but steady campaign with lots of cross-brand advertisement."

"What does that even mean?" I asked, frowning so hard my head hurt.

"It means we spark interest and get the ball rolling. I'm a genius at this stuff, if I do say so myself. I've been building my own brand for a couple of years. Check out my Instagram page. I have over a million followers, a number of sponsorships, and I don't really do anything. I just go places and take photos. I want to do something important. And when my dad asked me to run interference with you and Gray, it came to me. You're it. Your band...what's it called?"

"Zero."

"Oh." Charlie set his hands on his hips and cocked his head. "Really? Don't you want something catchier? Spider Invasion or Arachnoid Alien Zombies or—"

"Did you have a dream about spiders last night?" I

deadpanned.

"How did you know?"

"I think I'm beginning to understand you. And that's scary as fuck," I grumbled, taking another sip of coffee.

"It's fate! I'll need to meet with all of you to do a photo shoot. Do you have a sample recording we can use for your blog?"

"Uh. I can get you one."

"Good. If not, you can always record something here. I'm sure Gray won't mind. I bet he'd let you practice here too. At least occasionally. That would make my job easier while I'm finishing my classes. Now do you see why you should immediately say yes to the songwriting credit for the movie?" Charlie asked, sounding like a schoolteacher.

"Not really," I admitted. "But I'm still waking up, and I'm stuck on your spider dream."

"God, it was awful. Remind me to tell you about it another time." He stood abruptly and spun on his heels.

"Okay, so why am I supposed to say yes to the song?"

"Exposure. Gray can help you craft a beautiful song. He's a master. I can help you create your brand and then share your brand with the world."

"Why me? Why not Xena? She's flashier and prettier than me by a long shot," I huffed.

"She's a solo artist. I think she broke ties with Declan, who I understand is a very talented musician. He plays multiple instruments, including bass."

I shook my head. "Hard pass. Ky joined us anyway. We're set."

"Hmm. As I was saying, I want to work with a band. I want to create a family. And since I'm not likely to have children for another decade or so, I'll start with you. I think you're a good bet."

"Thanks. I'll talk to the guys about—"

"Excellent! We'll meet here after one of your practices. I'll talk to Gray about getting you time in the studio. You know, this would have been a lot easier if you had just agreed to take the job filing those albums. You would have had a built-in reason to be here a week ago. Time is ticking! Xena has already signed her contract. You need to secure a commission for yourself and then your band."

"I haven't told the guys about it yet. If it was for Zero, they'd be a lot more interested," I commented wryly. "This sounds like a solo gig. Like I'm defecting before we get started."

Charlie moved in front of me and nudged my arm excitedly. "Why not counter with a suggestion for Zero to perform a song for the soundtrack too?"

"Really?"

"Why not? The worst anyone can say is no."

"Huh. Maybe you're right."

"Of course I am. Use their interest in your favor. For Zero."

"Should I send an email or—"

"No. You shouldn't represent yourself. That's not how it's done in entertainment circles. You need someone to handle the business end while you handle the music. You need me," he said firmly.

"Hmm. Maybe." I nodded slowly. "I still have to talk to the guys, but this could be a good idea."

Charlie offered me his hand with a wide, radiant grin. "I look forward to working with you. Shall we commemorate this event with a selfie?"

"Fuck no," I huffed.

Charlie wrangled his arm around my neck and shot a series of photos. No doubt I had my mouth open in all of them. Then we shook hands like two seasoned businessmen. I wasn't exactly sure what I'd agreed to. The one thing Charlie and Zero had in common was that neither of us was a sure thing.

6

GRAY

People were everywhere. I didn't get it. An outdoor mall was the last place I'd think anyone would want to hang out on a Friday night in February. Sure, the weather was mild, but there had to be better things to do on a weekend. I'd been half joking when I suggested the mall, but Justin's reaction was so priceless, I had to follow through. Once the plan was made, I figured it would be a mini adventure and chances were high we'd have the place mostly to ourselves anyway. I was wrong. If we'd driven together, I would have moved on to plan B when I spotted the line of cars waiting to park in the multi-storied garage.

I left my Porsche with an attendant and typed a quick text to Justin on my way up the escalator to the main floor of the shopping center to let him know I'd arrived. I pushed Send before reading through our earlier correspondence.

Are we really doing the mall thing? he asked.

Yep! What time should I pick you up?

I'll meet you there.

You're not going to show, are you?

Oh ye of little faith. I'll be there at six. Meet me at the fountain.

Which one?

I have no idea. I've never been before. But every mall in the world has a fountain.

I grinned at the gif of Niagara Falls he'd posted, then started when my cell rang. I stepped off the escalator before answering.

"Hello?"

"Hey, I'm outside the pretzel shop on the first floor," Justin said.

"By the fountain?"

"Fuck, no. It's kid central over there. I love kids, but I can't hear myself think."

I smiled at his faux put-upon tone. "Got it. I'll find you."

Ten minutes later, I spotted Justin spread across a bench with his arm resting on the back and his knee bent on the seat in a pose that clearly said, "I'm not sharing." I nudged his foot and sat down before he recognized me. His annoyed scowl morphed into a sweet smile followed by an appreciative once-over.

He shifted to make room, then handed me a small paper bag. "I bought you a pretzel. Cinnamon sugar 'cause it's the best."

"Thanks. How much do I owe you?"

Justin rolled his eyes. "Don't be a dork. It's on me."

"Thank you." I unfolded the bag and sniffed. "Damn, I love the smell of cinnamon."

"Me too. It reminds me of Christmas." He opened his arms and gave me a comical look. "And this crowd is Christmas-sized. Did you know it was going to be like this?"

"No. I haven't been to a mall in years," I admitted.

"My mom dragged me to the one by her during the holidays. It was torture. You get lured in by the lights and the music and next thing you know, you're battling with an old lady over discounted slippers no one in their right mind would wear."

I chuckled. "You're a good son."

"I'm the only one she has now, so I feel like I have to be."

"She doesn't talk to your brother, right?" I asked, trying to remember what he'd told me about his family.

Justin nodded. "Yeah. But we aren't here to talk about my effed-up family. This is about love, right? Love at a mall. Color me confused, maestro. I have no clue what to look for. Show me the way."

I popped a piece of cinnamon goodness in my mouth and grinned before glancing around. We were in an ideal spot for people-watching. Our bench was in a corner facing an atrium. Ample seating surrounded the grassy area that I imagined was home to the Easter Bunny and Santa's house during the season. I scanned the crowd for couples and came up with a few good examples.

"First and foremost, we're looking for body language. Young, old...doesn't matter. You can tell a lot by how close a couple sits —if they touch, how much they touch, and how they look at each other. Check out those two." I inclined my head toward a middle-aged man wearing a red shirt and the younger blonde beside him. "They're infatuated with each other. Not in love."

Justin scoffed. "How can you tell? He's got his arm around her, and he's giving her a mushy look."

"They're sitting too close and smiling too hard. They're too attentive, if you know what I mean."

"No one knows what you mean," he quipped. "Isn't that all good?"

"Sure, but their language tells me their attraction is mainly physical."

"You gotta start somewhere. Sex is the best place to begin, if you ask me."

I chuckled at his adamant tone. "You're right, but that's not the song we're writing."

Justin hiked his knee on the bench again as he shifted to face me. "That's the million-dollar question. What kind of love song is this? There's all kinds of love. Tiers of affection too. You might really like your neighbor, but you don't feel affection for him. And you might feel a deep affection for certain friends without really loving them. Then there are special friends you'd give your left nut to if they needed it. You love those friends, but you aren't *in* love with them. Lovers are a whole other category. Some are sex-only partners, some are friends too, and others have that extra something that inspires a sappy song...like the one I'm assuming we're trying to write."

"We're going for authentic and genuine. Not sappy. Something that evokes longing and hope at the same time." I glared when Justin stuck his finger down his throat and gagged. "Behave."

"You gotta admit, that's kinda nauseating. Do you personally know anyone who's been in love like that?"

"My parents," I replied automatically before turning my gaze back to the seating area.

"How so?" Justin prodded.

"They just loved each other. Anyone could see it. They were married for fifty years. I was their surprise kid. I had a sister who died of leukemia before I was born. They were devastated and they didn't think they'd ever have other children. Then I came along."

"Oh. I'm sorry about your sister," he said softly.

"Thanks. I didn't feel her loss personally, but I think my folks were a bit more involved in my life because of what they'd been through. And I think they were more appreciative of one another too. My dad looked at my mom like she was the most beautiful woman he'd ever seen. She was pretty for sure, but he saw something no one else did. And because he saw it, she became it. Does that make sense?"

"Yeah. That's very...poignant," he said softly. We were both quiet for a moment; then Justin inched closer. "Was it hard being an only child?"

"No. I didn't know any different. Being an orphan at thirty-nine was harder. I don't have any family left. My aunts, uncles, and cousins have either passed away, or we just haven't kept in touch." I smiled wanly. "I miss my parents, but I don't mind being alone. I was the nerd in school who preferred reading comic books and playing piano to hanging out with kids my age."

"You look more like a former football player to me than a nerd."

I laughed. "I was painfully thin until my early twenties. I started going to the gym and bulked up a bit after I moved to LA."

"To fit in with the cool crowd?"

"In a way, maybe. It wasn't intentional. You go through times in your life when you try to be what everyone else wants. The obedient son, a hardworking citizen, a good boyfriend or husband…and then realize you're not paying attention to yourself. You lose yourself in everyone's expectations. It took me until my thirties to let that go and do what felt right for me."

"That's a nice goal. I think people get the impression I do that naturally. I don't." Justin kicked his feet in front of him and looked down at his sneakers. "Family expectations kill me. I'm neutral territory for my mom and my brother. And it's a lot of work being the go-between. It stresses me out."

"You should go to the gym," I teased.

"You know I hate the fuckin' gym."

I chuckled and put my arm around his shoulders and kissed his temple affectionately. "I remember."

He looked surprised, but he didn't pull away. "That's what music is for. And video games."

"And sex," I added.

"Good point. Let's see, you have an in-home gym, a music studio, a video console with a ton of games...and me. You never have to leave home." Justin grinned mischievously, then popped a piece of pretzel into his mouth.

I traced his ear with my thumb and nodded. "True. My friends think it's becoming a problem. I like staying home."

"Then it's not a problem. Hey, if I had a house like yours, I'd never leave either."

"It's cool, but it's not where I'm from, you know. I didn't grow up with a pool or a gym membership. I didn't have Nintendo or—"

"Well, that's because they didn't have video games back then. No PCs or cell phones. I bet it was kinda like growing up in the dark ages," he teased.

I gave him a dirty look before snaking my hand around his neck and rubbing my knuckles over his head. He batted me away with a laugh. All I could think was, *Fuck, I want him.* I swallowed hard and tried to remember what we were talking about. Oh, right...

"I grew up in the eighties. It wasn't exactly the dark ages. We had computers and cell phones, smartass. They were just big and weighed as much as you do," I huffed.

Justin made a funny face, then patted my hand and spoke slowly...and loudly. Like he was talking to a hard-of-hearing octogenarian. "Oh, that's nice."

"Very disrespectful. I oughtta turn you over my knee, young man," I chided playfully.

"I would not be opposed to that," he quipped, waggling his brows.

We both burst out laughing a moment later. I impulsively tugged at his arm and pulled him closer still, then rested my elbow on the bench behind him. "We're getting way off topic here. See that couple there...that's who I want to write a love song about."

Justin followed my gaze. "The old couple?"

"Yeah. And them too." I gestured toward the two men standing side-by-side in line at the pretzel store. "See what I mean about body language? Neither is touching, but you can tell they're in sync. The trick about writing a song like this is to stay away from lyrics that evoke longing. We aren't writing about what we wish we had. We're writing about what we know we're lucky to have. Appreciation, gratitude."

"And you're telling me that's possible to do without sounding cheesy...'cause I've got my doubts," he singsonged.

"I'll give you a sample line. This just popped into my head. I'm not saying we need to use it, but...'I want to feel your skin, touch your hair. I want to see you smile and know that you're there. I want you to be my forever,' " I sang in a low and melodic tone.

I didn't have the range or the sheer vocal power Justin did, but I excelled at writing hooks and forming songs from ideas. And another songwriter would recognize the hook instantly and might know how to build on it. Like playing volleyball with words. Justin was clever and quick-witted. I had a feeling he'd be good at this. I cocked my head and gave him an expectant look when he didn't reply right away.

"That's good," he said carefully. "But 'want' is a yearning word. Maybe we should tweak that last line to 'You are my forever.' "

"Yeah, I like that! It could be 'you are my forever' or some theme around 'forever' or—"

"Okay. Let me think." Justin tapped his jaw thoughtfully. "Forever friend, forever lover, forever baby, forever guy I want to kick out of bed for snoring, forever girl who posts too many food pics on Instagram. How are we doing here?"

"Less specific, but I think we're on the right track," I said offering him a high five.

"All right. Let's take notes."

We brainstormed on our bench, throwing out suggestions and one-liners in rapid succession before pausing to snack on pretzels and people-watch. Justin was funny, good-natured, easy company. Which surprised me because he was high-energy too. He frequently jumped up and paced when a new idea hit him. And he wouldn't sit again until he was sure I'd written it down. Or until a dog passed by. He must have stopped midsentence five times to pet a dog. The last one was a white French poodle. Her owner was a flirtatious college-aged girl with long brown hair and a winning smile who looked a bit dazzled by Justin.

"What's her name?" he asked, petting the dog behind her ears.

"Miss Sweet Susie Sassafras. Sassy Sue for short," she pronounced. "She's a sweetheart."

"Say that three times fast," he joked.

The young woman giggled like she'd just heard the funniest joke ever. I watched the interaction from a couple of feet away and found myself slipping into my familiar role of observer. It was what all good writers did. We pulled away to take notes and build stories. But just as my brain wrote me out of the scene to create an unlikely love match, Justin turned to me with a radiant grin. And just like that, I was part of his story.

When the young woman and her dog walked away, Justin nudged my shoulder and grinned. "Sassy Sue might be the best name ever."

"She liked you." I immediately winced at the note of jealousy in my voice.

"Dogs love me." He opened the pretzel bag and shook the leftover cinnamon into his mouth. "But I feel like I'm riding a serious sugar high right now. Between love songs, sugar pretzels, and Miss Sassafras, it's like I've eaten three bowls of Cap'n Crunch and now the roof of my mouth is raw."

"I wasn't talking about the dog. The dog's owner liked you. The girl. And you've got cinnamon on your face," I said, pointing to his mouth.

"Where?"

I leaned in without thinking and swiped my thumb over his bottom lip. Justin captured my wrist, then brought the digit to his lips and sucked. I went still as I stared into his eyes.

"Um..." I cleared my throat and glanced at my watch. "Did you drive here?"

Justin grinned. No doubt he knew he'd gotten under my skin and was loving it.

"No. I took the bus."

I gave him an incredulous look. "Why? I told you I'd pick you up."

"I came from the coffee shop. Tegan, Johnny, and I played this afternoon. It was really fun. We had dueling guitars and a bongo drum. We took requests and played oldies for the yoga moms and after-school crew."

"Sorry I missed it. I still would have picked you up."

"Thanks, but I didn't want you to. It would require explanation and I don't want to tell my friends about you or your proposal until I can hash out a few details that don't make it sound like I'm leaving them out to pursue a solo gig."

"It's not my proposal. I'm just the messenger. And there will be a contract involved to ensure you don't get screwed."

"Or to ensure I sign something I can't get out of that fucks my chance at a real career later. I can't afford a lawyer. I'm using every dime I have for rent and studio time."

"I told you that you can you use my studio."

"Yes, but that would require an explanation too. And like I said, they don't know about the offer."

"When will you tell them?"

He gave me a sharp sideways glance. "I saw Charlie this morning. He mentioned that he wants to represent or manage Zero. I don't know much about this stuff, but according to Tegan...and Charlie too, he has a big social media following and might be able to help us. I didn't say anything to the guys yet, but I know they'd be all for it. I wanted to talk to you first. What do you think?"

"I think it's a good idea. You'll have to rein him in a bit, but he's very creative and I think he's up to the challenge."

Justin nodded thoughtfully. "Cool. One more thing. I haven't contacted your friend yet, but...I want Zero to write and perform a song on the soundtrack too."

That stopped me. "You know I have no say in that."

"Yeah. I'm just bouncing an idea off you. I was talking to Charlie and—"

"Charlie," I sighed, massaging the bridge of my nose.

"It's not a bad idea."

"But you have a lot to gain by just writing the one song," I reminded him.

"Who cares? When you have nothing, you've got nothing to lose. I don't care about money. I just want to make music. As it stands, if I write a song with you, I'm choosing me for a short-term gain versus my band and a shot at something bigger than a possible one-hit wonder." He raked his hand through his hair and gave me a lopsided smile. "I know the contract isn't in your control, but I don't want to discuss it with them until it's real and Zero is in on the project. I don't want to get their hopes up and disappoint them if I can't deliver. I'm good at not following through on promises and...I don't want to do that anymore."

"Are you asking me to talk to Seb for you?"

"No, I'm a big boy. I can deal with him myself." He laid his head on my shoulder and turned his body so he was sprawled on the bench. "Let's not talk about it anymore. Tell me about your day instead."

I studied the top of Justin's head and tried to quickly process any possible red flags. He said he didn't want me to interfere, but he had to know bringing up my best friend and my godson would get my attention. However, I didn't detect manipulation on his part. I sensed that he was overwhelmed and needed to work through some ideas. That was all.

"Um...well, I worked on a couple of pop songs for a British songstress. If she likes them, I may have to travel to London. She hates LA."

Justin sighed. "I'd love to travel someday. The only place I've been outside of California is Las Vegas. Where's your favorite city?"

"Since I live in LA, I'll say it's my favorite. I also lived in New York and—"

"What's it like? Is it electric? What's the food like? Where's the best music? Where's the..."

I set my earlier misgivings aside, pushed my fingers through his hair, and started talking. I described the streets and scenery, the food and the people of some of my more memorable trips to Boston, Chicago, London, and Paris. I talked and talked...and just when I thought I might be boring him, he'd ask another question. I stroked his head while I spoke and let my gaze wander. But after a while, I got lost in the moment. I tuned out the piped jazz playing through the speakers, the sounds of children laughing and people chatting, and focused on Justin. The weight of his body against my shoulder, the way his voice reverberated through me when he spoke. Hell, just the sound of his breathing grounded me.

He stretched his arms above his head and twisted to face me after a while. "Are you still people-watching?"

"Sort of. I've been watching you."

"Me?"

"Yeah, you. Kiss me," I commanded.

Justin looked around the bustling atrium. There were plenty of couples holding hands or standing closer than friends might. But the lone same-sex couple we'd spotted earlier was gone. And no matter how enlightened or accepting anyone claimed to be, two masculine looking men locking lips always turned a few heads.

"Here?"

"Yeah. Here. I dare you."

He chuckled softly, then leaned in and sealed his lips over mine. It wasn't an overly amorous display. It was just a kiss. But it felt like a promise.

I pulled back and threaded my fingers with his. "Come home with me."

Justin

OF COURSE, he valeted. Gray snickered when I rolled my eyes and complained about wasting time and money. We chatted while we waited for his Porsche. We stuck to mundane topics like weather and traffic on the drive, but we both went quiet when he turned onto his street. The sexual tension built as we neared his house. It was subtle. We didn't touch and we barely talked. We listened to Top 40 radio and commercials on low. But we weren't lost in our own thoughts. We were both thinking of what we'd do the second we were alone behind a closed door.

Gray parked his car in the garage and paused at the door to wait for me before grabbing my hand and whisking me inside. He didn't stop and he didn't let go. He hurried down a wide hallway and led the way upstairs to his room. I gazed down at the blue lights of the pool and the cityscape beyond, but I didn't bother commenting. I wasn't sure I could use my voice anyway. My heart raced and a swarm of butterflies fluttered in my stomach. And yeah, my cock throbbed against my zipper like it had a pulse of its own.

The second he pulled me into the master suite, I hooked my fingers in his belt loops to stop his momentum, then crashed my mouth over his. Our tongues dueled in a frenzy as we unbuttoned, unbuckled, and unzipped. I paused to kick off my sneakers and pull my sweater and T-shirt over my head. Then I snaked my arms around his waist and lowered his jeans over his ass before squeezing the flesh with a porny sigh when his bare cock slid alongside mine.

"I want to be inside you, baby."

I whimpered when he reached between us and closed his fist over me in a firm grip. "Fuck. Yes."

Gray licked my lips, then traced a slow, teasing path along my jawline to my ear before whispering, "I want to see you this time."

Words failed me. I could only say, "Me too" so many times. I let out a needy groan before driving my tongue into his mouth again and tilting my hips in the quest for more friction. Gray got the message. He released me and pointed at the king-sized bed like a caveman. And of course I didn't hesitate. I pulled the fluffy white duvet back, then crawled onto the middle of the platform bed and wiggled my ass in invitation. Gray chuckled at my antics. I glanced at his reflection in the window and gulped. I may have leaked precum on his pillow. I couldn't help it. A naked Gray was a thing of beauty. He reminded me of a modern-day warrior. Tall, sexy, muscular, and inked in all the right places. And the touch of gray at his temples and in his beard made me a little crazy. But the sight of his raging hard-on sticking straight out in front of him made my mouth water. I wasn't gonna last long.

"You need to hurry."

Gray pulled a bottle of lube and a condom out of the bedside drawer before climbing onto the bed behind me.

"We have time. We're not going anywhere," he purred.

He pressed kisses along my shoulder and down my spine. He scooted back and smacked my right ass cheek and then my left before reaching between my spread thighs for my cock.

"Maybe you shouldn't do that. I'm already close. Just fuck me, Gray."

"Shh. I will. I want to taste you first. Open up for me."

I rested my head on the pillow then pulled my ass cheeks open per his instructions, exposing myself completely. It was funny that I didn't feel slightly vulnerable or awkward. I hadn't been intimate with many men. I'd certainly fooled around a bit, but I usually insisted on control in bed. I didn't take orders well, and I usually liked to be on top, but this felt too amazing and my brain had left the scene a while ago. I sighed in blissed-out pleasure and pushed my hips back to meet his talented tongue when Gray bent to lick the sensitive skin around my hole. He teased me mercilessly. He stroked my cock as he worked me over, licking my entrance and then pushing the tip of his tongue inside before repeating the action. Yeah, it was incredible, but it was torture too. And just when I was about to beg, he let go and reached for the lube.

"Want me to turn over?"

"Not yet. Hold on to the headboard. That's it, baby. How does that feel?" he asked as he pushed a single digit inside.

I shivered in response and rested my head on my forearms when he added a second. He spoke in a low, sweet voice as he finger-fucked me. He licked sweat from my neck and shoulders and praised me for being good. I should have laughed and made a joke of some sort to even the playing ground and not give him too much power over me. But I liked it too damn much. It felt oddly like being taken care of, and something in me responded like a thirsty man getting his first sip of water after a long drought.

"Mmm. I'm getting close."

"Not yet." Gray added a third finger, then bit my shoulder and growled in my ear, "Roll over."

He slipped a condom over his rigid pole as I flipped over. He scooted between my open thighs and bent to suck me. Thankfully, he kept it brief. I was a man on the edge. Literally. He shifted back and lined his cock up with my hole and pushed.

"Oh fuck," I cried as he made his way inside me, inch by inch.

He held my gaze the whole time, and he didn't stop until his balls rested on my ass. "You okay?"

"Yeah."

He smiled sweetly, then pulled out slowly, almost to the tip, before surging forward again. He repeated the maneuver a couple of times. And when I lifted my hips in a silent request for more, he delivered. I hooked my legs around Gray's waist and pulled him against me, gliding my tongue over his as he moved inside of me. The moderate pace gave way to an urgent one. I broke for air and grunted when he captured my hands above my head and slammed into me, bucking his hips over and over.

"So fucking good," he whispered, slipping his right hand between our sweat-slicked torsos to grab my dick. "So good. Look at me, baby. Tell me when you're gonna come. Tell me when you—"

"Fuck me. Now!"

Ropes of cum shot over his wrist and my chest as I fell apart underneath him. Gray didn't miss a beat. He released my cock and pushed my knees against my stomach and pistoned his hips until his own orgasm claimed him a few seconds later. He braced his weight on the headboard and roared like a wounded animal, trembling in the aftermath.

I laughed when he shook his head as if to clear the cobwebs. He pressed a sweet kiss on my forehead before slowly disengaging. He removed the spent condom and wadded it in tissue, then plucked a few more tissues from the box and swiped at the mess on my stomach.

"All better," he said, rolling to his side and pulling me along with him so we lay side-by-side.

I closed my eyes for a moment and smiled. "Don't let this go to your head, but that might be the best thing I've ever done."

Gray's slow-growing grin warmed me from the inside out. He pushed a stray strand of hair from my eyes and kissed my nose. "Me too."

I tried to think of a light, throwaway line to dim my ridiculous smile, but nothing came to me. My body was sated and my head was blissfully calm. Gray probably had no idea that he had this effect on me. I could breathe when I was with him, but I was never bored. Weird. He was a puzzle I wanted to put together, a song I wanted to write and listen to over and over. I wanted to collect those puzzle pieces and figure him out.

I didn't get it. But I couldn't deny that I wanted him. Not his talent, his connections, or his fancy lifestyle. I liked the mysterious guy with a nerdy side who seemingly had dozens of secrets he wasn't ready to share. I wanted them. But mostly, I just wanted him.

7

JUSTIN

Charlie called a couple of weeks later, demanding to meet the band. And he was very specific about the location.

"It has to be at Gray's studio. We have access to professional equipment there and can record a track to send to my dad's office immediately. We have to get the ball rolling, or the window of opportunity will close."

"Whoa. This is a little fast."

Silence.

"Oh. I see. And what are we waiting for?" Charlie prodded in a neutral tone.

"I just thought I had a little more time." I caught myself from adding anything dramatic like, "before my two worlds collided."

"You can't win if you don't play the game, Justin," he said gently.

"You're right. When do you want to meet?"

"Tomorrow afternoon. Four o'clock."

"We all have jobs, Char. I don't know if—"

"Make it happen. Time is ticking."

I stared at my cell after he hung up on me. I couldn't say why, but meeting at Gray's to record a song or two as a group felt like a big step. The second I introduced my bandmates to Gray and Charlie, I had a feeling something—maybe everything—would change.

I WAS RIGHT.

It was funny to see my band's reaction to Gray's place. Of course they were impressed with the house, but the studio blew them away. Tegan, Johnny, and Ky moved around the room, touching instruments reverently while Charlie looked on from the sofa.

"They aren't museum pieces. You're supposed to play 'em," he urged.

"Wait up. I don't really get this whole situation. Who are you?" Ky asked.

Ky was a quintessential California boy with longish blond hair, blue eyes, tan skin, and a lean swimmer's physique. He was a professional skateboarder turned bass player. Tegan went to high school with Ky. They lost touch for a while but reconnected after Ky saw one of Gypsy Coma's gigs. I didn't know him as well as Tegan or Johnny, but he was a good bassist, and we'd neared the point where almost anyone who could play was welcome.

"I'm your manager-slash-agent-slash-social-media-director. You all know the plan, correct?"

"Uh. Sort of. We're practicing here, and then I'm not sure," Tegan admitted before turning to me. "This is the place with the insane record collection?"

"Yeah. I'll show you after we play. So...here's the deal." I clapped, then rubbed my hands together before explaining that we wanted to present a track to the studio for consideration for the next Baxter movie. "Xena has already signed a contract with them. There's no reason we shouldn't give it a shot too."

My bandmates stared at me with matching "What the fuck?" expressions. Johnny spoke up first. "That sounds good. Maybe too good. How did we go from hoping to get invited to Carmine's to recording demos for a movie? Seems like we've missed a few steps. I mean, Ky just started playing with us. No one's gonna take us seriously until we've put a few miles on."

"Not with that attitude," Charlie snarked.

I waved my hands above my head. "Hey, I know it's a long shot. Nothing may come of it, but we're at the beginning where every opportunity is worth a try, right?"

"Okay, but whose house is this?" Ky asked.

"The guy Justin's working for. He's alphabetizing records or something," Tegan said. "Is he here?"

I caught Charlie's eye, wordlessly asking him to keep his side of the deal. I didn't want to share specifics about the studio's offer to write a love song or my relationship with Gray. In my mind, they were separate. I knew they'd come up eventually, but I'd already decided I wouldn't sign the contract for the love song unless I could finagle one for Zero too. And Gray was...mine. I wasn't ready to share anything about us. Not yet.

"No. He's at a project meeting," Charlie supplied. "And full disclosure, Gray is my godfather, and my father is the producer. Neither is a point in our favor. If you suck, my dad won't make exceptions to make his kid happy. Not his style. Speaking of style...what's yours? Are you rock or folk or—"

"Both," I said. "I think we should play 'The Ocean.'"

"I'm assuming this isn't a Led Zeppelin cover," Charlie said, pulling his computer out.

"You know Led Zeppelin?" Ky asked, raising his brow.

Charlie glared. "I do. Very well. Shall we?"

I grinned at Charlie, then gave Ky a "Don't be a dick" look before pulling an acoustic guitar down from the wall and adjusting the strap over my shoulder. Then I approached the mic stand, strummed the first few chords, and lost myself in the music.

We played for two hours straight and if I do say so myself, we fuckin' rocked. Gray joined us an hour into our session. He sat beside Charlie, and other than offering a minor suggestion on a chord change on one slower song, he simply observed. I introduced him to everyone and hung back while they exchanged pleasantries afterward. Then Charlie gave them a brief tour of the library, laughing when Tegan asked if I'd gotten any filing accomplished.

"Geez, Justin, it's kind of a mess," Tegan commented under his breath as Charlie stepped aside.

"And I'm kinda busy," I retorted. "There's a lot to it. You know, genres and languages and stuff."

"And remembering the alphabet. Hope he's not in a hurry," Tegan said, glancing toward Gray, who was in the middle of a conversation with Johnny and Ky in the hallway. "He's hot, by the way. What's he like?"

"He's cool," I replied nonchalantly before fixating on my cell.

Tegan shot a pointed look at me. "What's going on?"

"Nothing. Why?"

"Dude, you're the worst liar ever. Are you sleeping with him?"

I bit my bottom lip and gave him a weak smile in response. "Do guys really say 'sleeping together'? It sounds kind of old-fashioned."

"I'll take that as a yes." Tegan's tatted biceps stretched the fabric of his plain tee when he scratched his head. "Is that why we're practicing here? Or is he Charlie's connection? Or is Gray how you met Charlie and got us a place to practice and an opportunity to play on a soundtrack? And Johnny's right. Don't *you* think it's weird as fuck that a band who's only strung together a few shows at closet-sized venues would be considered for a deal like this?"

"Do you have twenty more questions, or is that it?" I huffed sarcastically.

"Just one more." He smiled at Ky and Johnny when one of them called his name; then he lowered his voice for my ears only. "What are you hiding? I know you, Justin. And I've noticed a few things. You're never home, you're always in a good mood, and you're not spinning in a million directions at the same time. Rory called me the other day to ask about you. He noticed it too."

"Rory called you?"

"Yeah. He wondered if you'd gotten back together with the dragon or if something happened with Dec."

"Never and no," I replied with a universal "yuck" face.

"I didn't think so. I can't figure out if you don't want to say anything because it's a gay thing and you like to keep your homo activity on the DL, or if it's something else."

"I'm openly bi, T. Everyone knows." Nice evasive maneuver, I mused.

"Oh, please. You make sure no one knows you like to suck dick. It doesn't go with your image. I know how that goes," he added with a self-deprecating shrug that defused the harsh words. "You're out—but when it's convenient. And it's mostly convenient for you to admit you're bi when you have a girlfriend. Just sayin'."

I rounded on him angrily. "Are you trying to start a fucking fight?"

"No, asshole. I'm just reminding you that I've been here from the beginning. We agreed after Gypsy Coma imploded that the only way we could start over was if we were honest with each other. No lies, no secrets. I don't care who you sleep with. But if your new boyfriend has something to do with this band, you might want to let me know."

"Hey, T, you gotta see these Elvis records," Ky called from the other side of the room.

Tegan nodded in acknowledgment before turning back to me. "I want you to be happy, man, but I don't get any of this. It seems...too good to be true. I hope I'm just being overly cautious. Somebody's gotta be."

"I might have forgotten to water your plants a few times, but I'm not completely irresponsible. And don't forget, you're the one who told me to call Charlie."

"Yeah. For social media help. I didn't think he'd be our manager." He let out a beleaguered sigh and stepped backward. "Hey, like you said, it's worth a shot—and maybe this'll work out. Crazier things have happened."

"It's true. T, think about it. If everything falls into place, Zero has a decent shot at being bigger than Gypsy Coma ever dreamed."

"That would be amazing. Gotta wonder what it's gonna cost us."

"What do you mean?" I asked, furrowing my brow.

"Get real, Justin. Nothing's free." Tegan gave a humorless laugh. He spread his arms wide as if to encompass the house, the people, the music...and then he moved into my space and tapped my shoulder. "Don't think I didn't notice that you avoided answering my questions. I'm gonna let it slide for now, but you're not off the hook. None of us are. If we're a band, we're in this together."

I stared after him for a moment, wishing I could offer reassurance or a guarantee. But I came up empty. I believed great things could happen here. This was a talented group of guys. We hadn't been together long, but none of us were novices. We'd paid our dues in other bands. We knew what it was like to play to uninterested hipsters in crappy clubs with worn-out sound systems. But in an age where YouTube videos launched careers for artists performing cover songs from the comfort of their own bedrooms, I had to believe Zero had a shot too.

Gray

I LOVED MUSIC. I loved writing scores and crafting songs, but writing throwaway content for box office hits wasn't creatively satisfying. Writing to order was boring, but I was good at it. If a music producer wanted to hire me to pen a signature song for one of their label's big stars, I needed minimal information to fulfill my part of the deal. Who was the artist? What was his or her range? What genre, what tempo, and was there a theme?

It was the same for a film. Seb knew he could give me a few key words and let me do my thing. Within a week or two, I could generally deliver what he was looking for and more. But I took my time on this love song because I didn't want it to end. And in the weeks after our first "research date," I wondered if the feeling was a metaphor. I didn't want an end date or a deadline with Justin. I wanted to go on and on.

Justin was my muse. I wrote a string of songs for a popular country singer's new album and started working on the score for a sci-fi thriller set to be released in eighteen months. But I didn't touch the love song unless I was with Justin. It was ours, not mine. In a business sense, of course. I was incredibly attracted to him, but I wasn't delusional. I'd had previous instances of "falling" for a muse for a short time. The singular obsession that led to intense spouts of creativity was a common theme among artists. But this felt different. In an artistic sense, he wasn't inspiration for a song; he was the silence in between the words. A gorgeous note followed by a poignant pause.

We saw each other a few times a week, depending on his work and practice schedule. I allowed Zero to use my studio to practice, but I made sure to be away while they worked. I didn't want to interfere with their vision or Charlie's effort to prove himself. My time with Justin was special, and I didn't want to share it with anyone.

We were cognizant of separating our "working" time with our personal time too. We wordlessly agreed not to discuss the band or the song or any possible contracts unless we were in the studio or on a "research date." It was easier than expected to lie with our feet entangled, playing video games in our boxer briefs. Or to go night swimming, or hang out on the roof, counting stars and playing guitar.

It might have been late March, but it felt like summertime in Southern California. Seventy-five-degree days and maybe ten degrees cooler at night. We could comfortably play on the roof, wearing shorts and sweatshirts. It was something I'd done since I was a teenager. But usually alone. Until Justin.

"What is that song?" he asked, resting his forearms on his guitar. He sat cross-legged in front of me the way he always did, with his back to the view, and watched my fingers on the fret.

" 'Kumbaya.' You don't know it? We used to sing it at church when I was growing up and at campfires." I sang the lyrics as I strummed along.

"I was kidding. I know it." He sang the chorus with me and chuckled when I jazzed up the arrangement. "You're good at that. I bet you were popular at campfire sing-alongs."

I snickered. "As a matter of fact, I was. We camped a lot by the lake when I was a kid. I have great memories of canoeing, pitching tents, making s'mores...and huge fucking mosquitos. Big as softballs. Seriously. We had to spray that awful toxic-smelling stuff on us to avoid getting bitten. That smell still reminds me of summers at the lake."

"Even with mosquitos, that sounds kinda nice."

"It was. Have you ever been camping?" I asked.

"Once with a friend from high school and his family. It wasn't all that fun. We slept on the ground in a tent with a hole. There were bugs everywhere. And not just mosquitos. They had a cool dog, though. Freddy. I was stoked that he liked me so much. He sat next to me in the van on the way there and back. It was all good until he ate something weird and had a fart attack on the trip home. Four hours in a van with a gassy dog, listening to sports radio 'cause the fucking Dodgers were playing. Why are you laughing? It was hell," he griped without heat. "I've never wanted to go camping again."

"But you still want a dog."

"Yeah, but my dog isn't gonna stink," he joked.

"How will you take care of a dog if you're on tour?"

"I'd get a small dog and take him with me." Justin's dreamy expression in the moonlight made me smile. "I can't imagine going on tour. Geez, I can't even imagine playing outside of LA. Seems too wild to ever be true."

"Anything's possible if you're willing to work for it."

"Is this what you wanted when you were a kid in Minnesota?" he asked, spreading his arms open to the city lights flickering below. "A house on a hill in LaLa Land?"

"No. I wanted a farm outside of St. Paul, and I wanted to raise chickens."

Justin let out a half chuckle. "Really?"

"Yeah. The plan morphed throughout my childhood, but I always thought I'd live near my folks. I left home for college when I was seventeen, and I never went back. I went for visits, of course, but...not to live. They assumed I got a taste of city life and fell in love. But that wasn't quite it. I figured some things out about myself in New York and then LA. Things I wasn't willing or able to change for them." I shrugged my shoulders. "It was better to keep my distance."

"You don't think they would have accepted you?"

"I know they wouldn't have. And they'd already lost a kid. I couldn't do it to them."

"Hmm. It's the same for me and my mom. I told her I was bi when Rory came out, but I didn't press her and make her believe me. She doesn't talk to him, but I made the cut."

" 'Cause you didn't have a boyfriend."

"Right. You're the closest I've ever had to one. I'm not giving you a label you don't want. I'm just being honest. I've never spent this much time with another guy and felt like it wasn't enough. This is new for me and I love it. But the hypocrisy weighs on me. The thing is…if she cuts me off, she'll be alone. Literally alone. She has no one but me and a few friends from work."

"That's sad."

"The sad part is that my brother is a great guy and his boyfriend is too. She's missing out. It's easy to say, 'Her loss,' but if she disowned me, I think the guilt would crush me. Does that even make sense?"

"All too well. I kept quiet for my parents' sake, but it didn't make me happy. If the timing was different, and my parents were from a more progressive era and hadn't lost a kid, I might still live in Minnesota. I loved growing up there." I pointed toward the heavens. "You could see the stars behind the stars at night. But I couldn't be myself there. Not really. I stayed in LA because it was the path of least resistance. It was easier to pretend I was exactly who they thought instead of letting them know I was different."

"Were you ever tempted to say, 'Mom, Dad, I'm bisexual'?" He waved his hands over his head like a kid on a sugar high.

"No," I deadpanned. "Bisexual has the word 'sex' in it. We didn't talk about sex in our house. Ever."

"Oh." Justin raised his eyebrows. "When was the last time you visited?"

"Five years ago. I haven't been home since they passed away. And I don't know that I ever will."

"You can go back when Zero's tour hits St. Paul," he said, kissing my cheek.

"Deal." I put my arm around him and nuzzled his neck. "Come on. Let's go inside. It's getting cold and—"

"Hang on. You said your parents passed away within weeks of each other. What happened?"

"My dad was eighty-five. He died of old age. Mom died twenty days later of a broken heart."

"Are you just saying that, or do you know or—"

"It's not on her death certificate, but that's what happened. She couldn't breathe knowing he wasn't there anymore. She couldn't talk knowing he wasn't in the room to hear her. She couldn't move, she couldn't feel, and for twenty days she didn't eat. She had no reason to be if he wasn't."

Justin sucked in a breath. "That's beautiful. That's what we have to write."

I held his face in my hands and kissed his lips. "We will."

WE MADE LOVE THAT NIGHT. Slow, sweet, and tender. I watched him closely as I moved inside him, noting the way his long lashes fluttered and how he bit his bottom lip when he sighed. He wrapped his legs around my waist and dug his heels into my ass cheeks, silently requesting more. But not too hard this time. Not too fast. We weren't in a hurry tonight. The gentle give and take felt like a conversation or a song. We moved in perfect harmony until our rhythm faltered and we fell apart in each other's arms.

The sheer beauty of being so completely in tune with a lover was a first for me. And the look of wonder in Justin's eyes made me think it was the same for him. We weren't ready to put the feeling into words yet. It might make this too real. And it was already a little scary. Like finding yourself at the edge of a cliff where the view was incredible...and so was the fall.

JUSTIN HAD a way of making everything feel like an adventure. We'd meet at the coffee shop, the park, or the mall and hang out on a bench or a table for two and talk for hours. But he was constantly in motion. He couldn't sit for long stretches without hopping up to pace or run around. If we were at Aromatique, he'd jump up and make a latte out of the blue. If we were at the park, he'd insist on bringing along some form of entertainment—guitars, a Frisbee, or skateboards. He'd apologize sometimes for what he called his "spacey brain," but I thought it was pretty genius that he knew himself so well. And if his quest for activity got me on a skateboard for the first time in a decade, it couldn't be a bad thing.

He freaked out when he found my old skateboard collection in a closet in the pool house...once he got over the shock that I actually knew how to ride one pretty well.

"When did you learn how to ride a skateboard?"

"Sixteen, maybe? I don't remember. It looked fun and mildly rebellious. My parents didn't approve, so I wanted it more." I flipped my board upright, then spun it before hopping on and taking a quick ride around the pool area.

"What did they have against skateboards? It's better than getting high every day. Or did you do that too?"

"No. I didn't rock the boat much. I topped out at skateboards and cigarettes. They disapproved of both. The skateboard was understandable. I could fall off a board, break my wrist, and end my budding music career. Smoking was just me being an asshole. My dad quit when I was a kid. I thought it was hypocritical of him to preach about health concerns when he'd done it his whole life. But my teenage perspective was limited. When Charlie was growing up, I made it a point to be more honest and open. I hated the "Do as I say, not as I do" rhetoric from my childhood."

Justin froze and then lowered his Ray Bans. Sunlight glistened on his smooth torso and accentuated his toned abs. He wore a pair of navy-striped board shorts and nothing else. Except a "What the fuck?" look. "When Charlie was growing up? You make it sound like you raised him."

"I was around a lot. Charlie's mom wasn't in the picture, and Seb's my best friend. I helped out. Took him to preschool, taught him how to ride a bike...that kind of stuff," I said with a shrug.

"Dad stuff."

"Godfather stuff," I corrected. "That's who I am."

He fixed me with a thoughtful stare. "He's lucky."

Justin switched topics and didn't bring up Charlie again until he mentioned a gig he'd landed for them downtown in late April. I thought about clarifying my relationship with Seb and Charlie, but then what? If he asked me, I'd tell him. But it seemed pointless to dig up old skeletons and frankly, I didn't feel like talking about the past. Not when the present was infinitely more exciting.

AFTER HE FOUND MY SKATEBOARDS, we started bringing them with us on daily jaunts to the park after his shift at Aromatique and before Zero practiced. We rode from the car to our favorite bench with to-go cups in hand one afternoon. Spring had been fickle so far—chilly and overcast one day and seventy degrees and sunny the next. Today was flat-out cold. No doubt we'd do more skateboarding than people-watching after we finished our coffees.

We sat a little closer than usual for body warmth, cradling warm drinks as we people-watched. This particular park had become one of our go-to spots because it was within walking distance of the coffee shop and a short drive to my house. We'd sit on a bench under a huge oak tree in the middle of a grassy knoll equidistant between a playground and a basketball court. It was a good spot to observe humans in the wild. As much as I looked forward to getting naked and horizontal with him, I came to love our "research dates" and my writing partner's random topics of conversation.

I'd learned to read him fairly well over the past couple of months. He was a deep thinker with frenetic energy. When he sat quietly for a long stretch, I could practically see the wheels turning in his brain as he gathered data. But he tended to process everything aloud. And while music might be his favorite subject, the guy could talk about anything. We had serious discussions about topics I wouldn't have thought were debate-worthy, like where to find the best sushi in LA or the merits of kombucha.

"That stuff is fucking disgusting," he huffed, sipping his coffee.

"What's wrong with kombucha?"

"It tastes nasty and that glob of gunk on the bottom of the bottle looks like phlegm," he replied.

"Gross."

"Right? My b-brother was talking about making his own. R-Rory is a good cook, and he's a mathematician. The combo leads to interesting experiments. Good thing Christian doesn't mind.

They're looking for a house in Long Beach to move in together after Christian's lease is up on his apartment. He keeps saying he needs a big window with lots of sunshine for his tea experiment. F-fuckin' weirdo," he said affectionately.

"Are you cold?"

"I'm f-fine."

I glanced up at the gathering clouds in the gray sky, then set my arm over the bench and motioned for him to slide over. "No, you aren't. You're always cold. That jacket isn't warm enough. Come closer."

"You sound like a parent," he huffed before obeying.

Well, sort of obeying. I tugged him against me and wrapped my arm around him.

"You sound like a brat," I retorted. "Better?"

"Yeah. Do you think you'll ever want to be a dad?"

I scoffed. "Where'd that come from?"

"This place." He gestured toward the father and son throwing a baseball on the opposite end of the playground. "I think our timing is off today. I see more families than couples."

"Hmm. Do you?"

"What?"

"Do you want to be a parent someday?" I asked.

"No. I don't think so. Never say never, but it's a big job and I wouldn't want to do it on my own."

"You don't know that you'd be alone. You might meet someone and fall in love and—"

Justin rolled his eyes. "Hmph. You know how I feel about that. Beside, I didn't exactly have a great role model. I wouldn't want to be anything like my father. What was yours like?"

I regarded him thoughtfully before replying. "He was a good guy. A little distant and hard to know but I think some of that was the parenting style my folks grew up with. Hover without getting too close. They were protective and sometimes overly invested in my achievements. When I was a kid, they checked every homework assignment. If I got a math problem wrong, they'd point it out and tell me to fix it. Maybe that's not a great example, but it was a theme. There's a right way and a wrong way. Do the right thing."

"What about your music? Did they make you learn piano when you were a toddler?" he joked.

"No, that was something I found on my own. Neither of my parents played an instrument but they wanted to expose me to the arts early, so they took me to museums and to the theater all the time. And concerts too."

"Rock concerts?"

I chuckled. "No. Glorified local talent shows at Town Hall. We had a few of them every winter. It was a good way to get the community together and keep spirits high when there was literally nothing to do besides play in the snow. The kids sat in the front on the floor, and I always made sure to get a spot by the piano. I'd watch Mrs. Murphy's fingers when she played. I started to memorize the notes and the corresponding keys of the songs in her repertoire. It was mostly simple stuff, ranging from easy classical music to "Over the Rainbow." At the end of one show, when everyone started mingling and feasting on cookies and punch, I hopped onstage and started to play. That was officially day one of my music career," I said with a self-deprecating half laugh.

"Wow. So you were a prodigy."

"I don't know about that. But I was drawn to it. Like the instrument called to me. Weird, isn't it?"

Justin shook his head. "No. It's cool. What song did you play?"

" 'Ave Maria.' "

"What? That's crazy!"

I snickered at his dumbfounded stare. "Don't be too

impressed. It's the same chord progression over and over. Fairly simple."

"Yeah, right! You might as well be from Mars. I cannot relate. My mom didn't have time to hover. If Rory and I had homework issues, we helped each other. He was a math whiz, and I was always good at English...*y español también*," he said with a wink. "I never even touched a piano until I was a teenager. I'm a poor kid from a beach town. I lived in apartments all my life. And not nice ones in the sky with views of Catalina and Palos Verdes. Our building had gang tag graffiti on the sides.

"Rory and I were latchkey kids who went to the YMCA after school to avoid the drug dealer who lived two doors down and was always asking if we wanted to work for him. When the neighbors fought or had parties or hell, had sex...you could hear through the paper-thin walls. We'd turn on our mom's old records and turn up the sound to drown out the noise. Fun fact... I joined my first band when I was fifteen so I could go to my friend Cam's house to practice. He had an actual house and a dog. He also had a pretty younger sister and a hot older brother. They asked me what I played, and I said guitar. Total fucking lie. I'd never even held a real one before then."

"So you found the guitar and your bisexuality on the same day. Nice."

Justin scratched his chin. "I guess that's true. I lied about both for a long time too."

"How so?"

"Well, I only half-assed play guitar and I only recently came out as bi. That makes me sound like a jerk, doesn't it?"

I frowned. "No. Why would it?"

Justin sucked in a deep breath and slowly exhaled. "I have all these big ideals when it comes to social justice and honesty, but I worry about my credibility and authenticity. You're the real thing. I'm a pretender."

"The best part about getting older is not giving a fuck what other people think. You fit in where you feel most comfortable, not where others say you should." I kissed his temple impulsively. "It's taken me every single one of my forty-four years on the planet to accept who I am and go for what I want. When I was younger, I played piano because I loved it and later because my parents loved it for me. They didn't like guitar. They associated it with a lifestyle they didn't approve of...drugs, sex, and rock and roll. They were very against me moving to California, but they approved of the commercial jingles. I was a pleaser. I kept my guitar playing and hell, even skateboarding mostly to myself. I might have pushed it once in a while, but I wanted to make them happy, so I showed them one side of myself and kept the rest secret."

"You mean about being bi?"

"Anything they wouldn't have approved of...and yeah, my sexuality was a big one. The unspoken rule was, if it's uncomfortable, we didn't talk about it. They never knew about any male lovers I had, just women they assumed were girlfriends... and my ex-wife."

"Did they like her?"

"Yes. They didn't know her well, but they liked the idea of me settling down and eventually having a family of my own. Mandy and I were married for ten years. All but one year was for show. She was bi and in a relationship with a woman. Both of them were high-profile movie execs. I was bi and mostly single. We were each other's beards at a time when coming out was career suicide."

"Even in LA?"

"Yep. A lot has changed in the last twenty-five years, Jus. I don't think I've ever been in a relationship where my partner has been able or willing to say, 'That's the guy who's important to me.'"

"That sucks."

I shrugged. "It does, but I got used to it. And I like my own company just fine."

"You sound like me."

"The difference is, you're younger and braver. You've come of age at a time where equality, social justice, and RuPaul are mainstream topics. It may be a struggle still, but the conversations are out in the open now. That wasn't the case when I was your age. And I really hate how old that just made me sound," I said with a laugh.

"You're not old. You don't act old. I think it's because you're creative. You push yourself to see things through other people's eyes. We wouldn't be out here freezing our asses off if you took the easy way out and just wrote the same tired shit every time."

"All right, all right. I get the hint. Let's go." I rubbed his arm and then shifted to stand.

Justin grabbed the bottom of my jacket and pulled me back, so I landed half on top of him with my leg draped over his thigh. "Stay like this."

"I'm sitting on your lap."

"Not quite...but I like it. You always hold on to me, let me hold you for a minute."

The sentiment touched me in a way I couldn't easily explain. I wanted to go home and write down how I felt and why. Then I wanted to twist my feelings into words I could give to someone else so the emotions didn't choke the life out of me and demand attention I wasn't sure I could give. But when I tried to move and reclaim my spot beside him, he tightened his hold and shook his head. My rigid posture slowly relaxed as he talked about practice...Johnny's awesome guitar riff, Tegan and Ky's perfect rhythmic timing. He was seemingly unaware of my turbulent headspace. And after a while, so was I.

According to Seb, the studio wasn't happy with the legal mumbo jumbo required to potentially include Zero on the soundtrack. In other words, they were stalling. I'd been around the business a long time and had become an expert at calling out bullshit. I'd bet big bucks they'd drafted a contract to Seb's specifications fit for an unknown artist and were waiting for him to give in. Justin told me he'd received an initial letter of intent inviting him to cowrite a song. It wasn't a contract, though. It was a lure. Something to let him know they were interested and willing to pay a one-time commission. The sum was peanuts comparatively speaking, but a high five figures was a lot of money to a guy struggling to make ends meet. Seb couldn't understand why he insisted on bringing the band into the equation.

"If he just signed as a solo artist, he could pick up his paycheck and get his band started in style. Why is he being so difficult about this?" Seb griped.

"He's seizing opportunity. You should approve, Dad," Charlie commented. "I, for one, think you should give his band a shot."

Seb furrowed his brow in agitation. "This is a big fucking movie. I don't want any mediocre BS associated with it."

"But you signed Xena," Charlie countered. "She's not special. She just looks the part. Gray, pass the ketchup, please."

I slid the ketchup across the island and groaned when Charlie liberally doused his french fries. "You just killed those."

"No, I preserved them for me. I'm not sharing," Charlie said before casting a wary gaze between his dad and me. "And I care about the Zero because...I'm going to be their manager."

"Excuse me?"

"You heard me. I want to use my social media platform to create a new brand-slash-band. Zero."

Seb gaped at his son, then turned to me. "Did you know about this?"

"Yeah," I admitted.

"And you didn't think to tell me?"

"Charlie is a grown man, Seb. It's his story to tell, his project to take on, and frankly, I think he's doing a good job of it."

"Oh. So this is already happening?"

"Well, yes. Zero practices here a couple of days a week. And they've started recording a few songs. I sent you the tracks. Didn't you get them?" Charlie asked, wiping his hands on his napkin nervously.

"No. I didn't. I received something from a C. Robertson. I didn't listen to it because I didn't know my son had anything to do with this. And since when is Robertson your last name?"

"It seemed fitting since Gray is...involved," Charlie said, glancing sideways at me. "Why aren't you eating? You love In-N-Out."

"I already ate. I didn't know you two were coming over," I replied, sneaking a fry from his plate. "And bringing drama with you."

"Should we have called first?" Charlie asked.

"Why would you do that?" I made a face as I reached for another fry.

"In case you had extracurricular company." Charlie's deliberate intonation and carefully chosen words had the same effect as a fire alarm ringing in the middle of a busy day. Everyone wanted to ignore it, but it just got louder and louder.

I flicked Charlie's ear and shot an irritated look at him. He had his dad's eyes and they shared a few mannerisms, but that was where the family resemblance ended. Charlie was slight, and his halo of blond curls gave him a deceptively angelic look while his dad was tall, lean, and looked like trouble.

I'd wondered when this conversation was going to come up. When I'd told Justin I had no family, I hadn't exactly been honest. Seb and Charlie were my family. Not by blood, but they were my chosen people and had been a major part of my life since Charlie was a toddler. They both had keys to my house and knew all of my security codes and a few important passwords. And vice versa. Charlie might not look like his dad, but he had a talent for finding innovative ways to get what he wanted, and he'd definitely inherited Seb's mischievous streak.

"None of your business, Char."

"Hmm. I don't want to get in the way of a booty call. Nothing throws a man off their game quite like an ill-timed Donna Summer hit blasting through the speakers," he said with a laugh before breaking into the refrain from "Last Dance."

I let out an amused huff, then glanced at Seb, who looked... upset. "What's wrong?"

"Why didn't you tell me you were still"—he put his hands over Charlie's ears and continued—"fucking him? I thought that was a one-time deal."

"Why would you care?" I snapped impatiently.

"I don't, but it's curious that you're fucking the guy who's trying to screw up my project by making ridiculous demands. Jesus, Gray, he's using you. He's using both of you to get to me!"

"Fuck you."

Charlie darted his gaze between us before landing on me. "*Gasp*! I was not prepared for fireworks."

"Then why did you bring it up?" I asked sharply.

"Because if you're in love with someone else, he should know." Charlie pulled his designer bag from the barstool and hiked it over his shoulder. "Work this out, dads. Remember the children."

If I wasn't pissed, I might have been amused at Charlie's over-the-top exit and Seb's openmouthed stare. But I *was* angry...at myself. I hadn't told either of them about Justin because I honestly wasn't sure what the hell I was doing anymore. We had more than enough material for me to put together a sweet love song with a catchy hook I knew would do well. But I wasn't ready to let him go, even though I knew saying nothing at all would come back to bite me. Like now.

Seb dropped his burger on his plate and pushed away from the island before pacing into the adjoining living area. His silhouette reflected in the window. He looked handsome and commanding with his broad shoulders and tapered waist in his designer suit pants and white oxford shirt. The great room's modern design and minimalist furniture added an element of sophistication, like his surroundings were further proof he was an important man. Except this was my house, not Seb's. And yes, Justin was my lover, but our liaison had nothing to do with him. I put together my "You have no right" speech in my head as he stared out at the pool. But when he turned to face me, he looked...hurt. It was hard to stay angry at hurt.

"So are you in love with him or something?"

"Really?" I countered. "I've only known him for a couple of months. We're working on—"

"I know what you're doing," he whispered. He kept his eyes locked on mine for a long, uncomfortable moment. "But while you're fucking him, you're kind of fucking up my deal."

"You know, that's almost funny. You wanted me to seduce him, Seb. You wanted me to get him on board so you could have the titillating ex-lovers' tale you think is going to sell tickets. You didn't count on him having a brain."

"If he had a brain, he'd have signed on, finished the song, and cashed the damn check already."

"But if he does this the way you want it, he's a flash in the pan by Christmas. He knows it. He figured it out on his own. I didn't put ideas in his head. He's smart as fuck and he knows what he wants."

"And what does he want?"

"A shot at the big time."

"So he wants to be Mick Jagger," Seb scoffed.

"I think he knows he's better off being himself."

Seb regarded me for a moment. "This is business. It's promotion only. Call me an asshole, but I don't care about Xena or Justin's future careers. That's for their agents, managers, or their mommies to worry about. Now suddenly my son is his manager or social media guy and you—"

"Watch it," I warned.

"I had one idea and it was a good one. Why do I feel I'd be fucking up my movie by doing your lover a favor?"

"I'm not asking for anything, asshole. You're the one who dragged me to Carmine's. Then you enlisted Charlie's help to lure Justin into this and—"

"I didn't ask you to fall in love with the guy," he yelled.

Silence.

"Why do you pull that shit? It's like you want me to feel guilty for something you did. Don't rewrite history with me....I wasn't the one who left."

Seb gritted his teeth and balled his fists at his side. "You know why I—"

"I do. I was there. And it was eighteen years ago, so it really doesn't matter anymore."

"Sometimes I wish we could do it over again." His breath hitched as he exhaled.

"We can't, Seb."

"I know."

I pursed my lips and then massaged the back of my neck before meeting his gaze. He looked sad now. Defeated. And *fuck*. I knew that feeling all too well.

"We like each other. Don't make it into something it's not. He's not using me."

He shook his head as he looked away. "I want to believe that, but it's a bit too convenient."

"You know, at some point we have to stop doing this. You have to let me be happy, and I have to do the same for you."

"I *do* want you to be happy," he choked.

"Then let go, Seb."

He let out a humorless half laugh and shook his head. "I can't. I love you."

"I love you too. But it's not the same. Don't make the memory into something more than it was. The reality was hard. The thing about us is, we'll always be together. Just not that way."

After a long moment, Seb rubbed his nose with the back of his hand and turned to me with a wan smile. "Okay. I'll see what I can do for him."

"Don't do it for me. Or Charlie. Listen to their recording. And then see what you can do. Like you said, it's business. It's not personal."

He nodded, then moved to the island and picked a fry from Charlie's plate. "Poor Char. He must be so fucking sick of us."

I set my hand on Seb's shoulder and kissed his cheek. "He's

tougher than he looks, and he knows we love him. I wouldn't worry about Charlie. And don't worry about me and you. We're gonna be fine."

We sat side-by-side, eating cold fries as we let the quiet settle over us like a fresh bandage. Once it covered us completely, we shared a smile and quietly reverted back to our new version of us. Just friends.

———

AFTER SEB LEFT, I locked myself in my studio, pulled my favorite Gibson from the wall, and played until my fingers bled. There was no rhyme or reason to my song choices. I played what came to me. But everything sounded like the blues. Sad, lonely, and a little bitter. When a drop of blood dripped onto the strings, I set my guitar on the stand next to the piano, licked my finger, and aimlessly tapped a tune on the keys with my free hand. And when the halting sound grated, I thought about going into the library to play a few albums and drown out the growing silence. I had everything I needed there, in languages I'd never learn. I could get lost for days.

I put a playlist together in my head. Muddy Waters, Patsy Cline, Peter Gabriel. And somewhere in the midst of my frantic list-making, I remembered a recent conversation with Justin about "go-to songs when you're feeling like crap." His words, not mine. I pulled my cell from my back pocket, scrolled for his number and pushed Call.

" 'Lo?"

"Hi, it's me."

"Hey. Are you okay?" he asked in a groggy voice.

"Yeah, I just—" I raked my hand through my hair and sighed. "What time is it?"

"Um...two a.m. What's wrong?" Silence. "Gray? Talk to me."

"Nothing," I lied. "I...hey, I'm sorry. I didn't know it was so late."

"Are you alone?"

"Huh? Yeah. Of course. I'm always alone."

"I'll be right over. Leave the front door open," he instructed before hanging up.

Fifteen minutes later, Justin showed up on my doorstep. He looked tired and concerned, but he didn't ask any questions. He opened his arms, wrapped me in a strong embrace, and held on tight. Then he led me upstairs to my bedroom, undressed and instructed me to do the same before pulling me against him. We fell onto the bed in a tangle of limbs, groping, sucking, and licking. His warm skin, soft lips, and the scrape of his stubbled jaw felt like a salve of sorts. His touch felt healing, maybe even empowering. Like he was replenishing strength I temporarily lacked. When he bit my bottom lip and thrust his erection alongside mine and whispered, "I need to fuck you," I simply nodded. I needed that too.

He reached for supplies in the nightstand drawer before crawling between my legs. He set a lubed finger on my entrance, then bent his head to swallow me whole as he gently pushed the digit inside. It wasn't the first time he'd fingered me. He didn't say it aloud, but I could tell he was used to topping. Every time he'd try a move that we both knew led to his dick in my ass, I'd stop him with a look. He'd back off and give me room to take over. Not tonight. I wanted...no, I needed to give someone else the reins.

Justin added a second finger, then a third as he alternately bobbed his head on my shaft and sucked my balls. I pulled my knees against my chest and writhed until I knew I couldn't take much more. When I tugged his hair, he released me before straddling my torso and setting the tip of his penis on my lower lip. He swiped precum from his slit and then slipped his thumb into my open mouth. I arched forward and sucked wantonly... first his thumb and then his cock. Not for long, though. We were both getting too close too fast.

He ripped open a condom and rolled it on in record time before lying beside me. I chuckled softly when he gripped himself at the base and waggled his eyebrows in wordless invitation. But I didn't hesitate. I climbed over him, set his cock at my hole, and slowly lowered myself. I took my time. I hadn't done this in a while, but I hadn't forgotten that it could hurt like hell before it felt amazing. Justin rubbed the inside of my thighs and languidly stroked me while he waited for me to adjust to his girth.

"You're thick...so big."

He flashed a goofy grin and chuckled. "Gee, thanks."

I laughed at the playful twinkle in his eyes and felt myself begin to relax. And then I moved. The slow roll of my hips gave way to gentle rocking, back and forth, back and forth. I splayed my hands over the angel wing tattoo on his pecs before tweaking his nipples and finally letting go. I sat up tall and rode his cock like a fucking pro. There was nothing hesitant or unsure in my movement. I was with the right man doing something I loved and damn, it felt good. And when he flattened his feet on the mattress and thrust his hips in a steady upward motion, I groaned loudly and pushed his hand away so I could stroke myself as I picked up the tempo.

"Fuck, you feel so good," I purred, biting my bottom lip.

"So do you, but I'm—fuck, I'm gonna come." Justin squeezed his eyes shut and bucked his hips furiously.

"Get on top of me. Hurry," I commanded.

He pulled me against him and rolled over me without losing a beat. When he lifted my right leg and kissed the inside of my calf, then gazed at me in wonder, I knew that was it for me. I clutched his ass to hold him close as I came. And Justin was right behind me. I wrapped my arms around him and buried my face in his neck, trembling in the aftermath.

We lay entwined for a while. I rested my head on his chest and listened to his heartbeat until it returned to normal. Then we headed for the bathroom to clean up before falling into bed. I fell asleep with his arms around me, his chest against my back. I wasn't a cuddler. I didn't really like to be touched at all when I was sleeping. But I liked this. A lot. Maybe too much. Because when I awoke the next morning and glanced over at the gorgeous man beside me, I wanted to pinch myself.

Had I really called Justin in the middle of the night to— what? Rescue me, comfort me, assure me I wouldn't be alone for the rest of my life? That wasn't like me at all. *I* was the comfort-giver and the one who kept their shit together when everything and everyone around me was falling apart.

I propped myself on my elbow and watched him sleep. He was more handsome than pretty, but he had lovely features: long eyelashes, high cheekbones, and full lips. I liked the contrast of his olive skin against mine. And I loved his ink. It complemented mine. I could imagine the rose vine on his upper bicep twisting around my forearm, tying us together. I smiled at the whimsical notion as he stirred.

" 'Morning."

Justin stretched his arms above his head and gave me a sleepy smile. "Were you watching me sleep? You know that's a little creepy, right?"

I brushed his hair from his forehead and caressed his face. "Yeah. I couldn't help myself. I had to be sure I wasn't dreaming."

"You asked me to come. Once last night, but I'm hoping for round two this morning," he said lasciviously.

"I think I can help you out there," I replied, snaking my hand under the sheets to palm his morning wood. I pressed kisses along his shoulder and up his neck, then whispered, "Thank you" in his ear.

"For what?"

"Being here."

"Mmm." Justin rested his hand on my hip and kissed me sweetly before pulling back with a scrutinizing once-over. "Are you okay?"

"Yeah. It's just..."

"What?" he prodded.

"It gets lonely sometimes. That's all."

He went perfectly still; then he reached for my hand and lifted it to his lips the way I sometimes did.

"I know."

We showered together, exchanging blowjobs under the warm spray and then sucking cum from each other's tongues before washing and rinsing a second time. I tossed a clean towel at him and dried off before stepping aside to make room for him in front of the floor-to-ceiling mirror propped against the wall like a painting.

Justin grinned at our reflection and squeezed my ass. "We gotta have sex in front of this mirror. What do ya say?"

"I say yes, but I need food first. You're killing me." I swatted his ass with the end of my towel and furrowed my brow in mock warning. "No old-guy cracks. C'mon, let's grab some coffee."

He widened his eyes comically and made a zipped-lip motion before following me into the bedroom to get dressed. Justin headed for the studio when I promised to bring coffee. I found him perched on a stool near the wall of guitars typing on his cell.

"Do you have to go to work?" I asked as I handed over his mug.

"Yeah. Johnny is covering for me for another hour." He stood and set the coffee on the stool as he continued to scroll through messages. "But I have to swing by Tegan's to pick up my—holy fuck."

"What is it?"

He looked at me with a wild-eyed expression that was part joy and part terror. "I just got an email from the office of Sebastian Rourke. A letter of intent. He says they'll use Zero on a track for the movie. I-I don't know what to say. It's not a contract, but he said the legal team is working on drawing one and blah, blah, blah. Fuck. I've gotta figure out a song. Wait. No, I think he'll choose the song, right? We've got a lot of material. We can fine-tune something and make it fit whatever they're looking for. And the love song is...I think we're close on that too and—you did this, didn't you? You and Charlie."

"I didn't do anything but suggest that he listen to your band." I motioned for him to show me the email. It was brief and noncommittal. Very Seb...very Hollywood. "It isn't a contract, but it sounds like one might be ready to sign in the next day or two."

"Fuck, yes!" He whooped and punched the air before running a lap around the studio, plucking at guitar strings and piano keys and banging on drums in a mini celebration.

I chuckled at his antics and set my coffee beside his on the stool. I moved to the guitar wall and pulled a gorgeous cherry-red Stratocaster down.

"This one is a beauty. Plug in and give her a try," I said, cradling the six-string like a newborn baby.

He flashed a lopsided grin before slinging the strap over his shoulder and strumming a few chords. "I have music in my head already. Ideas for the song. I don't play well enough to get them across but—"

"Sure you do. Play what you're feeling. Don't be tentative. Do it like you mean it." I sat behind the grand piano and splayed my fingers over the keys, prompting him with a jazzy tune, then backed off slightly to listen to his lyrics and try to catch the general idea of what I thought he might be looking for musically. After a few stops and starts, I embellished his elementary idea and crafted it into something a bit more sophisticated.

"Not bad!" he beamed with a Cheshire cat grin before going rogue.

I snickered appreciatively when he tilted the Strat vertically and hopped around the studio on one leg like he was doing a Chuck Berry impression. I joined in, swaying back and forth as my fingers flew across the keys, adding melodic filler to his mini rock concert. He ended with legs spread and one arm in the air in a time-honored rock god pose. I pivoted on the piano bench and clapped enthusiastically.

"Bravo."

Justin bowed before returning the guitar to the wall.

"Thanks. So...what did you say to him?" He straddled the piano bench and leaned in to lick my lips.

His jeans were frayed at the knees and worn thin around his crotch, and his black T-shirt hugged his biceps like a glove. He looked like a bad boy. A Latino James Dean with just enough geek in him to make him seem accessible and real. Magic combo for a rock star in the making.

"I told you."

"No, be specific. I mean, does he know about us?"

I hesitated for a second, then nodded. "Yes. Is that a problem?"

"Not for me. I haven't said anything to anyone...Tegan or Johnny. I haven't even told Rory. I want to. This is all good, right? Me, you, Zero, the song we've written."

"Well, we haven't quite finished, but—"

"I did. I mean, I've written something I think works, but...I get nervous when things feel like they're coming together. It never works out well for me. I usually fuck it up somehow."

"We're in this together, Jus. You won't fuck anything up."

I closed my eyes and pressed my lips to his. I memorized his scent as I breathed him in like a fine wine or a sweet perfume. Words like clean, new, coffee, manly, peppermint came to mind. I knew immediately that they were useless adjectives. They might remind me of this moment, but they lacked the poetry needed to describe him. Or to describe the way I felt about him. Or how nervous I felt that his beginning might be the end of us.

Justin

I WAS TOTALLY GOING to fuck it up.

Of course, I wouldn't mean to, but it was just my nature. I couldn't have nice things. I tried to tell myself that was the old me, and the new me wasn't gonna blow it. But I had my doubts. About a lot of things.

This might be the chance of a lifetime for Zero. But Hollywood didn't pursue no-name singer-songwriters or newly formed bands. So yeah, I knew any opportunity here was thanks to Gray and Charlie. Connections mattered. Everyone told me it was as much who you knew as how much you knew in this industry. But as I made my way to Vibes later that night, I couldn't help thinking I was missing something. And my brother agreed with me.

I adjusted my earbuds when Rory's voice broke midsentence. "...be prepared to slay. That's all you can do. If it's a legit deal, you'll soon find out. If not, you'll find that out too. But either way, you can't win or lose if you don't take a chance. Listen to your younger, wiser brother. I'm always right."

"I know that, dummy," I huffed.

Rory guffawed. "Say it again. I gotta record this. Go on...Rory is always right."

"Rory is always a pain in the ass," I said slowly. "Of course, I'm going for it. I'm just not sure what 'it' is. I trust Gray, but I don't think he really knows the behind the scenes BS grunt artists like us deal with. We're nobodies. The only reason the producer is interested in us is because of Xena. Gray says—"

"Whoa. 'Gray says this, Gray says that.' What's going on with you two?"

I stopped on the middle of the sidewalk and leaned against the stucco façade of a bank building before glancing at my watch. I had fifteen minutes to get to Vibes for my shift. Plenty of time to spill my guts. I filled Rory in on the project I was working on with Gray. I tried to downplay the note of hero-worship I heard in my own voice, but nothing much got by my brother.

"...a real contract for Zero and the other for me to cowrite the love song. It's a great song. Even if Xena sings it. The song is almost finished and Gray's a master at arranging music, so it shouldn't take long to—"

"Whoa! You're writing a *love* song? For Xena? Are you fuckin' with me?"

"It's not *for* Xena. Geez! It's just a business opportunity." When he didn't respond, I glanced at my cell to make sure he hadn't hung up on me. "Are you there?"

"Yeah, I'm here. Since when do you care about business opportunities? You're falling for him, aren't you?"

I fixated on a rainbow flag taped to the inside window of a barbershop and rolled my eyes, though the gesture was lost through the phone connection. "Why is it that people in love always assume everyone else is looking for the same thing? How's Christian doing, by the way?"

"He's great. But back to you. Are you fucking him?"

"Okay, we're done here. I gotta run. I'm going to be late for work and—"

"That's a yes." Rory sighed theatrically. "Justin, what are you doing? If you're romantically involved with the guy who's tied to a project where you're being asked to sell a piece of your soul, chances are he's got something to do with it. I could be wrong. I obviously don't know the guy. How are you gonna feel after you cash a check for a bogus love song? Sounds like dirty money and a big fuckin' setup. Just like that night at Carmine's. You walked out before she made a fool of you. You won't be able to walk away from a song on a movie soundtrack. If it's something you're proud of, that's great. But I know you. You get caught up in the moment, Jus. Make sure you know exactly what's going on before you sign your name on something you'll regret."

"You're a fuckin' downer."

"I'm a realist and usually you are too. What did Tegan say about it?"

I winced as I straightened from the wall and started down the street toward Vibes. "He doesn't know yet."

A cat meowed loudly from his side, no doubt saving me from a major lecture. "Even Buttons thinks you're a dumb shit. Christ, Justin. Get your act together. Be honest. Brutally honest if you have to be. With Tegan, Johnny, Ky...but mostly with yourself. Figure it out before something goes sideways. Oh, and one more thing. Call Mom. I ran into Agnes, the checkout lady at the YMCA. She was dropping off her grandson for camp and asked if Mom was okay. She said she looks thinner than normal. Mom's already too skinny. Will you check on her?"

"Yeah. Of course," I assured him.

Rory changed the topic to a recipe he'd tried for Christian, who'd just come home from his evening class. I appreciated the lighthearted banter after his whammy of realness. But the second we hung up, anxiety ate a hole in my stomach. Gray,

Tegan, a contract and a real shot for Zero...and my mother. Great. Just what I needed before working a five-hour shift where smiling was actually part of my job description.

I cranked an old Led Zeppelin tune and hightailed it down San Vicente to the heart of West Hollywood, LA's gay mecca. Everything in this section of town was fabulous. From the rainbow-painted crosswalk at San Vicente and Santa Monica Boulevard to the rainbow Route 66 sign. There were dozens of chic bistros, gay bars, and clubs within walking distance, and many of them had an upscale ambience that seemed to suggest that this was where the A-list queer crowd hung out.

Vibes was nestled between a dry cleaner who charged an ungodly sum per shirt and a fancy ice cream shop where Instagrammers and Hollywood wannabees posed for selfies with bougie ice cream cones. That was SoCal for you. I supposed people who spent ten dollars on a double scoop wouldn't blink at paying twice that to clean their designer duds. I never pictured myself living in WeHo. Yeah, I was bi, but I wasn't fabulous. And some days, I didn't think I was cool enough. But I loved the energy here. Under the glossy exterior was a sense of unapologetic pride that encouraged free speech and self-expression. It wasn't gritty or raw, but living and working in WeHo was a good opportunity to explore and truly embrace the gay part of being bi. And it didn't get much gayer than Vibes.

I nodded in greeting at the security guard and gave him a fist bump as he opened the back door for me. I could never remember his name. Ronny or Ricky or something. He was a big guy with short dark hair, a potbelly, and a birthmark covering one side of his face. We'd bonded over our Latino heritage on a cigarette break once. It must have been enough to seal a friendship, because none of the other bartenders got the nod *and* the fist bump.

I stopped by the employee break room to drape my jacket

and T-shirt over a chair before heading into the club, bare-chested and ready to pour. A steady dance beat pumped through the speakers, getting louder as I moved along the darkened corridors to the main floor. A decent-sized crowd bopped to electronic music under a rainbow glitter disco ball, but I knew from experience that it would be a scene within a couple of hours. Thursday was an honorary weekend night around these parts.

"Look who decided to show up."

Garrett softened his annoyed once-over with a flirty wink when I slid behind the bar. He was a beautiful African American model with short cropped hair, high cheekbones, and startling green eyes. He was six two, lean, and toned to perfection. Garrett was one of those weirdos addicted to spin classes and juice drinks. He claimed he only worked here to pay for his acting classes, but I had a feeling he was a victim of the LA lifestyle. Exclusive gym memberships, designer jeans, and BMW leases cost big bucks.

I washed my hands at the sink and smiled at the cute couple signaling they were ready to order. "Sorry. I—"

"Save it. Tegan covered for you." Garrett snapped a bar towel on my ass and winked.

"Where is he?" I asked, glancing around the dimly lit area.

The bar was a masterpiece of backlit glass shelving, mirrored backsplashes, and a fountain wall. The liquor was stored on lower shelves to give an unimpeded view of the cascading waterfall effect. Large flat-screen televisions hung high above the fountain and along the perimeter. Music videos played until the club got bumping. Then a video cam flashed footage of the sexy go-go boys shaking their ass on the catwalks above the dance floor. The bar was busy, but not overly crowded. And for the moment, everyone seemed content. Except the couple staring at us meaningfully.

Garrett flashed a friendly grin in their direction. "He's at the front door as usual. He was looking for you too. He seemed frazzled."

Garrett kissed my cheek, then sashayed toward the waiting couple.

It didn't take long to find my groove. Pour, flirt, clean...repeat. I'd been bartending for years and had learned a few things along the way. The friendlier and more engaging I was on a slow to moderately busy night, the better the tips. But when the press of bodies around the bar was three people deep and everyone was waving to get my attention, no one wanted small talk. They wanted a quick shot of courage before heading to the dance floor.

I pasted a smile on my face as I handed a cosmo to a cute twink wearing a cropped football jersey and pink lipstick. I took the twenty he gave me and was about to thank him for the generous tip when I spotted Tegan waving to get my attention a few feet away. I needed an excuse to leave the bar while it was this busy. I grabbed an almost-empty bottle of gin and tapped Garrett's arm.

"Hey, I'm gonna grab another bottle of Tanqueray from storage. You and Alex can handle it, right?"

Garrett glanced at the heavily tatted bartender working the opposite end of the space and nodded. "Hurry back. We need you."

I headed after Tegan, slipping through the crowd, winding my way through sweaty, scantily clad hotties and couples tangled in passionate kisses. I caught up to him outside the bathroom.

"Hey. What's—"

"She's here," he said in an ominous tone reserved for scary movies.

"Who?"

"Xena! Who do you think?"

I craned my neck toward the dance floor in vain. "What's she doing here?"

"I don't know. She came by around nine and asked if you were working tonight. Sean was standing outside too. He knows you were late again, and he's pissed. But anyway, she said she'd come back, and she did. She paid the cover, and she'll be at the bar any second. We can't have drama here, Jus. Sean will fire your ass. Stay here and I'll tell them you—"

I held my hand up and craned my neck toward the bar. "No. I'm not gonna hide. That's ridiculous. Just...cover for me and have her meet me in the alley."

Tegan frowned. "I can't leave you alone with her. Especially not here. You'll fight like you always do and you'll get fired. You're already on thin ice with Sean."

"I am?" I asked sarcastically.

"Dude, you've been late for every shift for weeks. Sean's asked me what's going on with you."

"Five minutes is hardly late, and he's just looking for an excuse to get rid of me 'cause he's a jealous fuck who thinks we're still—"

"Don't," he snapped. "Now is not the time."

I let out a weary sigh and nodded. "I think I see her."

Tegan glanced over his shoulder. "All right. Go outside and tell them to—"

"What's going on?" A gruff voice echoed in the corridor.

I didn't bother looking up. I always did my best to steer clear of my boss. He hated me, and the feeling was mutual. Sean Gruen was a divorcee with two kids who'd come out with a bang when he turned forty. He bought a few gay clubs and bars in LA and Palm Springs with a business partner and had made a name for himself in LGBTQ philanthropic circles. Most people would say

Sean was a great catch. He was wealthy, successful, and those who were into tall, bald, muscular types with designer wardrobes and flashy cars thought he was hot too. He did nothing for me. Except remind me that I should be thankful that he gave my sorry ass a job when I needed employment quickly a few months ago. I liked working at Vibes...as long as I didn't have to deal with Sean.

"Hey, boss. I'm taking a quick break." I gave him a phony smile and stepped toward the exit.

"You just got here, Cuevas."

"I've been here for a couple of hours actually." *Shit.* She was closing in. "I'll be back in ten minutes."

"I don't think so. Take that bottle to the bar and get to work," Sean commanded, gesturing to the nearly empty Tanqueray in my hand.

Tegan shot a distressed look between Sean and me and then over his shoulder at the raven-haired beauty heading toward us. I weighed the situation quickly before making one of my infamous snap decisions. The kind that usually got me into trouble. What can I say? Some life lessons didn't stick.

I unscrewed the top, lifted the bottle in a toast, and drained the contents like it was a beer bong. Then I swiped my mouth and angled my head toward the exit.

"It's gone now. I'll throw it out for you."

Sean clenched his fists and pointed at the door. "You're fired, Cuevas. Get the fuck out."

"You got it wrong. I quit."

I set the bottle at his feet, then winked before heading to the door.

The moment I stepped outside, I realized I'd forgotten my shirt and jacket in the break room. And it was cold. I couldn't go back in, and I couldn't ask Tegan to throw my stuff out here. Not yet, anyway. I thought about asking the bouncer, but he was busy talking to someone and before I could think of a plan, Xena was there.

She paused in the doorway and gave me a thorough once-over. I did the same. I hadn't seen her since that night at Carmine's, and I liked it that way. Though I had to admit, she looked great. Her red lips were her only concession to color. She wore a long, black flowing dress with combat boots. Her long hair fell in spiral curls over her shoulders. She reminded me of a Goth model in the middle of a photo shoot.

I felt woefully underdressed in my jeans and bare-chested state. But I bet any passerby would think we belonged together. Like the badass rock couple I'd once thought we could be when I figured looks and ambition could take us to the top. It was unsettling to realize how delusional I'd been.

Xena stepped into the shadow and folded her arms. "Hi, Justin. This won't take long. I heard that you—"

Tegan barreled outside and quickly inserted himself between us before growling at me. "I cannot believe you just fucking did that."

"Justin is always just doing things," Xena huffed. "Save your lover's tiff. It's fabulous to see you both again, but I've got better places to be."

"What do you want?" I asked. I was edgy, anxious, and call me crazy, but I didn't want to hang out in the alley—after unceremoniously telling my boss to fuck off—with my ex and my bandmate...oh yeah, who also happened to be my boss's lover.

Fuck, this was messed up.

"Sign the contract for the song and take the money, Justin. You need it and I need it. It's the perfect way to end our former relationship. And if we're lucky, we both end up with new careers."

"What is she talking about?" Tegan asked irritably.

Xena wrinkled her forehead. "You didn't tell your boyfriend the news?"

"He's not my boyfriend. And there is no news."

"Oh, that's right. You're fucking the songwriter," she taunted. "Or so I heard."

"From who?"

"Dec. He knows everyone. He's a good person to keep close. Did he tell you we're talking to an agent who thinks we can sign XenLA with a label?"

"XenLA?"

"Our band. We thought about going our separate ways, but my solo contract can help fund us. We have a new bass player and a drummer who can keep his dick in his pants," she said, shooting an evil look at Tegan before continuing, "But everything is at a fucking standstill because you haven't signed the damn contract. If this is about spite or greed, you've picked the wrong time to get even, Justin. Sign the fucking thing before we both lose out. You fucked me over once. Don't do it again."

I rounded on her with my teeth bared. "You got it wrong. You left me and the band and then—"

"And when I came back to get my stuff, I found you two were getting along just fine without me," she hissed. "Declan can be a real asshole, but he did us all a favor that day."

In a way, she was right. I hadn't felt that way when Declan let Xena into my old apartment. We were friends, or so I thought. And well before I'd met Xena, Dec and I were lovers. The casual kind that didn't stick around. But he must have wanted something more from me, because he'd been lurking in the shadows, eager to shine a spotlight on my every fuckup. Unfortunately, I gave him a lot of material.

"We were over. I didn't cheat on you." I annunciated each word and fixed her with a sharp, pointed look that unfortunately didn't faze her in the slightest.

"No, you switched teams and changed beds. You're a lowlife loser, Justin. You hang on till you suck the life out of everyone around you. I had to leave or I'd never get anywhere." Xena pushed her hair back distractedly and stepped into my space, pointing her finger at my chest. "So yeah...it's pretty fucking ironic and extremely unfair that I have to track you down to ask you to do the right thing by all of us. Sign the contract so I can finally get you out of my life for good."

"I repeat...what is she talking about? What contract?" Tegan furrowed his brow in confusion.

Xena cocked her head incredulously, then flipped her hair over her shoulder and let out an evil-sounding half laugh. "He didn't tell you? Wow. Lucky me. It looks like I get to see my boyfriend fuck you twice. Justin and I were offered a movie contract to write and perform a song. We can both walk away with a fat paycheck and a little publicity...when he signs the fucking thing."

"You mean for Zero," Tegan stated, turning to me for confirmation.

"Your new band?" she scoffed. "No. This one is for Justin only."

"Is that true?" Tegan asked.

"Yeah, but..." I pursed my lips and sucked in a deep breath. I couldn't go into any detail about what I was trying to do for Zero with Xena there. It was easier and probably safer if she thought I was greedy.

"But...he's trying to figure out how to screw me out of the deal. We're running out of time. Maybe you can talk some sense into him before he blows it for everyone, T. If you could make that phone call tomorrow morning, I'd really appreciate it," she said haughtily before turning down the alley.

I was aware of a lot of external noise at once...the clip of Xena's boots on the pavement, the bouncer talking to a few rowdy customers on a cigarette break, my phone buzzing in my pocket. But everything faded to a dull static when I caught Tegan's unrelenting stare. I shoved my hand through my hair and swallowed hard.

"Look, I'm sorry about that. I was waiting to talk to you guys tomorrow at practice but—"

"Are you quitting? We just started. I don't get it. I thought you were into this."

"I am!"

"Then what was she talking about? Don't sugarcoat anything and don't think about lying. Talk. And hurry the fuck up before I get fired too," he said gruffly.

"First of all, I didn't get fired, I quit. Second, I doubt your boyfriend is gonna let you go. And third, and most important...I didn't lie!" I yelled.

"No, you just push all the bullshit under a rug. You can't talk about anything important without freaking the fuck out."

"And you can?" I paced toward the trashcans and back again. "We've been walking on fucking eggshells around each other for months. We talk about the band and mutual friends and whose turn it is to buy toilet paper, but we can't talk about what we did. We don't say it was a bad idea or a good one. We don't say it was stupid or short-sighted or desperate. We don't even admit it was fun."

"You thought it was fun?"

"Sex is fun, Tegan. Of course it was fun. And you know what? I'm not sorry it happened."

"You're sorry we got caught," he snarked.

"Yeah. I am. Because we feel guilty and we shouldn't. I want to blame Declan for setting us up and starting the shitstorm that led to me unraveling and winding up on your sofa for eight months, but all that ugliness led us to Zero. We have a chance at something special, T. We have to get back to normal...me and you. I don't understand why it's so hard."

"Because I don't fucking trust you. And that..." He gestured toward the darkness before smacking my arm. "...is why."

"Xena?"

"No, asshole. The secrets. We're friends, we're in a band together, and until ten minutes ago, we worked at the same damn club. If you have some contract or a new boyfriend, shouldn't I know about it before your ex?" He threw his hands in the air and shook his head angrily. "I don't expect to know every detail of your life, but when you told me you wanted us to give one hundred percent to Zero, I thought you meant it. I rearranged clients at the gym to practice, and I've been working with Charlie to get us a couple of real gigs. And I got Ky onboard. I fed them every BS line you gave me about being the number one band in the world someday while you've been writing a love song with a Hollywood songwriter. A *love* song? What the fuck is that all about? Since when do you write that shit? That's not who Zero is, or is it?"

"It's a way to get a bigger contract, T. For the band. Not just for me. For all of us." I launched into a brief explanation about the letter of intent I'd received. "Read the email."

I pulled up the message and thrust my phone at him. Tegan scanned the message and handed it back.

"Interesting. Your boyfriend just texted you."

"He's not my boyfriend," I replied, glancing at the text. *What time are you off?*

I replied before stuffing my cell into my pocket.

"Whatever. I wish you'd told me about this shit sooner."

"I literally just got this email today. I wanted to—"

"That's not what I meant. I asked you about him when you let me think you had a job filing records for him. I'm not an idiot. I knew sudden access to his in-house studio had to be tied to something. I thought it was your ass. I didn't realize it was a sell-out contract," he huffed derisively.

"Fuck you," I hissed.

Tegan held his hands up in surrender and shook his head. "Hey, someone has to keep it real. Jus, has it occurred to you that they're telling you what you want to hear to get what they want? Nobody shows up and hands a contract over because they heard you sing a few songs at a dive bar. It's the same thing as showing up to Carmine's only to find they booked us to open for Xena."

"That's what Rory said, but it's not like that."

"It's exactly what it's like. You're losing sight of what's real because you're getting sex on the side. 'It's all good, man. Come on by. I'll suck your dick and we'll write a love song and you'll be famous one day,' " Tegan chided in a laid-back "dude" tone. "Un-fucking-real."

"You sound paranoid."

"Maybe I am paranoid, but you know what? I have every fucking right to be. She walked in on us, Justin. Not just you. I was there too. When she blabbed all over town that she caught her ex with a man. That was *me*." Tegan thumped his chest, then closed the distance between us until we stood toe to toe. "Me. And that was my reputation. And in case you're curious, it sucks that I can't walk into a club looking for a gig for our band without wondering if they're willing to give us a chance for the same reason those Hollywood assholes showed up to Carmine's in the first place. We're a curiosity. A flash in the pan cashing in on a so-called scandal. Just like Xena. She's right. Sign while you can. By this time next year, no one is gonna give a shit anyway."

Tegan's heated stare threw me off. This whole weird-ass chain of events threw me off. I was supposed to be the hothead, not T. He was strong and reliable, the friend everyone could count on, and the backbone of every band we'd been in together. If he was pissed, I knew I should listen up and try to make things right. But my gut insisted that in spite of all the warning flags, this was real.

"Wait," I called as he turned toward the club. "Look, I was going to lay all this out for you tomorrow. I'm not hiding anything. I'm just...trying to get it right this time."

"On your own. See, that's the problem. If you're in a fuckin' band, there is no 'on your own.' Being the idiot who follows you around with a set of bongo drums to play for latte drinkers after stepping over your underwear in my living room has lost its charm. You eat my yogurt, you never replace the toilet paper, and you only sporadically pick up your shit. Now it turns out you're leading a double life."

"Christ, I'm not leading a double life! I didn't want to over-promise and underdeliver. I was trying to do this the right way, but...I'm sorry. I'll buy you more yogurt and I'll—"

"I don't want that. I don't want anything but the truth. Why would you agree to write a love song in the first place if not for money?"

"I like Gray. And I'm writing the song because I like being with him. That's it. I swear that part has nothing to do with my personal aspirations or even the band. It's just him. He's smart and funny and yes, I probably learn something every time he corrects my finger position on the fret, but I don't care about that. When we get together to write or play music, I forget I'm supposed to have an end game."

Tegan cocked his head and gave me a funny look. "Are you in love with him?"

"I don't do love," I scoffed. "And I'm not a total idiot. I'm not signing away a song for Xena unless Zero gets one too. I've been holding out because I wanted to give you something real. A letter of intent isn't a contract, but it's more than we had yester-day. We can't give up now, T. We gotta practice like crazy and take advantage of every gig Charlie picks up for us. Not because we're banking on the studio offering us anything, but because we want to succeed. For us." I held eye contact for a long moment before continuing. "I know I don't make it easy, but I'm beggin' you to hang with me. We're in this together, man. I'm not going anywhere. I'm not deserting you. I promise."

I breathed a sigh of relief when he tentatively bumped my fist with his and then pulled me into a bro hug.

"I gotta get back to work. Some of us still have a job," he said with a lopsided smile before stepping aside. "I'll see you at practice tomorrow. Oh, and Jus..."

"Yeah?"

"You owe me two blueberry, two strawberry, and two honey yogurts. And buy the right brand."

"I didn't eat six yogurts." I scowled.

"I'm charging interest."

I shivered when a cool breeze swept through the alley, reminding me that I still had to grab my T-shirt and jacket from the break room. *Fuck.* I sucked in a deep breath and slowly exhaled. It should have felt better, right? It was good to get old shit off your chest. It helped you breathe easier. Or so I heard. I couldn't seem to swallow enough air at the moment. I felt dizzy, off-kilter, and completely overwhelmed. I pulled my cell from my pocket when it buzzed and pressed Call instead of reading the new message.

"What are you doing?" I asked.

Gray's soft laughter soothed me. It crept through the connection and wrapped me in a light veil that seemed to protect me from my self-destructive thoughts.

"Did you read my text?"

"No. What did it say?"

"It was poetry. To paraphrase, 'Come over when you're off work. I'll be waiting with two fingers in my ass, ready to go'...or something like that," he said.

I smiled. "That's so dirty...and kind of romantic."

Gray hummed. "If you want romance, I can turn on Barry White too."

"*And* stick your fingers in your ass? I might swoon."

"Don't swoon until after you get here. When are you off work?"

"Now. I quit."

"You quit?" he repeated. "Are you okay?"

"Yeah, I'll be fine. It's just been a weird night. I, um...I miss you." I winced. What the fuck was that? He was fifteen minutes away in the Hills. I didn't miss him.

Gray didn't reply right away. When he did, his voice sounded gravelly and thick with emotion. "I'm here. Come over, baby."

Our exchange grounded me. I felt a little less alone and unsure knowing he was somewhere waiting for me.

Fifteen minutes later, I entered the security code he'd given me for the front door and climbed the stairs two at a time and found him exactly where he said he'd be. Naked in bed, on his knees, fingering his hole.

"Wow," I gulped, tearing off my clothes as quickly as possible. "You have no idea how fucking hot you look."

Gray glanced over his shoulder and offered a sex-hazed lopsided smile. "So do you. C'mere. Let me suck you, Jus."

I set my precum-slicked cock on his bottom lip and kicked off my shoes as he swallowed me whole. My adrenaline level was already off the charts, and the sight of Gray on his knees, sucking and licking me from base to tip as he fondled my balls was nearly enough to push me over the edge.

"Are you ready for me?"

Gray straightened quickly and shoved his tongue in my mouth in response before turning around to present his ass to me. I stepped out of my jeans, rolled a condom on and added lube. Then I lined my cock up with his entrance and pushed into him from behind.

"Oh, my God." He groaned loudly as he stroked himself.

"You okay? 'Cause I need to fuck you hard."

"Do it. Fuck me, Jus."

Gray was as strung-out, horny, and demanding as I was. He bucked backward and urged me on with nasty commands to go harder and deeper. He loved it when I pulled his hair and smacked his ass. And when I slipped a finger in his hole alongside my dick as I reached around to jack him, he tumbled into ecstasy, crying out my name as his orgasm pulled him under. He shuddered beneath me, but I didn't stop moving. I couldn't. I pistoned my hips wildly and then gripped his shoulders before coming a moment later.

When I could breathe again, I cleaned up in the master bathroom and brought my lover a towel. Gray wiped the mess of sweat and cum from his junk and the sheets before flopping onto his back. I curled up beside him and propped myself on my elbow.

"Can I tell you something disgusting?"

Gray chuckled. "Sure. Why not?"

"I was just thinking how hot it would be to come in your ass. I'd love to pull out of you and see my cum drip—"

"That is hot. Graphic, but hot," he agreed.

"We should get tested. I mean...if you wanted to. I haven't been with anyone but you in months. And that's the way I want it to be."

Gray bit his bottom lip, then pulled me close and kissed me. "Me too."

"How old were you the first time you had sex with a guy?"

"Twenty."

"Top or bottom?"

"I don't think we had anal sex the first time but—"

"Blowjobs? Who did what first?"

"I don't remember," he said with a half laugh. "Does it matter?"

"No. I'm curious. I'm having a moment. Like there's an invisible angel on my shoulder telling me to let go of my ideas about how things are 'supposed to be.' I don't have to be the bi guy who goes out with as many girls as guys to prove he's masculine. I can be with the person who makes me happy without worrying about the ways I don't measure up."

"Me?"

"Yeah, you. I'm kind of crazy about you. And I've been thinking about love songs a lot lately for obvious reasons, but not for me. I mean in a broader sense. For example, I love my mom, but I resent her guilty hold over me. I love my brother, but I'm jealous of him sometimes. I love my best friend, but I hurt him. I don't know how to do that emotion correctly or purely, you know?"

Gray caressed my jaw, then let his hands roam to my hip. "No one does. We all just wing it, baby."

"Measures of kindness slip into place and allow us moments of purity...real affection, admiration, friendship. But is that love?"

Gray's smile dazzled me. "Did you write that?"

I squinted and replayed the question in my head. "Yeah."

"I like it."

"Thanks," I said distractedly. "I read Shakespeare's sonnets recently. For you."

"For me?"

"Yes. Do you know the line, 'It is an ever-fixed mark, that looks on tempests and is never shaken...'?"

"It's Sonnet 116. The one everyone uses for weddings," he replied quickly.

"That's the one. You really are a geek, aren't you?"

"Me? I'm a tough guy. Ask anyone," Gray joked, flexing his biceps.

I kissed his muscular arm as I rolled sideways, pushing my

leg between his. "Hmm. The concept of loving someone uncon- ditionally, without worrying if they'll ever love you the same way stops me every time. I don't understand it. I've never known anyone able to do it for a sustained amount of time. But every time we see a couple holding hands in the park or sharing an intimate look or a smile, I hope they make it. I hope they're brave and honest and strong. 'Cause it takes more than hearts and flowers and endless sunshine. I think it's work."

Gray lifted my hand and kissed it sweetly. "I think you're right."

I noted the sheen of tears in his eyes, but I didn't press. I didn't want to make a heat-of-the-moment declaration, but I had one more thing to say.

"I have no idea what love is, but you're the person I want to be with all the fucking time."

He gave me one of his signature slow grins, the one that turned me inside out and upside down. Then he pushed the hair from my forehead and pulled me close. "I feel the same way, Jus."

I REPLAYED last night in my head over coffee the next morning at the kitchen island. Gray was working out in his gym. He'd invited me to join him and laughed at my deadpan expression before leaving me to consume a fuckton of caffeine and munch on the contraband donuts Charlie left in the pantry. I had a sappy smile on my face as I wrote the final lines to the love song in my notebook. I stared out at the pool, admiring the sun's glitter-like reflection on the water when a new message from Charlie lit my screen.

The contract is ready for Zero to sign this afternoon at Rourke Studio at four p.m. Everyone needs to be there. Don't be late.

Holy shit. This was really happening.

A wave of doubt followed my initial burst of excitement. I cautioned myself not to plan Zero's concert tour yet. We had our first real gig at The Fix, a small indie club downtown next week. The idea of going from zero to one hundred was thrilling, but we had a ways to go. The movie soundtrack credit was a nice promotional tool, not a boost in the limelight. We had to prove ourselves and pay our dues just like everyone else. But I couldn't help feeling a little optimistic as I texted my bandmates. Maybe this really was our beginning.

WHEN THINGS SEEM TOO good to be true, they usually are. The second we were ushered from the sleek, modern reception area at Rourke Studios into Seb Rourke's private office, I sensed something wasn't quite right. I couldn't put my finger on it, though. Sure, I was nervous. I'd never been this close to Hollywood deal-making headquarters. At least I wasn't alone. Johnny and Ky sat on the edges of their leather chairs in the sitting area while Tegan paced the floor, pausing at the end of each lap to peruse the photos and movie memorabilia lining the walls. We'd all dressed in nice jeans with no holes, per Charlie's instruction, along with button-down oxford shirts. We looked like clean-cut kids rather than a kickass rock band, but I figured Charlie knew what he was doing. After all, he'd grown up in this world, and we were meeting his dad.

"What do you think is taking so long?" I whispered, plucking at my collar uncomfortably.

"Deep breaths, Jus. It's only been five minutes. Do you think Xena's with them in the conference room?" Tegan asked.

"No idea. It doesn't really matter as long we get what we're here for."

"Hmm. Check out some of these photos. Isn't this your boyfriend?" He pointed at a series of photos of Gray with a tall, handsome man I knew from my early Google research was Seb. In a few pics, they stood with their arms around each other with a small blond-haired boy. "Ha. I think that's Charlie. He was a cute kid."

I cocked my head curiously and studied the photos a little closer. Yeah. That was Gray. But a much younger version. Not that he looked old now, but he'd filled out, matured, and was more muscular now. This Gray was thinner and didn't have any ink. However, the photos spanned over a number of years beginning when Charlie was a toddler to recent pics that included another towheaded kid I assumed was Seb's younger son, Oliver. There were quite a few of Oliver on his own or with Charlie, but I was more interested in the fact that almost all of the rest featured Gray. That was weird. Best friends definitely deserved a place of honor on a photo collage wall, but every picture?

"Dad's finishing up a call in the conference room. He'll join us in a minute," Charlie announced. "Does anyone have any questions?"

"Yeah. Is this you?" I asked, gesturing at a picture of the two men and a little boy at Disneyland.

Charlie rolled his eyes. "Ugh. Yes. We should have waited in the reception area. There's nothing like a few embarrassing childhood photos to keep it real. I think I was five there, and I actually remember that day. I insisted I was ready for the Haunted Mansion. I said it was a baby ride and they didn't have to worry about me getting scared. Famous last words. I climbed into Gray's lap and held on to him in a chokehold throughout the whole thing. Poor guy."

"You spent a lot of time with him when you were a kid, huh?"

Charlie typed something into his phone before looking up at me distractedly. "Yeah. He was like a second dad to me."

"Right. He's your godfather."

"Mmhm. Dad and Gray were together for most of my childhood years, so in a way he's more than a godfather."

My stomach dropped, though I couldn't say what exactly bothered me. So Seb and Gray had been in a relationship. Okay. It had to be over years ago. They'd both been married to women and...I scanned the wall again. There were group pics that included women, some who looked vaguely familiar, like celebrities I should have recognized. But no single woman stood out. The only obvious couple was Seb and Gray. Fuck, I was jealous and for the life of me, I couldn't figure my way around this emotion.

They weren't together. Gray was with me. I'd slept in his bed, woken up next to him, drank coffee with him, and even showered and sucked his dick before this meeting. So why did this bother me?

"I don't get it. Were they married?"

Charlie shot a curious look at me and shook his head. "No. But gay marriage wasn't legal then. If it had been, they would've gotten married for sure."

"For sure?" I repeated.

"Yeah. We were a family. Two dads and a kid. My mom was a Hollywood hopeful who was a little too fond of disco snow. She dropped me off on Dad's doorstep when I was two months old. Literally. Not the drop part, but the story is, she left me in a basket with a note that said, 'This little guy is yours. Good luck!' like modern-day Moses. Dad had a paternity test done and sure enough, we were a match. Anyhoo, he met Gray when I was two and they were together until I was eight or nine. Let's just say, Dad has commitment issues. He hasn't been with anyone seriously in a while, but I think that's because he's still in love with Gray."

"Love." I pursed my lips and stepped aside to get away from

Charlie and give myself some breathing room. I was feeling more nauseous by the second.

"Yeah. I don't think they'll ever get back together again, but I'm not above using a twinge of jealousy to get Dad to cooperate."

"What do you mean?"

"Dad knows about you and Gray. He's a firm believer in keeping his enemies close." Charlie snickered. "Silly, I know. But you're hot and talented and he must feel a little threatened, because I doubt he'd give Zero the time of day otherwise. In fact, having me as your manager is a negative for him. He's still hoping I go into advertising when I finish my master's."

I nodded numbly and glanced at the photos one last time. A small one in the corner of the wall collage caught my eye. It was of Charlie with an older couple. "Who are they?"

"Gray's folks. That's from my high school graduation. I think it was the last time they flew to California."

"You knew them?" I choked, studying the burly-looking older man and his white-haired petite wife with their arms around Charlie.

"Of course! I think it was one of those funny situations where they probably knew Dad and Gray were more than friends, but no one said a word. So weird. People make things needlessly complicated," he scoffed.

"Charlie, your father will see you in the main conference room now," a young woman with long blonde hair announced with a sunny smile.

"Thank you, Trish. This way, boys!"

I couldn't move. My feet were stuck to the carpet and my mouth was bone-dry. I couldn't make sense of my emotions, and I couldn't exactly turn around and leave.

"You okay?" Tegan asked, glancing toward the door when

Johnny and Ky followed Charlie into the glass-enclosed conference room across the hall.

"Yeah. Fine," I lied over the grapefruit lodged in my throat. "Let's go."

I tried to focus on the view like Gray would. But the Santa Monica office was closer to the 405 than the ocean, and the energetic man who greeted us with a winning smile and a round of firm handshakes was hard to ignore. Seb Rourke was a good-looking man. Moreover, he was charismatic, friendly, and brimming with Hollywood-style enthusiasm. In other words, I couldn't tell if he was full of shit or if he really was excited at the prospect of signing an unknown entity. He shook my hand, looked me in the eye, and seemed perfectly sincere when he claimed he was happy to finally meet me.

"Take a seat. I'll get you in and out quickly. I know everyone's busy. I have to tell you, I loved the sample Charlie sent over. I'm sure you know I don't really have anything to do with the soundtrack as a whole. I'm just an idea guy. But I like your vibe, and I think your sound complements the film well. Once you sign the contract, you'll be working with our reps at the label to record. The sooner we get that ball rolling, the better. Go ahead and check out the contract. There should be one here for each of you and...two for you, Justin." Seb flattened his large hand over the paperwork and slid it across the glass table toward me.

Again, he held eye contact, but I didn't detect any animosity or negativity toward me at all. I did my best to push aside my angst and concentrate on business. This wasn't personal. This was for Zero. I flipped the paperwork over and skimmed the legal BS. It covered copyright clauses and some info about distribution and commissions. We'd agreed on a flat fee. It was more than generous, and it would go a long way toward setting Zero up professionally. I listened with half an ear as Seb presented the official document and set a few pens on the table. Tegan signed and Johnny followed. He handed his pen to Ky and—

"This isn't what we agreed to."

"What's wrong?" Charlie asked.

"This says we're supposed to play and sing backup on 'Karma.' That's a Gypsy Coma song. It's not one of ours," I said, pushing the contract away.

"Really? I thought it was yours. It's the perfect song for Baxter. It's got the perfect amount of tension and angst. I love it. I heard you sing it at Carmine's a few months ago. Just wonderful," Seb gushed.

I gave him my best "Are you for real?" look. "Yeah, it's a good song. But Zero has better songs. We sent you a few—"

"Yeah, but that's just not quite what we're looking for," Seb said cheerfully. " 'Karma' is the winner."

"I see. The verbiage here says 'backup vocals.' Who's singing lead?" I asked, flashing an obnoxious fake smile at him.

"Xena. Maybe you can work it into a duet or—"

"I don't think so." I stood abruptly, then reached for the paper in front of me and ripped it in half. "I'm not signing anything. I'm done here."

I heard my name in stereo as I flung the door open and headed for the elevator. I stabbed the button just as Seb rounded the corner.

"Justin. What are you doing?" he asked in a patient voice one might use on a wayward child or a mentally unstable person flitting too close to the ledge.

"I'm leaving. You don't get your way on this one. I'm not helping Xena unless Zero benefits too. I was pretty clear about it. I don't care about the money. I don't care about exposure. For all I know, it'll be rigged to make me look like the asshole who fucked up a great relationship because I couldn't keep my dick in my pants. That's not how it happened. But something tells me you can relate to that story, can't you, Seb?" I goaded.

All traces of warmth and friendliness drained from his face so fast, I felt it like a physical thing. A blast of frigid air on an already cold day.

"You know nothing about me," he hissed.

"Sure, I do. It's pretty obvious. You don't like that I'm with Gray. You're trying to buy me off and send me away. I'm not falling for it."

"Don't be a fool, Justin. It's business. Period. Gray has nothing to do with this."

"Bullshit. I'm not playing your game," I said before stepping into the elevator.

We stared at each other in an intense standoff I couldn't quite explain as the doors slid shut. I just knew I had to get away from him and out of this office building. I felt dirty here. This was a place for buying and selling a piece of your soul. This wasn't who I wanted to be. I didn't need or want the "get rich quick" scheme. I wanted an honest chance. I was pretty sure my bandmates would agree once they got over the strange turn in our meeting. But I wasn't waiting to find out.

THE DRIVER DROPPED me off at the bottom of the driveway. I hurried to the front door, past the succulents and perfectly groomed rock garden and entered the security code to let myself in. The soft strains of a piano floated in the air. Something melodic and soulful coming from the formal living area. Gray normally played in his studio. He claimed to like the controlled acoustics, but I suspected he liked having multiple instruments within reach just steps away from the pool house and his video game console. I didn't think I'd ever seen him play this particular piano. I was used to seeing him bent over the keys with his eyes closed, pausing frequently to make notes and correction on sheet music. Today, his regal posture and high chin gave him the aura of a concert pianist.

I paused a few feet away and wondered how I got here. With him. God, he was beautiful. The perfect combination of rugged and wild with a touch of geek. He looked hot in his holey Levis, an old NYU T-shirt, and bare feet. He lifted his hands above the keys and stared at them, no doubt twisting the note in his head before attempting it.

How could I know him so well and yet still be completely in the dark?

Gray glanced up and caught my reflection in the window. He grinned as he twisted sideways on the bench to face me. "Hi, there. You're back early. I was going to greet you with champagne at the door."

"No need for that," I said, moving into the room.

"Did you sign the contract?"

"No."

Gray frowned, then shifted to make room for me on the bench. When I didn't join him, he cocked his head and frowned. "What's wrong?"

I shrugged and let out a bewildered half laugh. I'd been running on a dangerous mixture of indignation, outrage, and heightened adrenaline for the past thirty minutes. I'd planned my self-righteous speech on the ride over, thinking I had every right to be pissed off. But the tension seeped out of me like air from a tire. I wasn't angry. Not really. I was sad. So fucking sad. And so overwhelmed, I could barely hold my head above water.

I bit the inside of my cheek and walked to the window. I glanced over at the pool house and the view of the city beyond before turning to Gray.

"The contract was for a Gypsy Coma song. Not one of ours.

It's still a vehicle for Xena and hey, good for her. But that's not going to work for Zero...or me."

Gray jumped to his feet. "What the fuck is Seb thinking? I'll call him. He can't—"

"No. I don't want you to," I said softly. "He can do anything he wants. I don't want his handouts. And I don't want him to do you a favor on my account."

"But he likes your voice and your sound. He wanted you *and* Zero. Why would he sabotage this at the last second?"

"He didn't want me, Gray," I huffed derisively. "He wanted my story. He can't have it. I'm not selling my past. It's mine. I'm plenty good at beating myself up. I'm not interested in whoring myself out and giving someone else the right to retell a slice of my personal history to line their pockets. The contract was for Zero to sing backup for Xena on a Gypsy Coma song, by the way."

Gray shook his head. "I don't get it. It doesn't make sense."

"Sure, it does. He loves you, Gray. He doesn't want me around. Get it?"

"No. That's not like him. We're friends. Best friends. Not lovers."

"But you were," I said. "I didn't know."

Gray regarded me for a moment, then nodded. "It was a long time ago, Jus."

"Yeah. Charlie told me." I paced to the other side of the window and crossed my arms. "He wasn't telling secrets or anything. I just happened to see the wall of photos in Seb's office and...I didn't know they were your family. Like close family. Your husband, your son. You made it sound so...removed. But it's not like that, is it?"

"Seb isn't and never was my husband. We were lovers, partners, and—"

"Parents too." I massaged the back of my neck. "Your parents knew. I saw that picture from Charlie's graduation and—"

"We didn't talk about it," he repeated stubbornly. "It wasn't... valid to them. Seb and I are both from strict religious backgrounds. We knew we had to keep quiet. Give them what they expected. Anything but the truth."

"So you both married women."

"We broke up after some big shakedown at the studio. Someone did a piece on the secret gay lives of actors and Hollywood elite. Seb was Assistant Producer on a big military biopic at the time. He was afraid to lose his job and his reputation. At the time, it seemed like the only solution. Unfortunately, it killed us as a couple. I moved out of the house when Char was eight. I met Mandy soon after, and we helped each other through a rough time. When she met her future wife, Seb and I tried again. But it was too late for us. We were better friends than lovers. We'd figured out how to co-parent along the way. Geez, Seb got married and had another kid. But 'we,' the me and him part...we haven't been a couple in years."

"He loves you."

"I love him too, but as a friend only." Gray grabbed my elbow and held my chin, as though I could look into his eyes and see that he was telling the truth.

I sucked in a deep breath and looked down. He was too close, and he had a way of consuming me that made me forget myself. No one had ever done that to me before. "That sounds heavy and complicated."

"Justin. Baby, look at me." He waited for me to comply before continuing. "I'm sorry I didn't tell you sooner, but honestly...I'm not used to sharing anything about myself. You're the first person I've let inside in a while. Maybe Seb saw that and felt threatened by it somehow. It doesn't sound like him, but I'll talk to him about the contract and—"

"No. I told you...I don't want that. I don't want his help or your help. I have to do this myself. No shortcuts. No special treatment." I gave him a weak smile and stepped away. "Thank you."

"Where are you going?"

"Home."

"Stay. Sit down, baby, and—"

"Gray, I can't." I swiped at my eyes angrily and moved out of his reach. "I don't belong here."

"Of course you do."

"I don't. I never did." I cradled my head and closed my eyes when my mind starting whirling. "My head is just spinning right now. Like a fucking merry-go-round that won't stop. It makes me feel shifty sometimes. I can't sit still. I can't concentrate. And when things go sideways, I go sideways too."

"What do you mean?" Gray reached for my elbow and tried to pull me into his arms.

I batted him away and paced to the window like a caged lion. "I am overwhelmed by the things I don't say. I thought music was my way of telling my truth. But I've lost myself. I've lost my truth."

"What truth?"

"Not just one truth. It's lots of little truths that add up. I'm bi, I'm ADHD, I'm a lousy communicator guilty of making bad decisions, I'm a—"

"Stop it."

I swallowed hard and widened my eyes against the sheen of tears. "I'm messed up, Gray. Sure, I'm bummed about the contract. I barrel into everything without thinking twice. I had no right to act on behalf of my band like I knew what was best for Zero, when in fact, I don't know shit. I'm angry with myself for not listening to my friends. This is my fault. Not Seb's. Not

Charlie's. I was blinded by what I wanted. But the worst part is... I've been lying about what I *really* wanted."

"What do you want?"

"Something I can't have." I shook my head and glanced out the window again. "I saw those photos in Seb's office, and I was fucking jealous of a life I have no right to know anything about." I gave a humorless half laugh. "Because it didn't include me. So I raced over here, telling myself I was pissed at you for lying to me and having a friend who still loves you who's not giving me what I want and wow...how fucking awful is that?"

"It's not awful. It's—"

"It's wrong. I have no right to that anger, Gray. You deserve better. I can't ask for what you can't give. I can't expect you to validate me or read my mind. It's petty and mean-spirited. It's unkind...and dishonest. And I just realized I have to let it all go. I gotta peel it back, start over, and be one hundred percent honest."

He waited patiently for me to continue, but I couldn't speak. I was tongue-tied and scared. So fucking scared.

"What is it?" he asked softly.

"I love you. I don't love you a little. I love you so much, my heart hurts and my head...my head is somewhere over Mars right now."

Gray opened his mouth and closed it. "Mars? Okay. That's good."

"No, it's fucking nuts. *I'm* nuts." I shoved a hand in my hair and tugged at it in frustration. "We're light years apart. You're smart and accomplished. You're well respected and wealthy and —I've got a ways to go."

"There's no rush. You're perfect the way you are."

"I'm not. I'm a jealous asshole who has some growing up to do. I hope you get your love song. You deserve it." I managed a ghost of a smile, then kissed his cheek before turning away.

"Wait. Justin!"

I passed through the sunlit rooms one last time and headed for the entry. I didn't pause to take in the view or admire the beauty around me. I couldn't see or hear well now. I couldn't speak and the thought of food made me ill. I felt myself shut down and begin to fade until I wondered if I could be partially invisible. Here, but no longer present.

10

JUSTIN

"**C**hrist! Where the fuck have you been? I've been worried sick about you, asshole," Tegan yelled.

I sank into a corner of the sofa and sighed. "I'm sorry."

He waited for an explanation but didn't press when I remained quiet. "It was very uncomfortable after you left. Charlie was pissed at his dad. Rourke was pissed at you. We couldn't wait to get outta there."

"No, I meant I'm sorry I walked out on the deal. Don't get me wrong, I'd do it again in a heartbeat, but I'd give you a heads-up first," I clarified.

Tegan inclined his head. "We're all behind you. It was the right thing to do. A less volatile exit would have been cool, but hey...that's how you roll."

"Yeah. I 'spose so. I guess we start over again from scratch," I said, rubbing my jaw.

"Well, sort of. We still have that gig next week at The Fix. Charlie's trying to nail another one down for the following weekend."

"He still wants to work with us?" I asked.

"Of course he still wants us. We're gonna make him a gazillionaire someday. Carmine will be begging us to play his club next month and we'll have to say, 'Sorry, man. We'll be at the Troubador.' C'mon, Jus. Shake it off. It's a bump in the road. We'll get over it together and move on."

I didn't think it would be quite that easy for me, but I nodded in silent agreement. "Hey, any chance we can switch cars tonight? My engine light is on, but it'll get you to Vibes and back."

"Sure. Where you goin'?" Tegan asked, looking slightly worried again.

"Home."

I SHOWED up on my brother's doorstep an hour later. He welcomed me with a fist bump and a bro hug and put me to work chopping vegetables. We sat on the sofa, eating stir fry when Christian arrived, and watched some weird documentary about haunted houses. During commercials, I filled them in on my craptastic day. When Christian went into the kitchen to feed their cat, Rory leaned in and spoke softly.

"You love him, don't you?"

"Who, Christian?" I asked in mock confusion.

Rory smacked my arm. "No, idiot. Christian's mine. I'm talking about the music man."

"What makes you think that?"

"You hardly ate, and you've got a mopey, sad look on your face."

"I'm not sad," I lied, staring at my worn Converse. "I just wish it was simpler."

"Don't we all? But the real thing is worth working for." Rory patted my knee and shifted on the sofa. "I'll grab you an extra blanket and a pillow."

The steady creak of bedsprings woke me in the middle of the night. I put the pillow over my head and tried to go back to sleep, but my brain immediately revved into fifth gear. I replayed the day over and over. And all the associating emotions came along for the ride. The excitement and nerves of actually signing a real-life contract with a band I founded followed by the slow, sinking sensation that something wasn't right. I'd been angry and disappointed too, but the only feeling that stuck with me was a bone-deep sadness. The longer I lay there, the more agitated and unhappy I became. I couldn't fix this. I couldn't erase his past or reshape it to make room for myself. But I couldn't be an opening act in my own life. I had to be the main event.

I had to be honest.

I rolled off the sofa, folded the blanket, and set the pillow on top with a short thank-you note. Then I snuck out of the apartment and headed home.

———————

THE COMBINATION of excessive sunlight and humming from the next room woke me up the following morning. My eyes felt gritty from sleep. I rubbed them as I stretched before slowly sitting up and looking around the childhood bedroom I'd shared with Rory. It was like a time warp from the late nineties peppered with teenage mementos from the next decade. Power Rangers figurines and old board games were stuffed into bookshelves and posters from our favorite rock bands adorned the walls. Green Day, Foo Fighters, The Strokes, Arctic Monkeys.

The chambray comforters on the twin beds matched, though Rory's had faded more from sun exposure. His bed was under the window, mine against the wall opposite. I remember talking all night when Mom turned the lights off and made her way to her own room next door. Stupid stuff that seemed important at the time...kids we liked and loathed at school, our chances of getting Nintendo for Christmas, Cartoon Network's lineup. The conversations changed as we got older. We talked about sports and cute girls. But one night, I told him I'd kissed a guy. I wasn't going to say anything ever to anyone, but my secret had been eating me alive for months. I'd braced myself for the worst before blurting it out, then waiting for my little brother's disgust or concern or a sign he no longer thought I was the coolest guy he knew.

He went quiet in the dark and, after what felt like five minutes, whispered, "Did you like it?"

"Yeah. I did. But don't be weird about it. I'm not queer or anything. And whatever you do, don't tell Mom."

I wished I could take those words back. Not for myself, but because I had a feeling my desire for anonymity had been mistaken as advice. Rory and I eventually came out to each other a few years later when he was in college. Even then, our conversation was laced with anxiety and a desire not to share our news with our mother. She hadn't navigated our teen years well. She fought her own demons and I wasn't so sure she'd won when she put the bottle down and joined a conservative church. But when Rory said he was done keeping secrets, I told him I was too. We came out to her together and it was a mega disaster. She hadn't spoken to Rory in almost two years now.

And yet this room hadn't changed. She hadn't erased him from her life. She'd preserved him. Kept him small and knowable.

"Justin, honey, do you want pancakes? I have to leave for work in half an hour. I whipped up a batch. Oh, and the coffee is fresh. Come get some!"

"I'll be right out," I called through the closed door.

I got my ass out of bed and used the bathroom before meeting my mom in the kitchen.

"Good morning."

" 'Mornin'. Smells good," I mumbled, making a beeline for the coffee machine.

"Bacon always does," she chirped happily. "I always keep some on hand in case you or Ror—you stop by. And here you are. Patience pays off. Take a seat. This will be ready in a minute. You can tell me what's going on with you while you wait. You scared the heck out of me last night!"

I studied my mom over the rim of my Harry Potter mug. Another remnant of my youth, I mused, noting the new lines at the corners of her mouth. They made her look older than fifty. Melanie Germaine was still pretty, but at one time, she'd been beautiful. She was tall and thin with long blonde hair and a killer smile. Time and alcohol had taken a toll. She was too skinny, too pale, and her once lustrous, long hair had a strawlike texture that seemed to suck the life from her face. The nondescript brown uniform she wore for her job as a checkout girl at the local grocery market didn't help. Somewhere in the last ten years, my mom had given up. Maybe she forgot who she was, or maybe she didn't care anymore.

She set a plate piled high with pancakes, scrambled eggs, and bacon in front of me, then patted my shoulder before taking the chair beside me.

"Thank you."

"You're welcome. Are you all right?" She squinted as though it might help her see without having to ask twenty questions.

"I'm fine. I started a new band," I said as I picked up my fork.

"Oh." She sipped her coffee, cradling the mug in both hands. "Don't take this the wrong way, honey, but aren't you getting little old for this band business? Maybe you should go back to school and get a college degree, eh?"

"Hmph. Yeah, maybe. But I'm doing this instead. And this is where you're supposed to wish me luck or tell me to break a leg or something," I said around a mouthful of eggs.

She smiled. "Break a leg. Did you really drive from LA in the middle of the night to tell me about a band?"

"No. I had a bad day and I wanted to come home."

"What happened?" she asked.

"Just...life. I had dinner at Rory's last night. He's doing really well, by the way. He still works at the Y."

She glanced out the window and sighed. "I know."

I decided her wistful tone was a green light to keep going, so I did. "He tutors too. That's actually how he met his boyfriend. Christian's a great guy. You'd like him. He's a quarterback at Chilton."

"I heard about that mess. His poor parents."

The pancakes in my mouth turned to sawdust. I gulped my coffee to wash it down as I pushed my chair noisily across the linoleum floor. I set the plate and cup on the counter and warned myself not to lose my shit in one go.

"His 'poor parents' are missing out. Kinda like you are. But hey..." I put my hands up like a traffic cop. "We don't talk about that stuff, do we?"

She shot an angry parental look at me. The kind I associated with getting my butt swatted or being grounded when I was a kid. She pushed her mug aside and stood slowly.

"No, we don't. I don't appreciate you stirring up trouble for no reason. If you came to borrow money, tell me what you need. I'll leave a check for you, but you can't cash it until tomorrow."

I raked my hand through my hair and let out a frustrated growl. "Jesus, I don't need your money, Ma."

"Don't use the Lord's name in vain. If you have something to say, be quick about it. I have to go to work. I'm not in a band. I have a real job and I have to be there on time," she huffed, folding her arms over her chest.

"All right. Remember when Rory came out to you? We were sitting right here. He didn't want to tell you 'cause you'd been on a holy kick for a while."

"What is that supposed to mean?" she asked sharply.

"It's like an exclusive club for saints and pious assho— people only. I told him not to worry. I'd be there and I'd come out too. You didn't believe me, but you believed Rory. He had a boyfriend, and someone said they saw them holding hands or something." I gasped theatrically. "Imagine that. You told him you didn't want to see him again until he found Christ. Well, he found Christian. That's a start."

"That's not funny."

"No, I guess not. But you know what else isn't funny? I've been sitting here in the neutral zone. I've been playing it safe, waiting for something to change. I love being in a band, but I've been playing the wrong instrument because playing the right one meant I'd have to stand up and make my voice heard. I stayed with the wrong woman a few months too long because admitting I was in a nowhere relationship meant I'd have to speak up and potentially hurt someone I cared about. So I waited and let her hurt me instead."

My mother's face softened. "Oh, Jus...I'm sorry. I—"

"No. I'm not done. See...my problem is I talk a lot, but I don't talk about what matters. I save that for my songwriting and let real life issues pile up until it's like a stack of bills so high, I know it'll take a lifetime to pay 'em. Maybe twenty-six is too old to join a new band, but Ma...I need to be heard. I have things to say. Some of them are important. This is my chance. But I gotta start here."

"Justin..."

"When I told you I was bi, I wasn't kidding. I am bi. Just like Rory. You chose not to believe me because I had a girlfriend. That's what you said, anyway. I think the truth is, you really didn't want to know. You didn't want to lose both of us, so you made a choice. And that choice sucks." I paced the edge of the old wood table and back. "I didn't bring up my own bi-ness again because I didn't want to have this conversation. I didn't want you to choose between me and your church. I told myself I didn't want you to lose both of us. But you know…I think I was afraid you'd choose faith over me too. And it made me realize how stupid I've been. I feel like such an asshole. I let Rory take the fall on his own. I should have insisted you listen to me too."

"I don't know what you mean. He made his own choices, Justin."

"So have you. So have I. You're still working the same ol' job you've hated for thirty years and living in the same crappy apartment in a sketchy part of town. And I'm still trying to put a band together. He's happy, Mom. He's good, kind, smart and…he'd forgive you in a heartbeat because Rory is the best man I know."

Her lower lip trembled, but she'd lost some of her righteous bravado. She dabbed at the corner of her eye and cleared her throat before speaking. "I love him. I love you both. But he's got to be right with the Lord, Justin. It's the only way."

I stared at her for a long moment, then blurted, "I'm in love with a man."

She blinked in surprise and waited a few beats, like she was sure I'd take my words back. "You're just saying that."

"No. It's true. I don't know if he loves me, but he likes me. I wish that was enough, but I'm greedy. I want things I never thought I could have now. But they don't seem to matter if I can't have him."

"Why are you telling me this?" She put her hand over her mouth and shook her head.

"Because I'm tired of lying...or telling half-truths. It's making me miserable. I love you, Mom. And so does Rory. We're the older versions of the kids who taped those posters up in the room down the hall. Things have changed, but we're still us."

She dabbed at the corners of her eyes furiously and then gasped as if in pain before the first sob wracked her body. I moved to her side and pulled her against me. "I love you, I love you. I can't lose you too. I can't..."

"Shh. It's okay. I'm here. I'll always be here," I chanted, holding her close. "But you gotta talk to Rory. You can't do this to him. To us."

"Yes," she sobbed. After a minute or two, she pushed at my chest and let out a ragged breath. "I'm a mess. I have to fix myself before work, and I'm gonna be late. There's money on my dresser. Take what you need and lock up behind you. And... what's his name?"

That stopped me. I narrowed my eyes and stuffed my hands into my pocket. "Gray."

My mother stared at me for a long moment. Her eyes glistened with tears. I could practically see her struggle to compute and comprehend something she didn't understand as I held my breath and waited for judgment.

"Okay. I love you."

She grabbed her purse from the counter and hurried into the next room before I could respond.

I couldn't tell if it went well or not. She said she loved me, which was a good thing, right? I thought about warning Rory but decided that was their story. I had my own to untangle and rewrite. I just wished I didn't have to do it alone.

11

GRAY

This wasn't my first heartbreak. I'd had a few. Some were relatively small and easy to get over, like the time Sherry Hansen told me she liked another boy in second grade. Sure, I'd been crushed, but bigger hurdles awaited. Like losing Seb. I'd loved him blindly. He was dynamic and self-possessed and so damn handsome. And best of all, we shared a need for secrecy. I hadn't wanted to come out officially and rock any boats. It might not have affected my career, but it would have ruined my relationship with my parents. Maybe they suspected there was more between Seb and me, but we didn't talk about it because saying the words aloud would give them power. They'd need validation or condemnation. Either would change us...and not necessarily for the better.

But losing Justin was worse.

I couldn't say why. It didn't make sense to me that I could fall so hard for an unpredictable, headstrong barista-slash-bartender who was eighteen years younger than me. Age wasn't really a factor—it was an excuse. It allowed me to push him aside into a neat box where I could be the mentor. The one with all the experience and connections. I misjudged the power of sheer bravery. Justin wasn't afraid to stand up and face his fears. He didn't second-guess himself or assume someone else's viewpoint could work for him. He was true to himself and...he loved me.

At least, he said he did.

"I like that piece," Seb said. He sat on one of the Eames chairs in my living room, cradling a beer between his spread thighs. "Do I know it?"

"No. But you will."

"Okay." He went quiet before trying again. "Is it for *Baxter's*—"

"I'm not talking about that," I snapped.

"How long are we going to do this? I said I'm sorry twenty times. I told their manager...aka, my son, I'd draw up a new contract and I apologized. You're all acting like it's the end of the world and it's just a fucking song!"

I flattened my hand over the keys, sending a clang of uneven notes through the room as I shoved away from the piano and rounded on him furiously.

"You don't fucking get it, do you? You lie and apologize over and over again, Seb. This isn't a movie. This is real life and real people. I told you to leave Justin alone, but you had to have his story. Did you get it? Did pitting him against his ex make him seem more exciting? Did it give you ideas to sell to the masses? Did it make you feel powerful?" I spat angrily.

Seb gaped at me before slowly standing. He set his beer bottle on the piano bench and held his arms open in a helpless gesture.

"What are we doing? Where is this coming from, Gray?"

"I'm tired of doing things your way. Keeping quiet, keeping the peace. I love you, but I haven't been *in* love with you for years. It happened gradually. Every time I couldn't touch you in public, every time I had to step aside for a Hollywood starlet to take my place at a movie premiere, every time I had to fudge the truth with Charlie so he wouldn't think for one second our incredible dysfunction meant he wasn't loved...has led us here.

"Zero doesn't want your contract, Seb. They're gonna do it their way, and I bet they'll be amazing. They have an incredibly talented manager, who might not know the ins and outs of the business but is willing to give it his all. They're going to be okay."

"What about us?" he asked in a small voice.

"We'll be fine too. We have no choice. We know each other far too well," I huffed.

"What about you?"

I met his gaze as I splayed my fingers over the piano keys and picked up the melody where I'd left off. "That, I don't know."

Seb sat beside me on the bench and nudged my elbow until I stopped. "So you *are* in love with him. Why didn't you admit it when I asked you that same fucking question a month ago?"

"I didn't know. And now, I do and I'm...I don't know what I am without him. I guess I'm just...empty."

"Can I fix it?"

I jerked my head in surprise. "No. It's not your fault. It's mine."

"Then you fix it," he replied irritably.

"Gee, thanks for the advice," I snarked.

"I wish I'd tried to undo the mess I made when I lost you. I wish I was brave enough to put you first when I still had a chance to make it right."

"Seb..."

He smiled. "I know. It's different now, and it's probably for the best, but if you think he's special, find a way before you're left with an empty house again and a fuckton of regret. It's not too late. You just have to be brave."

ONCE UPON A TIME, I was very brave. At least when it came to music.

My access was limited when I was growing up. I had to search for it in record stores, libraries, and at school and church. There was no internet. No fast exchange of ideas and words, but it didn't matter. Music found a way. It called to the quiet only child in me and encouraged me to spread my wings and fly. That might sound corny, but it was true. I'd always admired people like Justin. The reckless, hungry souls who couldn't hide behind their talent if they tried.

I wasn't like that at all. And now I lived in a glass house with a view of the city where I could observe life and lovers and write their stories from above where they couldn't touch me. I craved the anonymity Justin joked about the first night we met. I'd been burned by the spotlight. The scars weren't the kind that faded. They were deep wounds that conjured painful memories. At forty-four, I wasn't interested in tempting fate again. Sex was one thing, love was another.

But I couldn't get him out of my head. I couldn't pretend to be indifferent or unfazed. When I saw Justin onstage at Carmine's, I knew he was special. I didn't realize then that he was my missing piece. I might survive, but I could never be whole without him. And what was the point? Now I knew what it felt like to skateboard with my best friend, play guitar on the roof, and make love with my eyes wide open and my heart fully exposed. Scary as fuck...but exhilarating.

I had to get him back.

———

"THEY'RE GOING on in five minutes. Want a drink?" Seb asked, gesturing toward the bar.

"Yeah, sure." I nodded distractedly, then scanned the area,

stepping sideways to avoid bumping into a drunk patron carrying three beers to his friends.

The Fix was a half step up from a dive bar. It was set up like most clubs, with a raised platform area that served as a stage, a sticky bar in the back, and a standing-room-only policy. On the plus side, it was slightly bigger than Carmine's, and the crowd was young and enthusiastic. They seemed to know Zero too. I overheard a couple of college-aged girls discussing them with a reverence that made me smile.

"I love that song, 'Funny Feeling.' It's kinda sweet and edgy at the same time. Like Justin. Oh my God, he's so hot."

"So is Ky. Never mind, they're all freaking gorgeous."

I smiled at their star-struck tones and nodded my thanks when Seb handed me a gin and tonic.

"You'd think Beyoncé was making a guest appearance. This place is bumping," Seb commented, sipping his cocktail.

The lights went down before I could reply, and the crowd went wild. When a single spotlight shone over the microphone stand, it got a little louder. And when Justin and the boys walked onto the stage, the noise rose to stadium concert levels. Okay, maybe that was a slight exaggeration—but only a slight one. The sound of cheering, wolf whistles, and applause reverberated through my body.

Justin gripped the mic with his right hand as he adjusted his guitar strap with the other. He wore a snug black tee that accentuated his ink and basic blue jeans. He'd cut his hair, but it suited him. He emitted a badass, sexy vibe before he even opened his mouth. If he was nervous, I couldn't tell. He looked poised and proud and fuck...he looked like a rock star.

"Hey there. We're Zero and this one's called 'Everywhere.' One, two, three..."

Tegan set a steady beat on drums, Ky followed on bass a few seconds later, and Johnny on electric guitar. I'd heard them play often in my studio and thought they were good. However, performing live was a whole other art form. These guys sounded as though they'd been playing together for years. And when Justin joined in on vocals, anyone could tell Zero had true star power.

They played new material for thirty minutes before pausing for Justin to introduce himself and his bandmates. The audience hung on his every word, clapping and cheering with their arms raised. When they continued with a bluesy number, everyone swayed to the beat. The follow-up rockin' anthem, "My Way" had everyone jumping and dancing. The energy was frenetic. Magical, even.

When the club darkened after a ninety-minute set, Zero left the stage to the sound of thunderous applause.

"Damn, they're really good," Seb gushed.

"Yeah. Here. Hold my drink."

He furrowed his brow as he took my glass. "What are you doing?"

"Honestly, I have no idea. Wish me luck."

I moved through the crush of bodies to the nearest exit. The heavy door opened onto a wide driveway at the side of the club between the main street and the parking lot. I immediately realized that I didn't know where to go. I hadn't asked enough questions. *Fuck.* I'd been like this for days. Full of ideas but unsure about how to execute them. I swiped my damp hands on my jeans and went to search for my car, which of course was sandwiched tightly between two expensive-looking vehicles.

I took pity on the attendant's panicky look when I asked for my keys. "It's okay. I can wait. I just need to get something out of my car. Thanks."

"Phew. Here you go, sir."

My Porsche was parked under a streetlight behind the club. I sidled between the vehicles and miraculously was able to wedge my arm in the passenger-side door and grab the roses. A few red petals tore from the buds and scattered in the light spring breeze, but they still looked good. I shoved a couple of stray stems into the bouquet and turned toward the back door just as it opened. I spotted Ky and Tegan first. Then Johnny. But no sign of Justin.

I waited a couple of minutes more before inspiration struck. I shimmied back to my car and climbed on the roof just as the door opened and a triumphant cheer filled the air. The four members of Zero clasped hands and whooped. I grinned when they lifted Charlie and ran around the small clearing near the building. I was too far to hear their conversation, but I didn't mind. I was skilled at the art of people-watching.

Charlie spotted me from his perch and waved excitedly. Everyone turned, or maybe no one did. The only one I saw was Justin. He froze for a moment and stared at me. Then he smiled. Even from a distance, I could tell it lit his eyes before stretching from ear to ear.

My heart pounded in my chest. I licked my lips and sat a little taller. I started to slide down to meet him, but he was faster and more agile. He slipped between the cars and then hopped onto the Porsche's hood.

"You're here," he said.

"Yeah. I couldn't miss Zero's debut. You were incredible, baby."

"Thanks." He pursed his lips, then brushed his nose with the back of his hand before inching forward. He gestured toward the bouquet beside me. "Are those for me?"

"Yes. They're boyfriend roses."

Justin grinned. "Oh yeah?"

"You said they should be bigger and these were the biggest ones I could find. I should have bought more and maybe a different color," I babbled nervously.

"No. They're perfect."

"Come sit with me. Please."

He glanced at my outstretched hand before threading his fingers with mine. I moved the roses to give him space and set them in his lap. "Thank you."

I bit the inside of my cheek and nodded like an idiot. I couldn't find the words I needed. They were right there on the tip of my tongue, but they wouldn't come. Even if they did, I wasn't sure I could speak around the lump in my throat. After a long moment, I took a deep breath and gave it my best shot.

"I love you," I whispered. "I love you. I love you. I love your beautiful smile, the sound of your laughter. I love that crinkle you get between your eyes when you're concentrating. I love your sense of humor and fuck, I love that whirling brain of yours. As crazy as it sounds, I feel like I've waited my whole life for you. Forty-four years. It's a long time. But I bet I've got another forty-four to go....And I don't want to spend a minute more without you. That's my truth, and you're my beginning and my end."

Justin held my face in his hands before sealing his lips over mine in a passionate kiss that spoke volumes. He pulled back slightly and rested his forehead on mine.

"Fuck, you say pretty things." He wiped at a tear on his cheek and glanced up at the sky before beaming a radiant grin at me. "You know, I had a plan tonight too. I was gonna do a kickass show and then show up out of the blue at my boyfriend's house and serenade him with the song we wrote. I want him to know he's the best thing that ever happened to me."

I nodded. "You should definitely tell him."

Justin bit his bottom lip and grinned. "I love you. I want to be your story. I want to be your love song. And I want you to be mine."

"Yes. Starting now."

We kissed under the stars like we were the only two people left on the planet. The city lights, the traffic noise, and the conversations of passersby faded to a dull static. Time didn't matter; the past had no place here. This was true music. The silence in between the notes marked the beginning of our love story, starting from zero.

"Where words fail, music speaks."—Hans Christian Andersen

Justin

BAKING WAS SUPPOSED to be fun. Sugar, chocolate, and butter were magical ingredients, so anyone who could read directions should be able to make a damn cake. The state of our kitchen suggested that might not be the case. Five mixing bowls, a KitchenAid appliance that was supposedly ideal for the task, and a variety of ingredients littered the island. And a mixture of flour, salt, and something sticky was all over the hardwood floors...and me. I studied the recipe again before glancing at the puppy sleeping in his crate in the living area.

If Chester woke up, I'd have a legit excuse to leave this mess and order dessert like I should have in the first place. I tossed the wooden spoon into the bowl. Nothing. I picked up a measuring spoon and "accidentally" dropped it on the counter. He snored and let out an adorable whimper, but he still didn't wake up.

"Hi baby, what—" Gray stopped in his tracks and opened his mouth in a comical O before shaking his head in bewilderment. He massaged the back of his neck and tried again. "What are you doing?"

"Making a cake for the party," I announced proudly.

Gray craned his neck to check on our sleeping baby before circling the island with his hands on his hips. "And how's that going?"

"Not well," I admitted.

"Let me be the judge." He stuck his finger in the metal bowl and then tasted the cake batter and shuddered theatrically. I threw my head back and laughed at his antics, which of course woke the dog.

"I'll get him," I volunteered.

Gray raced me to the crate and opened the latch for our ten-week-old French bulldog, Chester. "Hey there, little fella. You should see the mess Daddy made while you were sleeping. Come here. Come to Papa."

"I can't decide if that's really cute or if we're turning into weirdo dog owners," I deadpanned before crouching beside Gray. I put my arm around my boyfriend and chuckled at the silly "baby" noises he made.

Gray kissed my nose. "What time is everyone coming?"

"Two o'clock. So…I've got three hours to either remake the cake or order one. What's your vote?"

"Order," he replied immediately. "What made you decide to bake anyway? That's not like you."

"I don't know. I'm feeling very homey, though. I think it's Chester's fault. Isn't it, little cutie patootie cookie cake?"

Gray rolled his eyes and snickered before ushering Chester

outside to do his business. I watched my boys with a goofy grin. There was something crazy sexy about my big tattooed hunk taking care of a pint-sized pup. Some days I couldn't believe this was my life.

I moved into Gray's house in the Hills in early May, a week or two after Zero's first show at The Fix. Gray insisted and I couldn't argue. This was where I belonged. We had a few minor adjustments in the beginning. Gray was used to living alone, and I was used to bunking on a sofa. He was a neat-freak and I was... not. No doubt, he'd taken Chester out to give me a chance to clean the kitchen before he was tempted to take over and make everything spotless for our family and friends.

It was early October, but it was seventy-five degrees and sunny in LA with crystal-blue skies. A perfect day for an impromptu celebratory barbeque. Zero had just finished playing a successful series of sold-out shows in the LA area. Charlie had turned out to be an amazing manager-slash-social-media-guru. Zero was a local band on the rise. Our fan base had skyrocketed over the past six months. We'd had a few record labels voice interest, but Charlie was adamant about controlling our artistic vision. We trusted him to help us find the right fit.

We had a ton of material for an album, including the song Gray and I cowrote. It was a great song. Possibly the best I'd ever written. It was honest and it read like a story of us...from the heart. I choked up every time I sang it. Part of me wanted to keep it for ourselves, but Gray insisted that it was mine to use for Zero's first album. His exact words were something like, "Don't be ridiculous. When you have something beautiful, you need to share it with the world. Show everyone that love is real. I love you. I want everyone to know you're mine."

I could hardly argue.

Timing was important though. Sure, we could have asked Gray or Seb to step in, but after our attempt at taking a short-cut went sideways, we decided to do things on our own. I tried to ignore the rumors, but I knew Seb scratched his plan to use Xena for the Baxter movie. She'd made money off the contract that I assumed would help Declan and her fund their new band. No doubt Charlie would keep his eye on them. I didn't want to know. I just wanted to make music.

We were already doing well enough to quit our day jobs and concentrate on our music. And it left us more time to hang out with friends and family. Like today. Johnny, Ky, and Tegan would be here soon. Maybe with dates. I didn't ask for a headcount, but I knew Ky had a new girlfriend and Tegan was kind of, sort of seeing someone. He'd been very secretive about his new man. I didn't press. He seemed happy, and that was all that mattered. I teasingly asked Gray if he thought Tegan and Charlie were secret lovers. Gray shook his head and reminded me that Charlie couldn't keep anything to himself. True. He must have inherited that trait from Seb.

I'd wondered if things would be awkward between Seb and me after I moved into Gray's house. It wasn't necessarily smooth sailing. We were both demanding and boisterous, and Gray was our touchstone. We still had to figure out how to move around the past without coming to blows. I supposed we'd get there eventually. Gray told me Seb had helped him get Chester for me, so hey...we were making strides. No doubt he'd come by to play with our pup before everyone arrived.

My brother and Christian were supposed to carpool from Long Beach with our mom too. They'd started a slow healing process. Nothing would be fixed overnight, but no one was hiding anymore. All of our scars and mistakes had been acknowledged. It was time to move on.

I hopped to my feet and headed outside to join Gray on the lawn with Chester...my birthday present. And yeah, our kid. He'd only been living with us for a couple of weeks, but we were both in love with the little furball. And I was madly in love with Gray. He calmed me and excited me in equal measure. He was my best friend and my biggest fan. He saw me for who I was and allowed me to see him. I didn't take a single second for granted. I wanted us to be the little old couple someone else pointed out to their lover one day. I wanted them to say, "Look at those two old men. They look like they've been in love forever."

I kissed the back of Gray's neck and then rested my head on his shoulder. "If I were going to buy a dessert, what should I get?"

"Brownies, cookies...no one will care, Jus. They'll be happy with beer and burgers."

"So I should break out our ice cream supply?"

"Hell, no. That's ours," he huffed in faux annoyance. He wrapped his arm around my waist and pulled me close before showering me with kisses. "Hey, Jus..."

"Hmm?"

"I love you."

I flashed a megawatt grin at my lover and kissed his lips. "I love you too. And my head is still on Mars."

"I know," he chuckled.

A love song is a very personal thing. No two songs are heard the same way. We look and listen for what we want in life. And every so often, we get exactly what we need. I was grateful for a new beginning with Gray, starting from zero.

"This is Love" by Justin Cuevas and Gray Robertson
   You in the moonlight, under the lamplight
   You with the city behind you and a million stars above
   Everything changed and time began
   The moment you smiled at me
   And for the first time I wondered, is this love?

One night and I was hooked
We talked for hours
You came when I needed you, and you stayed
I can't imagine a night without you now
And for the first time I wondered, is this love?
Measures of kindness slip into place and allow us moments of purity...
real affection, admiration, friendship
I don't need words, I don't need music,
I just need you
And for the first time I know, this is love

OUT IN THE FIELD- COMING JUNE 2019

EXCERPT FROM OUT IN THE FIELD BY LANE HAYES (JUNE 2019)

Phoenix twisted a piece of plastic ivy on his sash and regarded me thoughtfully. "This is a very confusing tête-à-tête. Do you have a crush on me, Max?"

I let out a ragged sigh and glanced toward the crowded corridor. "Yeah, I—maybe."

"Hmm. If it's makes it any easier, I like you too. But I'm seeing someone. It's not serious, but—"

"Then you can see me too, right?"

"Where? In the closet?" he snarked.

"No, smartass. We can meet for coffee or something."

He regarded me thoughtfully then shook his head. "I should go."

"Wait." I grabbed his arm and accidentally pulled him against me. I ran my fingers from his elbow to his wrist before stepping backward. "I've been lurking around the food court and walking by the theater even though my classes are on the other end of campus because—"

"Because what?" he prodded.

"I wanted to see you again. I can't stop thinking about you. It's been like this for a while for me. It was bad enough when I thought you lived in LA, but I figured I'd snap out of it eventually. But now that I know you're in the same city, at the same school...I'm going kinda crazy."

Phoenix regarded me skeptically. "You could have called me."

"I thought I'd try catch you after your final show instead. Except...not with your sister," I said with a wry laugh. "I swear to you, I met her five minutes before the lights went down. This was never a date. This was a group of friends using extra tickets to the last night of the school play. I'm sure your sister felt the same way."

"I doubt it. Those were Sonny's tickets."

"Uh...really?" I asked lamely.

"Yeah. I gave them to her. She told me she was going to invite her friend, Sarah, and her boyfriend and then ask them to invite the cute baseball player she has a crush on."

Oh. Fuck.

"You knew your sister had a crush on me?"

"Of course not! I only knew the lucky guy played your sport. I assumed you knew him, but I didn't think you *were* him. Geesh!"

I scratched my jaw thoughtfully. "That's a little awkward but hey...we're even now."

Phoenix huffed indignantly. "Even? How do you figure?"

"'Cause neither of us planned on this, but here we are. It's like fate or something."

"Nice try, but I don't think your reasoning adds up at all. Look, I—"

"Coffee," I intercepted. "Let's meet for coffee or wine or—"

"Yogurt," he pronounced.

"Yogurt?" I wrinkled my nose in distaste.

He nodded. "There's a new place I've been wanting to try on Grand Street. It's actually a juice bar, but they have frozen yogurt too. Text me. We'll plan a casual encounter. I mean...if you want."

"I want." I fixed him with a slow-growing grin then stuffed my hands in my pockets to keep myself from touching him. "You look hot, by the way."

"Thank you." He wrapped his arms around his chest and shivered. "Not much to this costume though. I should grab my sweater."

I shrugged my navy sport coat off and laid it over his bare shoulders. "Here. Take my jacket."

"That's sweet of you, but my bag is in the dressing room and—"

"Just take it. You can give it to me next time I see you," I said.

He cocked his head curiously. "Okay, but won't your friends wonder why I'm wearing your stuff?"

"We're leaving. Or I am anyway. They won't notice."

Phoenix slipped his arms in the sleeves and snickered. "This is a true fashion statement. How do I look?"

Ridiculous. But in a charming way.

My jacket was ginormous on him. The fabric hung halfway to his knees and swallowed his hands. He should have looked clownish. But that smile was everything. It was brilliant, bold, and captivating. It rendered clothes a silly distraction. No wonder I didn't want to leave his side the night we met. Sure, he was pretty and fun. But pretty, precocious twinks weren't my usual type. Phoenix had to be the exception because I couldn't get him out of my head. Every time he smiled, he pulled me further into his orbit until I forgot myself and did stupid shit; like show up to a college play to moon over him like a lovesick teenager.

"You look amazing," I said in a raspy voice I barely recognized. "Just amazing."

ABOUT THE AUTHOR

Lane Hayes is grateful to finally be doing what she loves best. Writing full-time! It's no secret Lane loves a good romance novel. An avid reader from an early age, she has always been drawn to well-told love story with beautifully written characters. These days she prefers the leading roles to both be men. Lane discovered the M/M genre a few years ago and was instantly hooked. Her debut novel was a 2013 Rainbow Award finalist and subsequent books have received Honorable Mentions, and were First Place winners in the 2016 and 2017 Rainbow Awards. She loves red wine, chocolate and travel (in no particular order). Lane lives in Southern California with her amazing husband in a newly empty nest.

ALSO BY LANE HAYES

Out in the Deep

Out in the End Zone

Out in the Offense

Leaning Into Love

Leaning Into Always

Leaning Into the Fall

Leaning Into a Wish

Leaning Into Touch

Leaning Into the Look

Leaning Into Forever

A Kind of Truth

A Kind of Romance

A Kind of Honesty

A Kind of Home

Better Than Good

Better Than Chance

Better Than Friends

Better Than Safe

The Right Words

The Wrong Man

The Right Time

A Way with Words

A Way with You

Made in the USA
Middletown, DE
02 November 2019

77878911R00137